THE GRACE GLEASON FILES

the BLUE WALL

THE GRACE GLEASON FILES

the BLUE WALL

DONALD REICHARDT

JOYCE OSCAR

GLEASON FILES LLC

ISBN: 978-1-0818-8013-2

Printed by Kindle Direct Publishing

Available from Amazon.com and other retail outlets, online outlets and book stores.
Cover design by William David (WilliamDavidCreative.com)
Other novels in The Grace Gleason Files series:

Justice On Hold

Unholy Mind Games

For more information visit: www.GraceGleasonFiles.com

ACKNOWLEDGMENTS

THE AUTHORS WISH to thank Valerie Clark, author, agent and filmmaker, for her counsel and support; Investigator Joe Baeza, of the Laredo, Texas, PD and the late Don McAfee, retired officer of the NYPD, for their advice and expertise; John Staton, our Beta reader, for his suggestions and ongoing support; Bill Reichardt, Juli Niemann and Mary Poole Reese for their contributions to the story; The Atlanta Black Tie Club for their continued support; and the vast majority of the men and women of the Atlanta PD who do their work honestly and ethically, risking their lives every day to serve and protect.

Donald is thankful for the support of his sons, Bill and Scott, and of course Zeina and Lukas. He thanks his late parents, Walter and Agnes, for paving his way. Donald is grateful to Ann Arensberg, Roy Moskop, the late Dr. Green Wyrick and the other mentors and teachers along the road. And Maggie the Doberman, who befriended Joyce and BooBoo during our first "business meeting" in East Roswell Park.

Joyce thanks her late parents, Edward and Gertrude, who taught her how to work hard and achieve the American dream. She also wishes to thank her husband Jerry and children, Jennifer and Jeremy, who encourage her every day not to take life so seriously. And she acknowledges writers everywhere who keep the art of storytelling alive and inspire us to perfect our craft.

INTRODUCTION

THE BLUE WALL is set in the present day. It is inspired by true events that occurred in Atlanta, Georgia during the early nineties. The authors have accurately identified Atlanta and many of its landmarks, street names and institutions. But several cities, organizations and businesses have been intentionally changed because of the sensitivity of the material or the fictional nature of the story. All the names of characters in *The Blue Wall* are fictitious.

PROLOGUE

NICK PONTELLIS SEEMED EDGY as he left the Silver Rush Showbar. The deafening, driving beat of music and boisterous hooting of drunken customers quickly faded as he hurried from his office down the corridor. He slipped out through the strip club's darkened side entrance and glanced right and left, walking with an urgent quickstep.

Pontellis wore a hand-made, gray silk suit and carried a metal brief case. As the brisk winter wind met his face, he hunched his neck and shoulders into the jacket.

Bret Larkin, an off-duty Riverwood cop, held open the driver's side door of Pontellis' pearl orange Lamborghini Aventador. Nick nodded at him and slid in, setting the brief case on the passenger seat.

"Sure you don't want me to ride along?" Larkin leaned down and asked. His black tee shirt strained at his hulking, muscular frame. The word *Security* in large silver block letters stretched across Larkin's massive chest, the obvious result of intense workouts. Larkin appeared to ignore the raw weather the way professional football players show machismo by going sleeveless in Green Bay during December games.

"Damn it, Bret," growled Pontellis. "I've already told you twice. I'm good to go."

"I know, boss. But that's an extra load of cash you're hauling tonight. I just thought, since you've already been hit before…" He paused and waited.

Pontellis' deep brown eyes narrowed and his tan, rugged

1

face drew up in a scowl. He looked into the rear view mirror and smoothed his thick, silver hair. "Those bastards won't go after me tonight. They established their M.O. when they robbed me the last time on a Saturday night. They won't suspect I'd be loaded on a Tuesday. Besides, if you tagged along I'd have to deliver you back here once I got it into the safe. I'd rather sit back, have a nice Scotch and maybe get lucky with my wife." He grinned at Larkin. "I'll be fine."

Larkin pushed the car door shut and Nick eased out of the parking lot crowded with high-end SUV's, sedans and pickup trucks. The security man stood watching as the LP 700-4 screeched out onto Peachtree Street and roared away.

It was early morning, and the city was still buzzing with nightlife. Restaurants and bars were closing, and the party crowd, tipsy and loud, spilled out onto the streets of Buckhead. Drivers careened out of parking lots, pushed past the speed limit and weaved their way recklessly through traffic. The din of vehicle sound systems with their bass speakers set on high thumped through the chaotic streets.

Pontellis drove carefully, slowly, staying in the right lane as traffic whizzed past him. He turned up Paces Ferry Road and passed the multi-million dollar mansions of the corporate movers and shakers, top dog politicians, even the governor.

As he gazed at some of the homes, he let out a guttural groan. When he had bought the club two years earlier and moved from Florida, he had asked his real estate agent to find him a house in this area.

"You wouldn't like living there," the agent had told him emphatically as they left her office to look at houses she had lined up for viewing. "These guys are in the inner circle, the movers and do-

2

ers. They would take a dim view of a nightclub owner in their midst. They would make your life miserable." She hesitated, scanning his expression below his gray Stetson.

His eyelids narrowed and he stopped walking and crossed his arms. "You're not showing me anything in Buckhead?" he said, his voice loaded with annoyance.

"You know as well as I," she cautioned, "that neighborhoods are just as political as governments and more prejudiced than any other institution."

The agent held out some photos, and he scanned them. She pointed at one of them. "Ten minutes from there you'll find un-believable buys on homes like this one, just as elegant as Buck-head, and right on the Chattahoochee River." She grasped his el-bow and steered him toward her car. "Besides, you'll be getting a lot more value for your money."

Nick grimaced, but he never again broached the subject.

He was taking the familiar shortcut through the community that wouldn't have him. As Paces Ferry Road dead-ended, he pulled onto the interstate which would take him to his neighborhood, Riv-erwood Heights.

Riverwood was one of those areas where the second ring of influential people lived. They were not those who made the momen-tous decisions that fueled and dictated the character of the city. But they made the inner circle's decisions possible through business success, legal prowess, fund-raising reputations and connections to the rich and famous of entertainment, sports and the underworld.

The neighborhood was easily accessible to arterial surface streets that splayed into the city in every direction. Yet ninety-five percent of the metro residents had never been through it nor had much of an idea how to get there.

Those who did happen to pass through it, for whatever reason, were no doubt unimpressed. There were no sidewalks where children played and no adjoining fences where neighbors gossiped back and forth or shared barbecue pits. The oldest homes, built in the seventies, were close enough to the winding, tree-canopied streets to be seen. They were stately but relatively modest.

The majority of the houses had been built recently and were more ostentatious. They sat far back off the roads, at the end of gated, winding driveways. There was little neighbor interaction, no block parties or swim-overs. Residents of Riverwood Heights kept to themselves and their own private circle of friends. Hidden from view by clumps of oaks and pines lining the street, the homes were further walled on either side by massive hedges or rows of gigantic Leyland cypress.

Pontellis lived in a mountainous Georgian mansion one could only see when nearly upon it.

"I'm glad that real estate agent talked me out of Buckhead," Nick told his wife Jasmine one morning at breakfast two months after they had moved in. "Over there, everybody knows everyone else's business. Here, you don't ever see the people next door."

Arriving home, he steered around the gentle curve of the long, uphill drive. It forked one way toward a circle in front of the huge porch running the width of the structure, and the other direction to a four-car garage at the end of a massive turnaround. Just as he turned toward the garage and raised the door with the remote, his head yanked sideways as the shrubbery nearby appeared to rattle. But Pontellis shrugged it off and pulled the car inside.

He watched his rear-view mirror, and immediately the form of three people took shape. Without hesitating, he grabbed his cell phone and punched a speed-dial number, then swiftly reached up

4

and activated the garage door, lowering it as the last of the three intruders dashed inside.

Nick calmly opened the car door and held a bare hand up, as if to signal surrender. But in the next instant, he sprang from the car. As his handcrafted calfskin cowboy boots hit the floor, he fired his .38 caliber special three times in rapid succession.

The invaders, dressed in black clothes and ski masks, fell back, startled. One dropped to his knees clutching his face. Split seconds later, the garage was a torrent of sound and smoke.

"Son of a bitch! Dirty bastard!" burst out in desperation, mixed with the deafening thunder of gunfire.

Pontellis got off one more wild shot as he turned and scrambled toward the door into the house. One of the robbers fired his 9mm semiautomatic pistol, emptying it at the club owner.

The shots riddled Nick's back with one impact after another. His body recoiled. As he went down, he managed to squeeze off a final round. Another trespasser staggered.

The shooting stopped. The cacophony was eerily replaced by utter silence. The acrid sting of gun smoke saturated the air. Pontellis lay motionless, his sidearm still clutched in his bloody hand, his expensive silk suit splotched with multiple scarlet wounds. Spent shell casings littered the floor. Sirens wailed outside, at a distance but rapidly growing ever-louder.

"Christ, let's get out of here," one of the men screamed, blood oozing through his mask. He gurgled and coughed as he yanked it off, gasping desperately. He reached up and grabbed the handle to manually raise the garage door. He tugged, but was too weak and the door didn't budge.

"Screw that," the unwounded intruder yelled. He pulled down a mallet hanging on the garage wall, and with a grunt bashed the door, shattering it. With two more swings he had pummeled a hole large enough for them to climb through.

Two sets of cruisers turned from the street into the long drive toward the house, blue lights flashing and sirens blaring. The three men, even the one limping, raced at full speed toward the woods surrounding the Pontellis property and disappeared.

The patrol cars skidded to a stop. Four officers dashed to the garage. The first to reach it gazed in through the gaping hole with thick smoke filtering out. "Holy crap!" he exclaimed. "It looks like the Iraq war was fought in there."

1 THE ATL

IN THE SPRING before Nick Pontellis was killed in the garage of his Atlanta home, the weather was milder than any in recent memory. Soft rains had fallen throughout April. May had exploded with a showy array of pink, white, red and violet azaleas so profuse that out-of-towners drove through residential neighborhoods to marvel at them.

As Grace Gleason drove toward the Channel Six building, she noted the rainbow of colors in her new city—The ATL or Hotlanta—the city too busy to hate. The resting place of Dr. Martin Luther King, Jr., site of the world's busiest airport and the 1996 Olympic Games, headquarters for a worldwide cola company, hub of two major airlines, cradle of the Handy Harry home improvement chain.

And nightmare traffic. Grace crept down Peachtree Street, one of the thousands inching their way toward work, even at the early hour of six-thirty. Her first meeting would be at eight, but on her initial day she wanted to get settled beforehand.

During a test run on Saturday, she had driven the route from her townhouse in fifteen minutes. Today, Monday, it was forty minutes and counting.

Almost there, she thought. *This afternoon I'll look into the mass transit routes.* She peered upward through the windshield. *At least this turtle's pace is giving me a chance to look around at the buildings.*

Looming ahead was Trans-United Bank, the tallest building in any U.S. city that wasn't New York or Chicago. It was built in the early nineties, she had read online. But it was now in bankruptcy. The building boom that had brought 100,000 new residents a year to Atlanta for a decade had faded with the folding economy. Not only was the housing market in financial distress, but so were commercial properties such as this magnificent structure.

Grace turned up the winding, tree-lined drive toward her new workplace. She felt her heart racing a bit. Even a seasoned news reporter could suffer a tinge of apprehension at the unknown.

The News Beat Six station, number one in the metro market, had sought her out. There had been no submission of audition tapes, no formal interviews. A surprise call from Vivian Ellis, recently named news director for the powerful outlet, had turned into an hour-long phone conversation. Then came a visit by the fast-talking, aggressive Ellis to Dallas where Grace was covering crime for the top station.

They had lunch at a small diner where Grace often met with a detective she had not only developed a professional relationship with, but had also grown close to.

"I know your work," said Vivian, a trim black woman with short-cut, blond high-lighted hair and almond-shaped eyes framed by neatly threaded eyebrows. "My closest sister lives near Dallas, in Arlington, and I watch your station when I'm visiting. Your tenacious reporting gets an A in my book. I'm curious. Why haven't they made you an anchor?"

"It's a long story. Suffice it to say I really like what I'm doing."

Vivian had wolfed down her sandwich in about four bites and took a swig of sweet tea. "Grace, I'm trying to create something new and exciting in Atlanta, and I think you're the person to help me."

Grace was intrigued by the unconventional overture. "What's it about? And why me?" she asked.

"You know as well as I do the news business is changing. We see young kids coming in right out of journalism school who don't know a subpoena from an archeological dig. Can't spell and can't write. They hustle, rely on questionable sources, sometimes do their own camera work and don't give a hoot about objectivity. They commandeer footage coming in off the street, some of it awful quality but much of it still relevant. And they're getting hired at the expense of veterans, because that's how a news director keeps control."

"It's not all that haphazard, is it?" Grace challenged.

Ellis broke into a smile, showing perfect white teeth against her mahogany skin. "Of course not. I'm sometimes accused of hyperbole. But it's a trend that will snowball, even on the nets and cable systems. Television news will putrefy like last week's table scraps. I'm worried that our station is going down the slippery slide just like everyone else.

"But I don't want to hit bottom. I want my tenure as news director to set a tone. News Beat Six in Atlanta can take these trends in the right direction. We'll keep the hustle and the fearless attitudes of the kids, but balance it with some experienced objectivity and responsibility at the same time."

She paused and gazed into Grace's eyes with the dead-serious demeanor of a soldier going into battle. "I'm new at Channel Six, but not to Atlanta. I grew up in the city, and I know what will work there. We'll have a hard-hitting reporter staff that our viewers look up to and not switch over to the cables. News hawks who will push the anchors to a higher level. I have a unique plan for this."

She paused, half-smiling, waiting for Grace's curiosity to bud.

"Which is?" she bit.

"It's still percolating. But basically it's continuous coverage of a critical crime or political corruption story throughout the week. A serial story, so to speak, pregnant with intrigue. It would be covered in regular news reports and then capped off twice a week by hard-hitting, ten-minute segments as part of our news programming. These segments would pull the subject matter together for our viewers, complete with opinions and finger-pointing."

"You mean a crime-stopper show like everyone's doing?" Grace tried not to sound underwhelmed, she realized too late.

Unfazed, Vivian shook her head and leaned forward, her dark

eyes sparkling with enthusiasm. "No. Much more, Grace. Crime stoppers hop from story to story. One day, maybe two, and they're gone. I'm talking about getting into the weeds with the cops, the perps and prosecutors. Digging up intelligence nobody else has. Taking chances. Reporting on it every day in one of our newscasts until it has everyone's attention. Then going for gold twice a week with compelling insights no one can turn off. My working title is *Crime and Corruption*, but I'll get the host's input on that."

Grace liked this woman's tenacious attitude. She whistled lowly. "You're passionate about this."

"To my husband's chagrin," Vivian chuckled. "He thinks I'll be working eighty-hour weeks and then get run out of town. When I was a young girl, an editor for Atlanta's daily newspaper was fired because his investigative work hit too close to some unassailable institutions. I was too naive to understand at the time, but it became the stuff of lively discussions in journalism school. That newspaper is part of the same company that owns our station, but I'm not going to let past disputes influence my decision-making."

Ellis leaned forward with her elbows on the table, the index fingers of both hands pointed directly at Grace. "I need a strong personality to pull it off. Someone who's not afraid to look the bad guys right in the eyes and report on it. You're the person I want to help me launch this baby." She leaned back and took a huge breath. "What do you think?"

"This is coming at me pretty fast," Grace gasped in bewilderment. She was fighting a huge grin. *If this woman is true to the talk,* she thought, *we could be a lot alike.* "It's intriguing," she said, "but I have a daughter in college here and a several other reasons to say no."

"Couldn't your daughter move with you? Atlanta has colleges," Ellis said, a positive, playful glint lighting up her expression.

Grace looked down, considering her response carefully as

she decided how much to say. "It's…complicated," she offered. "Megan has decided she wants to go into architecture, so there's the issue of where she could get in. Who would transfer her credits? Beyond that, if I'm living close to her, I'll be much more at ease. I did a story here once that inadvertently put her in horrible danger."

Ellis waited, but Grace offered no further explanation. She wasn't about to open the healing wounds of covering a criminal who had wreaked havoc with their lives.

"That's why I came to you…I understand it's a life-changing decision," Vivian said. "But Grace, this is your chance to expand dramatically what you do—to appeal to a wider audience. As you got traction, they would not just be our followers, they would be yours."

Grace hesitated, impressed, running her fingers through her hair in contemplation, knowing Vivian wanted an immediate response. "Can you give me a week? And then let me call you with the thousand questions I can't think of right now?"

The news director gave her a warm, reassuring smile. "One week."

**

Grace took the bait. In less than a month, she had given notice, bought an Atlanta home and agreed to today's start date. Pulling into the Channel Six parking lot, she remembered how a first look at her new building the previous weekend had evoked an involuntary gasp. Channel Six wasn't the utilitarian, concrete block type of structure that so commonly housed broadcast stations. It was called The Plantation, aptly named for the stately antebellum homes it resembled.

And then there were the trees. The Plantation's colossal structure was surrounded by a plethora of green. Massive oaks. Spreading maples. Full, magnificent magnolias reaching fifty feet skyward. Grace paused momentarily near The Plantation's impressive entrance and took a deep breath.

She had thought hard about making this change. Megan's situation had been paramount. Then there was the rationale for leaving what she considered a great job. In Dallas, she had fought hard to win the acceptance and support of her management. Yet she was still just one of the news crew, albeit valued. She knew she had made a difference on some level. She had definitely contributed to the station's top ratings. But if Vivian Ellis' ambitions were on target, Grace might have an opportunity to sway an entire community—to change how a city viewed itself.

She reached the huge double-doors. Inside, Mrs. Nicholson smiled up from her desk in the front of the cavernous atrium. Grace had spoken to her several times on the phone. The receptionist had sounded pleasant enough, but not especially warm. The gray-haired, plumpish woman greeted her with a firm handshake.

"Come with me," she directed and walked briskly back to the newsroom door. The place was still nearly empty and quiet. "This is your workspace," she gestured, her stark-blue eyes gazing at Grace over the rims of reading glasses. "Log into the computer and create your own password. There's a company cell phone in the drawer. Coffee is over there," she pointed. "Let me know if you need anything." She pivoted and disappeared.

Grace had barely arranged her desk and logged onto her computer when the familiar, ardent voice of Vivian Ellis floated toward her cubicle.

"You're here early. All settled?" the news director asked with highly caffeinated energy. From their first meeting, Vivian had struck Grace as friendly but abrupt and systematic, oddly masculine for an attractive woman—but more from an assertive mien than appearance. Hard-charger, Grace would have described her if anyone had asked.

"I'm getting there," Grace smiled.

"And what about your daughter Megan. Any decision?"

"It's hard to pull her away from her home state," Grace sighed. "The Texas A&M architecture school offered to transfer most of her credits. But Georgia Tech has been very positive, and it's in everybody's top twenty. I was able to convince her to come up here so we won't be miles from each other."

Ellis smiled knowingly. "That guy? The murderer you covered who attacked her?"

Grace stared, her mouth gaping open.

Vivian emitted a spirited laugh. "You don't think I would hire someone without knowing everything about her, do you?"

Grace didn't want to have this conversation right now. Every time she thought about a killer going after her daughter, she choked up.

"I might need a couple of days to help her move," she said.

"Of course." Vivian nodded and started to leave. "See you at morning meeting." Then she turned back. "Oh, Grace, Jackson Davis."

Grace raised her eyebrows, inquisitive.

"One of our anchors. I'm just getting to know him, but it's obvious he has contacts all over town. He has already hooked me up with some of the people I need to know. Might be willing to do the same for you." She sped away through the newsroom like a Kansas whirlwind.

**

An hour later, at five until eight, Grace snatched up her electronic tablet, pulled up a note-taking app, and exited her cubicle to rush to staff meeting. In her haste, she almost ran headlong into a tall, square-faced man emerging from the cube across the aisle.

He guffawed boisterously and extended a hand. "Jackson Davis," he introduced himself in a deep and unctuous voice.

"Hi, Jackson. I'm Grace Gleason." She smiled, noticing his sandy-colored hair was so carefully combed and sprayed it resembled wax.

They walked together toward the conference room.

"Welcome to Big Six News Beat," he intoned with the flamboyance of a man always yearning to be noticed. "I'm one of the anchors. Let me know if there's anything I can do to help you get started around here." He stepped back and motioned her, regally, into the meeting space.

"Thanks," she smiled, trying to be sweet. "You can count on it."

Morning meetings were held every day. Reporters, producers, most of the editors and some of the daytime anchors participated. Grace was eager to learn if the meetings were less contentious and political than those at her last station where she had regarded them as total disasters.

"First," said Vivian Ellis in a business-like tone, "everyone say hello to Grace Gleason. As you probably know, she comes to us from Dallas." Grace was greeted by a series of waves and a handshake from a young Hispanic woman next to her.

"And across from her, meet our newest hire out of Georgia's School of Communications, Scott Matthews. He just finished his master's in journalism and won national honors reporting for the university's daily newspaper," she said. They repeated the greeting ritual. Grace was taken aback at how young Matthews looked, an impression made more acute by a tuft of a beard so thin it bordered on absurd.

Then she realized he was not much older than Megan. She wondered if she was that much older or if professionals in the news media were getting younger. These questions were bubbling up with alarming frequency.

"Down to business," Ellis said with trenchant impatience in her voice. "Tom?"

Grace quickly inferred he was the assignment editor.

"Okay. Reviewing what's been covered in the early shows…" Tom started, and ran down the list of murder, accident and fire stories they had aired. He concluded with, "Might want to carry that DUI story as filler later today, since the arrested party is on the city council up in Maryville."

After Tom had exhausted the list of stories, Vivian took firm control of the meeting. "Jackson shared a story he has picked up through a contact," she began. "Surveillance on some houses up in Gwinnett County the cops think is a crystal meth factory. Grace, I want you to take it."

Grace nodded and jotted a note on her tablet. She glanced at Jackson who smiled with what she considered a patronizing expression. She knew that anchors sometimes shared such leads with the news director to garner favor, as they changed stations every two or three years in the big markets. Since Vivian was new, Grace imagined Jackson needed to cement a relationship quickly to prevent the news director from supplanting him with her own favored replacement.

Grace also knew these were the types of stories news directors passed to their new reporters in hopes of launching their success.

She smiled back at Jackson, trying her best to appear grateful.

"Now, let's go around the table," Tom said. "What story ideas do you have to share?"

"I'm checking out a tip that the Creekside area might push the state legislature for cityhood," offered a bespectacled Asian reporter Grace thought was probably in his fifties. "There's a pro group and an anti group, so there's a fight brewing."

"That's pretty interesting," chimed in a young woman Grace pegged as a producer. "I might want to put that in my show."

"It sucks," hissed Vivian bluntly. "These cityhood fights go on for years, and they're boring. Forget it. Can't you chase down something with more urgency?"

The reporter failed to respond, instead staring down deject-edly at his notes.

"Maybe you're right," the producer backed down meekly in the face of the news director's vitriol. "We'll hold off until it goes to court."

The exchange astonished Grace, since it seemed out of char-acter from the Vivian Ellis she had observed to this point. It was then she realized that whatever Vivian's good intentions might be, she was a product of her job. Most news directors were bullies who chewed their staff up. Back in the day, news directors respected their anchors and reporters and trusted their skills. Now, people were struggling to hold onto their jobs, hoping they weren't considered to be over-priced talent that provided a reason for management to dump them like a CEO opting to outsource production for cheaper labor rates in Asia.

Complicating the battle of nerves, the directors worked from fear that if a general manager noticed stories on other newscasts they had missed, they could be the ones walking the unemployment line.

Grace was relieved when the meeting ended. She had es-caped drawing anyone's ire, and she had a great story lead. She grew excited as she sped through the hallway toward the newsroom.

Jackson Davis caught up from behind and slowed her down, lightly grasping her arm the way a docent steers a visitor around a museum. He was sporting his constant, condescending grin. When Grace stopped and stared at his hand, the anchor removed it sheep-ishly.

"Men have been sued for that in the workplace," she warned politely.

He examined her expression, appearing to determine if it were a joke.

She didn't smile.

"Sorry," he muttered, sounding befuddled.

"Anyway, thanks for the story lead." She dug deep to overcome a negative first impression and to sound cheery.

Davis brightened and feigned confidentiality. "Eduardo Cruz," he said.

"That's your contact?"

"I'll give you his phone number. Always happy to help the newbie in town."

She grimaced mentally but managed her best to maintain a pleasant demeanor.

As they neared their cubicles, Jackson swept his hand toward the wall above them, lined with photos of the station's news talent, mostly women. "The wall of shame," he said, mocking.

She cocked her head, curious.

"There's Maggie Martin," he blustered. "Sleeps with half the guys in the state senate. That's LaShana McIntyre, busted at a marijuana party. That's…"

"Enough," Grace interrupted, feeling her face grow florid. "I have to get to work."

He fixed his eyes on her for a moment and shrugged. "I'll get that phone number."

As Davis disappeared into his workspace, Grace wondered how long it would take this overbearing boor to add her to his "wall of shame."

    **

Ten minutes later, she forgot all about Jackson Davis and his disdain for the women on the wall when she called Eduardo Cruz.

"I'd like to meet you and learn about the drug war you're fighting," she said.

"Sure, can you drive up here?" He sounded young and pleasant.

"How about lunchtime? Tell me where your station is, and I'll come pick you up."

"No, we need to meet," he answered quickly, and she realized he wanted to maintain privacy. He gave her the name and address of a restaurant. "See you at noon."

Grace hung up and smiled. She would be digging into her first juicy story for Big Six, and she was as jubilant as a child who discovered a new swimming hole.

2 EDUARDO

RAUL CRUZ, Eduardo's father, grew up outside Monterrey, Mexico's third largest city. His family had labored in the fields for decades before moving into the city to work in the steel mills. Raul and his eight brothers and sisters worked alongside their parents for meager wages. They were part of the poorly educated, low-skilled laborers that lived in squalid conditions across the city from the upper class in a divided society with little middle class.

Raul was twenty-eight years old when he married a co-worker's sister in 1979. He and his wife Juanita had their first child, Eduardo, a year later and Christina came along the following year.

By then, Raul was thirty, and although he had little formal schooling he was street smart. First he told Juanita they must not have more children, that they could not afford to feed more than two. And he began to consider how to better their condition. Every day, as he trudged to work in the hot mill, he thought there must be greater opportunity someplace else. The so-called Mexican Miracle, a period of unprecedented economic growth and prosperity, had pulled wages up and expanded industries. But by the time Little Eduardo was a year old and Christina was on the way, the country's fortunes had reversed. Payments of foreign debt were suspended. The peso was devalued. Inflation ran rampant, and families such as Raul's, already living day to day on low pay, increasingly struggled.

Raul told Juanita one morning before work they should consider a move to improve their fortune.

"But where would we go?" he posed in his native Spanish. "And how, with two babies?"

"I don't know," his wife shrugged helplessly. "Eat your breakfast."

That Friday afternoon, several co-workers, stopping with Raul for beers before going home, put an idea in his head. Raul pointed out their rich counterparts sitting across the barroom, divided from his group like the class-separated city and country they lived in. The affluent drank the crisp, clean Corona from bottles, the only way it was produced. Raul and his amigos consumed the cheaper, denser Tecate drawn from a tap.

"I actually prefer Tecate," he told his amigos. "Even so, I would like to have the choice. I just can't afford Corona. We need to do something."

"Los Estados Unidos," one said. *The United States.* The others nodded enthusiastically. *"Si. Los Estados Unidos."*

When his friends suggested slipping across the border to improve their lot in life, Raul thought about it seriously.

He talked about it all weekend until his wife said she had tired of the topic.

"If we're going there, do something about it," Juanita scolded.

"First we will need to save some money," he answered.

He had heard the stories. Mexicans had crossed into the U.S. freely during several eras since the Treaty of Guadalupe had ended the Mexican-American war and ceded much of Mexico to the U.S. In the 1800s, they were virtually invited to the northern republic to help build the railroads. During both world wars they were welcomed to American manufacturing sites. For more than a century, with only brief periods of resistance, unspoken agreements to permit border crossings brought cheap labor to United States corporations and agricultural concerns.

When Christina reached her first birthday, Raul Cruz packed up his wife and their two *ninos pequenos* and traversed the Rio Grande.

The Cruz family crossed at night, part of a group of two dozen people. When they arrived at the riverbank, a paid guide called a coyote met them.

"Two hundred dollars, U.S.," the man told Raul, who was surprised their helper was a local, probably sixty. He had heard most of the coyotes were young Americans.

"They told me one," Cruz protested.

"One to get to Texas, another one hundred for the truck on the other side. And for knowing how to avoid the authorities."

Raul glanced at Juanita with a frown; he had planned for such a complication, but the extra money would leave them with very little. He shrugged and paid the man.

The crossing point was shallow enough to wade across, but there was still concern. An acquaintance who had made the trip several times told Raul to brace against the current and be careful not to fall into a border canal where some had been swept to their deaths. Raul had fashioned a makeshift float from an old inner tube to carry the children. As he guided it across, Juanita followed, lugging three plastic bags with their clothes and other possessions.

Safely across, the sopping wet contingent clambered into the back of the old truck waiting for them not more than a mile from the Laredo bridges. *"Vaya Con Dios,"* Go with God, the coyote said with a wave and slammed the metal doors shut with a bang. It was crowded and dark and smelled of must and river water. No one spoke. Raul knew some people died in these passages, but usually from heat and lack of fresh air. Tonight it was cool. They would be okay.

The rickety vehicle raked into gear and rumbled across the bumpy road toward the highway. Soon they would be in a San Antonio safe house and become anonymous.

Raul and Juanita spoke little English and had no job. But they mingled with thousands in the same predicament. Information about jobs and opportunities spread among them more quickly than the Internet could ever accomplish decades later.

It was November 1981. Raul and Juanita had no idea how fortuitous was the timing of their move to America, for a bill in Congress four years later would bring them and three million of their fellow illegals incredible good luck. Within months after arriving in the new land, the young Cruz family found themselves living in a house on the Whitworth ranches near San Antonio, Texas.

Sam Whitworth owned two spreads less than one hundred miles outside the growing city. He didn't live on either. The foreman he had hired to oversee the entire operation, consisting of nearly 30,000 acres, lived in a huge stone house on the larger of the two properties. The main house and other buildings on the second ranch had become home for the several dozen undocumented immigrants paid to tend to the upkeep of the property. The men repaired fences, rounded up strays and corralled the longhorns to worm and vaccinate them. The women cared for the children and houses, did the gardening and cooked for *los hombres*. The foreman came around every day to see that his workers were performing their chores.

Raul and Juanita lived in the big house. There was only one room for them and the children, but they had access to the living room and kitchen, as all the other workers did. It was not much of a life, but even so, the pay was decent and meals were free. They learned very little English, working alongside others who were not bilingual. It was only after Eduardo, and then, Christina, became school age that the parents began to absorb some of the language.

Every day, the foreman had a bus pick up all the children and transport them to a schoolhouse on the edge of San Antonio. But as the Cruz children progressed through the elementary grades, they left their parents in the dust, linguistically.

The law that would bring them grace was the Immigration Reform and Control Act of 1986. Among other things, this legislation granted them amnesty, since they had moved to the United States before January 1, 1982. They were permitted to apply for temporary

22

residency, permanent resident status after that, and eventually green cards and a path to citizenship.

The Cruz family might have stayed in Texas for the rest of their lives, except that an extraordinary opportunity presented itself. A city to the north, Atlanta, Georgia, was selected in 1990 to host the 1996 Olympic Games. Word spread quickly construction workers were needed to prepare the city and open it to the world.

Raul had squirreled away enough money to get them there. Without any assurances, in early 1991 he bought four bus fares to Atlanta and said goodbye to the Lone Star State.

**

The informal immigrant network had supplied them with enough information—where to live, how to find work—to get them started. They quickly found an available two-bedroom rental in one of Gwinnett County's growing number of nondescript apartment complexes. The county population had once been virtually all white and black. But increasingly it was becoming brown.

It was five years until the Olympic Games would be there, and Eduardo's father was earning nearly one thousand dollars a week working construction projects. He and Juanita were also taking English classes, for they now aspired to be citizens, buy a house and stay in Atlanta until they died.

But young Eduardo, who was eleven at the time they re-located, faced problems he had never dealt with before.

"Hey, kid. You're new, right?" a next-door neighbor teenage boy said to Eduardo, falling in beside the newcomer. Eduardo was bouncing a basketball, walking home from shooting hoops in the nearby park. He gave the boy a "so what?" glance and continued walking and dribbling.

"You need to join up."

"To what?"

"*Los Lagartos*. We are family. We look out for each other."

23

The older boy pulled out a pack of cigarettes and pushed one toward Eduardo, who shook his head no. The teen shrugged and lit one up. "Listen, when I first came here I was about your age. Everyone picked on me. We didn't have numbers then, we were on our own. But now we do. And we have each other's backs. No one screws with *Los Lagartos* no more." He pulled up his sleeve and displayed a tattoo of a lightening bolt running through double L's on his forearm.

Eduardo stopped walking and stared at the marking. "I just want to play basketball and ride my bike," he replied innocently. "School will start in two more weeks."

The older boy took a puff and scoffed. "School is where it is the worst. You'll learn. When they start beating you down, taking your lunch money, you'll come running to us. *Comprehende?*"

Eduardo shrugged, not grasping fully this thing called *Los Lagartos*.

Two weeks later he had his first lesson in civics. Dusk was falling as he rode his bicycle home from a quick trip to the store for his mother. The nights were getting cooler, and he shivered a little from not wearing a shirt.

The apartment complex had one way in and one way out. As Eduardo pedaled through the entrance, trying to ride faster to beat the setting sun, something hit his bicycle hard, throwing him off. He realized someone had run from behind and kicked it. He lay sprawled on the grass as several bigger boys descended on him, pounded him with their fists and kicked him mercilessly.

Each blow seemed harder than the preceding one. Young Cruz tried to scramble away and run, but there were too many and they were too big. He took a dozen blows before a car pulled up and they all scattered like seeds in the wind.

It happened in a furious moment. There had been no time to think, just react.

24

Except that he had noticed something. One of the fists that had pummeled him was attached to an arm sporting the "LL" logo with a lightning bolt. The tattoo was his clue the people *Los Lagartos* would supposedly protect him from had not attacked him. It was the gang's own brand of recruiting by intimidation.

The car was a police cruiser. As Eduardo painfully picked himself up and began to examine the damage to his bicycle, the officer who was driving stepped out.

"You okay, son?"

"Yeah. My wheel's bent."

The policeman approached him and knelt down to examine the damage. "You can straighten it out. Who did this to you?"

"I don't know them."

"What'd they look like?"

"It happened too fast."

"Listen, kid, my name is Officer Ortega. If they do it again, see if you can get a description and then call me at the police station. I know all the gang-bangers in this neighborhood. They know I won't put up with this stuff."

Eduardo nodded and watched the patrol car pull away. He liked the policeman. He was serious, but nice. His uniform was cool, and he was carrying a gun. Eduardo thought he might want to be a police officer someday.

**

On the drive toward the Chattahoochee Mall, Grace realized for the first time how out-of-water she was. Everything in Dallas had become second nature to her, and now she would need to feel her way through a strange city. New sources. Different relationships. Unfamiliar routes to destinations. She hadn't felt this lack of confidence in years.

She pulled off the interstate onto the four-lane avenue misnamed Gwinnett Highway. As she entered the busy thoroughfare, not really a highway at all, the neighborhoods seemed invisible to her. Although she was passing through one of the metro area's busiest and most over-developed business districts, the housing areas abutting it were completely obscured by a thick veil of oaks and pines.

Thank the Lord for GPS, Grace thought as she spotted a small sidewalk café near a gargantuan mall, the state's largest. She parked in front and saw a police officer seated at a small table outside on the corner. She knew immediately it was Officer Cruz.

Her reporting experience had trained her to absorb a lot of information immediately. She soaked in many impressions as she walked toward the officer. Dark, smooth face. Buzz cut, no sideburns. Crisp-looking short-sleeved uniform, highly polished shoes. Bulked-up shoulders and muscular arms. There was a full cup of coffee in front of him. He had obviously just arrived.

"Grace Gleason," she said, sounding friendly as she extended her hand.

He half-rose as he shook it. "Officer Eduardo Cruz. Nice to meet you," he said with the self-conscious mien of a schoolboy.

"Sorry I'm late. I'm a transplant, and I'm still finding my way. Had to rely on GPS.'"

He laughed and leaned back, seeming to relax. "Things are in the saddle and ride mankind." His English carried only a modicum of accent.

"What's that from?" she asked curiously, sitting down across from him.

"I think it was Ralph Waldo Emerson describing machines."

"Emerson. Do you read a lot?"

"Some," he responded. "We had a great English teacher at Gwinnett County High. But these days, most of what reading time I have, I devote to the Bible."

"You're a Christian?" she asked.

"Catholic. 'Go into all the world and preach the gospel to every creature,'" he recited. "That's from Mark. Jesus was saying it to his disciples, but I also think he was speaking to me—to all of us." He smiled at her lightly intrigued expression. "And you? Do you have a church?"

The question didn't startle her as much as her answer did; she hadn't given her spiritual views much thought in a long time. "I did when I was growing up," she reminisced. "Good Chicago Catholic family. But I sort of got away from it when I went to college and then out on my own."

"You're not alone. That's sort of the way the world is these days, isn't it?"

There was an uncomfortable silence.

"So, you're from here?" she asked to break the awkwardness. "Gwinnett County?"

He nodded. "Moved here when I was a kid. I've seen the metro area spread out and swallow up my little hometown of Shoreville. Gwinnett isn't your father's sleepy little county anymore. I don't mind the crazy, out-of-control growth so much. I just hate the crime that has come with it.

"There were gangs when I moved here, and they could get rough sometimes. But they were more like social families that stuck up for each other. The worst they did was shoplift, penny-ante property damage, fights with other organizations. Somewhere along the line the gang scene changed. They became vicious and dangerous and entrenched in drug warfare. They amassed huge sums of money and killed for revenge."

The waitress arrived, a disinterested young woman with tattoos, nose ring and orthodontic braces. They both ordered hamburgers and fries.

"As I told you on the phone, Jackson Davis gave me your number," Grace said as the waitress retreated into the building. "I'm launching a series of news reports on crime, and he thought you might help me get up to speed on the drug war here."

The officer responded, "He told me yesterday you would call."

Yesterday? Grace thought. *So Davis had this whole thing rigged with Vivian before I hit the office.*

Cruz continued, "Jackson's my brother-in-law."

"You're kidding," Grace reacted.

"The other anchor he's married to—Christina Cruz—is my sister."

"Oh, my gosh," exclaimed Grace. "I just met your sister this morning. Her workspace is next to mine and across from Jackson's. I didn't realize they were married."

"Ten years," Eduardo told her.

The waitress brought the hamburgers. "Anything else?" she asked, gazing at the passing traffic with the enthusiasm of a dishrag.

They both shook their heads no, and when the woman laid the bill between them, Grace put her hand on it and slid it to her side.

Cruz made no gesture of protest. "I'll let you take it since we're here on business," he said. "But understand I'm not on the arm."

"What?"

"On the arm. It's cop-speak for the guys who take free meals and gratuities for just doing the job they're paid to do."

"That's a new expression for me," she admitted.

"My initial experience with it came from a run-down little Shoreville restaurant on my first post. I paid for my six-dollar lunch with a ten. The owner, who was also the cashier, gave me back a five, four ones and four quarters in change. In other words, he was giving me a meal on the arm."

"Did you take it?"

"I walked back to the table and left six dollars on top of the tip I'd already left. That sent a message back to the owner." He bit into a huge bite of hamburger and chewed slowly as he talked. "There are some cops who think the blue uniform and shield are their right of passage. But I never felt that way."

Grace felt uncomfortable listening to his story. A detective in Dallas she had worked with and admired greatly had regularly accepted free coffee and sometimes meals. She changed the subject.

"I've been researching the drug problems in Gwinnett County," she began.

"What have you learned?" he asked.

"Only what little Google turned up. That it's one of the hottest spots for smuggling illegal substances in the United States. That the Latino gangs are getting out of control again, even though you crippled them with a huge raid ten years ago, that you guys, and the DEA and FBI are having a hard time tracking down all the crystal meth labs hiding in the quiet little subdivisions."

He squinted. "I grew up fishing the streams here before it got overrun with development. This place was as American as apple pie and baseball, not some damned outpost on the Mexican cartel trail..." his voice faded, his eyes lowered to his coffee mug. He took a deep breath. "The Hispanic population in Gwinnett twenty years ago was just over eight thousand. I was one of them. Now, it's over one hundred thirty thousand. Most of them are good, hard-working, law-abiding people. They labor in the chicken factories up north, clerk in grocery stores and gas stations and—yes—some percent are illegal and clean houses or mow yards. But what has changed more than the population is the amount of crime. My sons kick a soccer ball down the street and I don't know if it's rolling past a crystal meth house or not. Of course, I keep a careful eye out in my own neighborhood. Even though these facilities can be easily hidden, there are also ways to detect them."

Grace took her tablet out of her purse. ""We're off the record here," she assured. "I just need some memory joggers for interviews. How big a problem is the drug business here?"

"One DEA consultant told us that in recent years, the feds have seized more drug money in Atlanta than any other region of the country." He grinned like a trivia show emcee. "I'll give you a test. Until the past few years, do you know what the meth production capital was of the United States?"

"I have no idea. Spanish Harlem?"

"Iowa," he said, laughing as she sat up, startled. "So it's happening in the most unsuspecting places. We don't know how many labs we have right here in our backyard, but I believe we have now become the capital."

Grace typed on her tablet briskly. "This is exactly the kind of story I was brought here to uncover," she said excitedly. "Officer Cruz, do you think there's enough here to carry it forward for an entire week?"

He leaned back and chuckled. "Are you kidding? There's enough to run for a decade if you want. We are busting these guys, but we're always one step behind them. A decade ago we put together a team—us local cops and federal agents. We broke up the biggest gang, *El Grupo Leal*, or EGL, which controlled the drug trade here. Now other groups are filling the vacuum, and even the remnants of that organization are recruiting like crazy. It's a running war, as vicious and menacing as anything in Mexico. Just more secretive."

"How can we get started?" she asked, laying some money on top of the check.

He considered for a moment. "I need to know if I can trust you."

"Of course you can," she promptly responded, a little insulted.

"You must think about that question. I have information that can get me fired if you give me up. And get both of us killed if anything comes out in the open. This isn't like chasing down an arsonist or an alcoholic politician. This is dealing with the guys who cut off heads south of the border and hang their enemies from a bridge with their hearts cut out."

The image sent a tremor down Grace's back. "I've seen some of the video," she said.

"Then you know that if I tip you on a story, it must be an honor system between you and me."

"Cruz, I'm a news reporter and I learned one thing covering crimes in Dallas. I can be more effective if I cooperate with my cop sources."

"Quid pro quo?" he asked.

"I won't cross any lines," she responded. "But where I can help by pulling a punch—not jumping the gun on my source of information—and ultimately getting a better story, I'll do it."

"Tell you what," the officer responded. "No promises, but if I can, I'll let you know when something is going down. I won't compromise an operation, understand?"

She nodded agreement.

"But if it will help us nail these drug-peddling criminals who ruined my county and give you a story at the same time, so be it." He held out a dark, muscular hand, "Give me your card. If I have anything that might help you, you will hear from me. All I ask in exchange is discretion in handling the story so it's not obvious you were tipped off."

"I can do that," she answered. She extended her card. He took it and shook her hand with a firm grip, holding it for several seconds. His black eyes burned into her face, searching for final commitment.

"Why are you willing to help me, Cruz? If something goes wrong…"

He interrupted, "If all goes well, it will be you helping me. And my fellow officers. The public needs to understand what's happening here, what we're up against. They can be our first line of information about events occurring in their pristine, quiet little subdivisions."

He stood and looked down at her as she gathered her bag and tablet. "You will hear from me soon." He paused for a moment. "'Prepare yourself and be ready, you and all your companies that are gathered about you; and be a guard for them.'" He grinned at her puzzled reaction. "That's Ezekiel."

He turned and walked to his squad car, climbed in and drove off quickly. As she stood and watched him leave, Grace was simultaneously exhilarated and frightened. The emotions that had gripped her many times in pursuit of a murderer in Texas, less than two years ago, now were raging through her once again like a river in the middle of a spring thaw.

Officer Eduardo Cruz seemed like a straight shooter. And his sister and brother-in-law were now her colleagues. But his words darted through her brain, chilling her optimism: *"…can get both of us killed if anything comes out in the open."*

She realized from his very first phone call, she needed to treat her relationship with Cruz as if it were the Holy Grail.

3 CRIME AND CORRUPTION

FOR TWO WEEKS Grace worked with Vivian Ellis, planning the format for her news segment and gathering content material. Ellis had set the opening date for mid-June and turned the promotions department loose on a citywide publicity campaign. The news director obviously considered Grace's introduction to the market a big deal, and the station's expectations were high.

To Grace, that meant she had to pull good ratings, not just on the afternoon newscasts, but especially on her twice-a-week specials.

The date loomed in her mind like the countdown to a new year, ripe with excitement but also apprehension over the unknown.

Only two days before lift-off, Grace was on her computer, intent on gathering some compelling facts, when Vivian appeared at her workspace with two people in tow.

"I want you to meet your producer," Vivian enthused. "This is MaryAnne McWherter." The producer nodded slightly, seeming unsure.

Grace had assumed her segment would fit into the newscast's regular staff. Instead, they were assigning someone to her. It hadn't occurred to her this position was considered important enough to merit such consideration. She was surprised by a sudden burst of pride. Grace had garnered accolades for her work in the past, even received regional Emmy nominations. But her boss' announcement that she would get her own producer was far beyond expectations. It was an achievement she never could have imagined as a young journalism graduate fresh out of the University of Texas hoping to get a job.

She blinked back tears and looked astonished at Vivian, who grinned in acknowledgement.

Grace shook MaryAnne's hand eagerly. She recognized the young woman as the producer who had surrendered submissively at that first morning meeting rather than stand her ground with the new boss. Although Grace had formed an immediate, negative impression of McWherter that morning, she was ecstatic about not having to share her.

"I plan to work your butt off," she warned MaryAnne.

"No problem," the producer responded. "I'm excited to work with you."

"And this guy…" Ellis reached back and tugged playfully at the elbow of a shy, barely thirty-year-old man, thin, bearded, bespectacled, "…is David Williams, the best information tech in the business. He has already saved me several times from computer disasters."

"Hello," Williams nodded, his voice surprisingly deep and soft.

Grace nodded.

"Come on. We want to show you your set," Vivian said energetically, turning and moving swiftly through the newsroom. MaryAnne and David stood back as Grace followed the news director, but Vivian suddenly stopped. She swept her arm around the newsroom, smiling broadly at Grace.

"What?" Grace asked, confused.

"This is it. Your set," the news director announced triumphantly.

"The news room? I'm doing the show from here?"

Vivian turned toward the IT guy. "Tell her, David."

He stepped forward and motioned toward a corner of the room. "You've probably noticed some construction that's been going on over there," he said, pointing out a space that had been cordoned off. Two workers stood by, waiting.

"I assumed they were installing a new cubicle or something," she answered unknowingly.

Williams nodded toward the workers, and they quickly removed several screen panels to reveal a huge video monitor. "We've been installing the most modern, versatile multi-touch display in the world. No other local station has this kind of technology."

They moved to the screen.

"This is a ninety inch pro-cap—that's short for projected ca-pacitive—LCD display. I won't go into all of the technical specs…"

"Thank you for that," Grace interrupted, laughing.

"…but let me show you what it can do. It's similar to what some of the bigger networks use, but this is the latest version with all the B's and W's."

"B's and W's?"

"Bells and whistles," he answered.

"Well, if you're going to use a lot of technical terms…" she joked. He chuckled sheepishly, and Grace could tell she would enjoy working with this geek.

He continued, "Okay, so this baby has a storyboard software application, which is used to find out what the story is and analyze the information at your disposal. It can give you quick and easy access to any sources you have, power points, PDF's, maps…"

"Remote video?" she interjected, energized.

"Sure. It can access twelve live video screens. And apply touch cast technology so you can manipulate the information on the screen, such as a map. Watch this. I can pull up Google Earth from over here, focus it on Metro Atlanta, then reach up here and pull down a map of Channel Six and embed it into the Google version to give added detail. Now watch." With a few deft strokes of his fingers, David manipulated the conjoined maps one way, then the other, and then turned them into a three-dimensional view of the city and their station building.

"That's fantastic. Could I do this with Gwinnett County—embed specific neighborhoods to show what they look like?" Grace asked, trying hard not to sound giddy, her brain swimming with possibilities.

"You could do it with downtown Beirut if you wanted to," Mary-Anne broke in. "Watch him handle all this content with the software, use a link of a map within a map to tell a compelling story, then reach over there..." she nodded at David.

He pulled additional elements toward the maps.

"...and access different video," the producer continued, "or B roll footage or even a live feed, to link everything together to give depth to your story."

"It's easy to access all your video sources, interact with them, start and stop, switch around for emphasis," David said.

"All the time delivering your story," the producer finished David's thought. "It will be at your fingertips."

"Where will I sit?"

MaryAnne smiled. "You won't, much," she said. "We'll have a small table space in front of the screen, like those counters in stand-up lunchrooms. You can put notes on it and live guests can come in and park across from you. We'll put some tall stools there for convenience. But I envision you moving around dynamically, interacting with this LCD monster, switching from one app to the other, then getting in the face of your guests. Put your viewers in the newsroom with you. Create a sense of immediacy."

Grace was surprised at her producer's take-charge attitude, given what she had witnessed at the staff gathering. She realized she might have initially misjudged the young woman.

She turned to Vivian. "I'm sold." Grace watched them all smile at her approval. "But I'm also scared as hell," she added.

"Of what?" Vivian asked.

"Of...this. The technology. The prospect that a fuse might blow, or a widget could fail. We'll have to discuss how to handle glitches. It looks like a lot of very expensive hardware and software, and it'll be a challenge to use it expertly."

Vivian assured, "You're right—it's expensive, beyond what most local stations are willing to spend. This will be a test case for us, and management's counting on you and your ratings to justify the cost."

"Thanks for the added pressure," Grace joked.

"I hoped you'd like the idea of being in a different environment than the traditional anchor desk," McWherter probed.

"I do," Grace responded. "But David, your work is cut out for you. You have to teach a forty-something how to play Donkey Kong."

They disrupted the newsroom with spontaneous laughter. Grace enjoyed this collegial moment.

"You have forty-eight hours before your first program," Vivian reminded her. "Besides pulling the show together, you'll be rehearsing the use of this new gear with David and MaryAnne at your side."

She was terrified at the prospect of having to steer this complicated ship, with or without them.

**

In the next two days, she practiced using the screen and software several times, with David coaching. Although introverted people usually tested her patience, Grace liked him. Unlike techies who wear their superior knowledge like a badge, his demeanor was one of a joyful teacher, she thought.

After the second rehearsal session, she had gained confidence that she would use her new set to a huge advantage.

Yet there was the nagging prospect of equipment failure. Like all newscasters, she had experienced every kind of on-air faux pas ever imposed by a video glitch, or a wrong switch flipped, or some freak of nature visited on an unsuspecting field reporter. But this was different. This was the Titanic, new and shiny and full of promise. She prayed it didn't run aground.

Meanwhile, she knew the true challenge of the show would be her news judgment and how she delivered on it. Throughout the hours of story preparation, makeup, voice warm-up exercises and last-minute script edits, she felt a flood of anticipation cascading through her body.

**

Zero hour. The evening anchor, Christina Cruz, delivered the lead-in from the production studio. Grace's nerves automatically blocked out Christina's intro until the final words seemed to come out of nowhere: "...our newest addition to Big Six news, Grace Gleason."

Like a sudden cloudburst, everything went into overdrive. The red camera light flashed on and MaryAnne pointed toward her with authority.

She felt an adrenaline-infused onrush of energy. "Good evening. I'm Grace Gleason, and I'm excited to be the newest member of the Big Six News Beat family." She tried to ignore the chill surging through her. "This is 'Crime and Corruption.' I will report to you daily on elements of Metro Atlanta's underbelly. We'll expose the gangs, dealers, criminals and unscrupulous politicians who make your neighborhoods and the community dangerous and less livable. Then, twice a week, I will expand my report, posing all the hard questions you would want asked and bring in the folks who should have the answers. We will take our cameras into the dark and murky waters where the demons that threaten your well-being lurk."

Grace peered seriously into the camera. "Tonight, we examine the gang and drug wars that are destroying the peace and progress of Gwinnett County."

She slid quickly from her stool, stepped to the screen and touched an icon—a photo of a new Shoreville middle-class home. She pulled down a Google map of the neighborhood and embedded the photo into it. The two-story brick house was freshly painted and neatly landscaped. When Grace touched it, the image exploded full screen and activated a video scanning the neighborhood, then moved out to a nearby business district where people bustled into and out of stores in a mixed-use mall.

"Neighborhoods in this northern metro group of suburbs have been infiltrated by Latino gangs who have turned Atlanta into one of the key stops in the Mexican cartels' supply line of drugs and arms."

Grace tapped the screen and pulled the video to one side, then touched a different icon and a new video came to life. The camera panned across a cluttered, crumbling neighborhood with boarded-up buildings and gang graffiti scrawled across broken concrete walls.

As the video zoomed in and filled all ninety inches of screen, Latino youths flashed gang signs, flexed heavily tattooed biceps and mugged with sophomoric exuberance at the camera. Several young men and women raised their middle finger in obscene gestures, which was blurred out.

Grace pulled up a different video, a street scene on a dark street of a dozen squad cars parked in random disarray, blue lights flashing. Their high beams illuminated several officers cuffing suspects they had forced to the ground. A helicopter circled overhead, its rotor noise and searchlight adding to the drama.

"This is almost a nightly scenario in Gwinnett," Grace declared tersely. "Since the first of this year, police have arrested some seventy people on felony drug charges, recovered nearly three hundred fifty pounds of crystal meth, twenty-five hundred pounds of marijuana and three hundred pounds of cocaine. Police actions have netted nearly three million in cash, more than fifty assault rifles and pistols and countless truckloads of drug-making paraphernalia."

Touching the screen, she froze the scene behind her, depicting the close-up faces of the arrested gang members radiating defiance. *Well,* she thought thankfully, *at least the video worked the first time around.*

Grace returned to perch on her stool. A man and woman walked onto the set and slid into adjacent seats across from Grace.

The bearded, bespectacled gentleman could have easily been mistaken for a high school biology teacher. He wore blue jeans and a wrinkled navy blazer. The other, glancing darts at him, was a large black woman who held her head high with fire-breathing fight in her dark eyes. She wore a neat business suit and flowered scarf draping her neck.

"Travis Bolton is a community activist whose organization, Safe Streets, meets regularly with local police and county commissioners to push for more active law enforcement," Grace told her audience. "Mr. Bolton, what is being done in Gwinnett County to stem the swelling tide of gangs and contraband?"

"Not nearly enough!" the activist blurted in a strident tone that belied his mild-mannered exterior. "The local and county police departments up here don't have a clue. With help from federal agents, they took down a major gang ten years ago, but in the world of cartels, that's ancient history. Look where we are today—the epicenter of crystal meth production in the Southeast."

Grace started to interject another question, but Bolton raced on.

"Drug trafficking through the region and on out to the rest of the U.S. begins and ends right here. We've become their major hub. Sherman's march to the sea through Atlanta doesn't compare to what's happening right here, right now. And the Gwinnett County Council, with its weak courts and law enforcement policies, is helpless to do anything about it."

Grace asked, "Gwinnett police tell me their arrests and recovery of drugs and arms have increased every year. And you say?"

Bolton answered, "The county commission has budgeted diddly-squat for this conflict. They don't understand we're in a war. And the county police department's lack of coordination and cooperation with state and federal authorities has been pathetic."

"Let's get a point of view from the Gwinnett County Commission," Grace turned to her other guest. "Rashada Morton, you are the longest tenured commissioner. You've been here to see many of the changes Mr. Bolton spoke of. How do you react to his criticism?"

"Travis Bolton has stirred up unproductive trouble in Gwinnett County long enough," she spewed. "It's easy to show up at the council meetings and criticize the authorities when you don't have any responsibility..."

Bolton cut her off, "That's bull. My organization has put forward a comprehensive..."

"As I was saying," the councilwoman broke in, "we are working hand-in-hand with the ATF..."

"The Alcohol, Tobacco and Firearms Agency of the federal government," Grace clarified.

"Yes, and with the FBI and the Georgia Bureau of Investigation. We took down *El Grupo Leal*—The Loyal Group—the largest collection of gangs in the metro area."

"That was a decade ago!" howled Bolton. "We're right back where we were before. What have you done for us lately?"

"I'll tell you what," Rashada snapped, leaning in toward her adversary. "Our county has a gang task force which talks every day to our city police departments. We're making daily arrests, but there's a constant stream of contraband and cash coming in. It's a problem we're all dealing with just like every other city in the United States..."

The activist interrupted again, "Then why is Atlanta the biggest narcotics source in the South? Why do the county authorities you speak of so highly find us in the middle of the biggest problem in our history?"

Morton's voice rose as she pointed a finger at Bolton's chest. "You're trying to undermine everything we do. We will win this battle if loudmouths like you stay out of our way."

"Do your job and I'll go away," he erupted.

"No, you won't. Grace, gadflies like Travis Bolton make noise so their donations won't dry up."

"I totally resent that," the antagonist shot back, half-standing from his stool and tilting almost face-to-face with the councilwoman.

Grace broke in, terrified she was losing control. "Unfortunately we're out of time for this evening. Thank you Travis Bolton and Rashada Morton for being here. I'll have more tomorrow. Back to you, Christina."

Grace watched the monitor as her camera shut off and Christina Cruz's image reappeared from her anchor desk in the news studio.

"Thank you, Grace Gleason for that 'Crime and Corruption' report. More after this," she said, and a commercial came on.

Bolton slipped down from his stool, shook Grace's hand, muttered a hasty, "Thanks," and was gone.

The councilwoman sat simmering across the table, seemingly trying to regain her composure.

Grace offered a smile. "I promise you as I dig deeper into this story, I'll have you back, Rashada."

The woman's expression softened. "Fine, just so I don't have to deal with that man," she said and headed for the exit.

Grace heaved a sigh. She leaned back, pulled the microphone from her lapel and gave the producer and staff a quick "Thank you" with two thumbs up. She didn't let on that she felt a massive letdown. She had approached her debut with excitement, but her enthusiasm had dimmed about mid-segment. She realized it was long on bluster but short on compelling television. Grace had always set high expectations for herself and bore the brunt of self-criticism when she failed to measure up. Now the stakes were higher than ever. She was not simply reporting. She had a starring role, and she couldn't afford the luxury of trial and error. Every segment had to be golden. If she failed, she could not live with herself.

Christina wrapped up, *"Sunny skies tomorrow with a high of eighty-one. That's the news for this first day in June. We'll see you right back here tomorrow. Good night for Big Six News Beat."*

As Grace gathered her script, Christina appeared at the newsroom set. "Nice job," she said. "You really got your guests going at each other."

"Thanks," she tried to sound genuine, but as Cruz turned and left her spirits sagged. She knew two old warhorses squaring off against each other wasn't what her spot should be about. She wanted to lay out problems and offer answers. If she didn't breathe some substance into these segments, she would not only kill her own opportunity, but she might also bring Christina's newscast ratings down as well.

She felt like bursting into tears, but losing her composure in front of the crew would be disastrous. She left the set and walked slowly toward her workspace. It occurred to Grace that Vivian Ellis was absent. *Is she that disappointed?* she wondered. *Is she worried we've laid an egg, or is she in management's office defending a disappointing start?*

Arriving at her cubicle, she sank into the desk chair and stared at the blank computer screen feeling empty and dejected. She absently picked up her cell phone checking for messages.

"Grace, It's Eduardo Cruz," she heard her new source say. She sat up alertly at the Gwinnett officer's voice. *"Call me as soon as possible. Something's going down."*

She couldn't seem to dial the number fast enough. "Officer Cruz?" she tried not to sound overly ebullient. "It's Grace Gleason. What's up?"

"Something kind of sudden," he answered. "We're going to raid a crystal meth lab early tomorrow morning. The chief assigned me to the task force and said I wasn't to tell a soul."

"You know the information is safe with me," she reassured.

"I'll give you the details, but we need to agree on how you'll cover it. This is your chance to make good on your promise. If you jump the gun, our deal is dead."

4 METH BUST

THE BRIEFING ROOM at Gwinnett County Police head-quarters was an austere box with gray tile flooring surrounded by plain white walls. A dozen folding tables and chairs were set up for task force officers and agents, a small podium, computer and large screen for the briefing leader.

Deputy Chief Roosevelt Jones shuffled through a stack of papers on the rostrum. Jones had once been a formidable defensive end for the University of Georgia, but he eschewed a questionable run at playing professional ball for a career in law enforcement. His parents had named him after his father's favorite football player—Roosevelt Grier. Grier was the so-called "gentle giant," a member of the Fearsome Foursome of the Los Angeles Rams who later wrenched the gun from the hand of Robert Kennedy's assassin, Sirhan Sirhan.

Now Roosevelt Jones was physically just a memory of the rock-hard, three hundred pounder who for four years had dealt havoc on offensive linemen in the Southeastern Conference. He was forty pounds lighter and six inches wider around the girth. His brown skin sported dark age spots. Though he was not the athletic phenom he once had been, all of the officers in his unit showed him respect for his serious pursuit of criminals and stellar leadership.

On this morning, Roosevelt's chubby, aging face was furrowed into a frown of concentration. Gwinnett County officers, Atlanta police, federal marshals and FBI agents poured cups of coffee at a table in the back, then found seats. It was five-thirty a.m., and most of the task force members were still bleary-eyed from waking at the early hour.

Jones cleared his throat and tapped the podium. "Listen up, guys," he said in a deep, somber tone. He waited for the din of the group to settle. "I know we called you in unexpected. The force has been surveilling several suspected meth locations for weeks, but we didn't expect we could move this soon. We got some wiretap and stakeout information on one of these places, and now we have evidence another crime has been committed. So there's a reason to move in. We got a warrant and decided to act this morning."

"Do we have a no-knock?" a county officer asked.

"No," Deputy Chief Jones answered, to groans. He raised his hammy hands to signal silence. "Look, that's the judge's discretion— you know that. No-knock warrants are hard to get. Just ID as you hit the door. We want a minimum amount of time after giving notice. Surprise is our biggest advantage." He shuffled through the papers and briefed the team. "I've done the drive-by with the investigator and we're on the same page." He handed out a stack of the written raid plan to the front row to pass copies back. "This will give you more of the details."

Jones picked up a remote and activated the television. "This is the drive-by video we shot." It depicted a nondescript one-story ranch on a corner lot in a middle-class neighborhood. The moving image turned onto a side street for a block-and-a-half. The deputy froze the frame. The camera had captured a huge parking lot adjacent to a Handy Homer home improvement store.

"This area over here, just at the back side of the Handy Homer, is the staging site for the raid van and support vehicles. This early the only people around might be some delivery trucks, but the docks are on the other side of the building. We'll have privacy here." He paused and looked around at the group. "Most of you guys have worked together before so you know your roles. But look over the material to be sure you understand everyone's assignment. Also, who rides in what vehicles, and who's primary and secondary on entry."

The officers rifled through the plan.

Jones clicked his remote and pulled a diagram up on the

large screen. "Here's the house layout as best we can figure. You've got a copy in your material." He directed a laser pointer as he went on. "Primary entry door. Secondary entry." Pointing. "Windows here and here if necessary. Check the rooms and hallways. All these houses in this subdivision are pretty much the same."

He paused and took a sip of coffee. "Questions."

"Children?" asked an ATF agent.

"We don't know. No toys in sight. No sightings during surveillance. But some of these guys are pretty crafty, and they don't give a damn if they're endangering their own kids. I don't think so, but don't assume. At least six adults have been observed coming and going frequently. All the other traffic has probably been customers. There is a dog on the premises, probably inside for the night. Be alert. This raid is considered high risk."

"What about the other suspect locations? No coordinated raid?" Eduardo Cruz asked.

Jones frowned and shook his head. "Not enough evidence yet. The judge wasn't satisfied," he sneered, agitation in his voice. "Maybe hitting the one place, which we think is the biggest anyway, will influence them to shut down."

"Officers on the scene?" asked an FBI operative.

Jones nodded. "Shoreville police are there as we speak, staking it out. Two of you are on your first meth raid. Just remember your training. Be very careful with the evidence—chemical bottles, hoses, pressurized cylinders. Some of this stuff will be toxic and dangerous. Wear your helmet of course. We're taking masks but won't wear them until we see what we've got in there. First and foremost, we don't want them confused about who the hell we are. Let them know we're police right away."

He paused, his puffy brown eyes scanning the group. "All right. You have fifteen minutes to get your gear in order. Let's be safe, okay?"

The team members pulled on fireproof coveralls, gloves and boots in silence. They filed out to an adjoining lot where their transportation waited. They organized the equipment to be loaded in the vehicles—air purification respirators, self-contained breathing equipment, battering tools to break down doors.

The officers' apprehension took shape on their faces—clinched jaws, tight lips, squinting eyes—as they equipped the trucks. They couldn't know if these would be simple arrests with no gunfire, or a dangerous conflagration.

**

Traffic was building on the street near the Handy Homer. The task force vehicles were on the backside of the building, out of sight of the residents commuting to work. Also parked nearby were two Channel Six News Beat vehicles, a van and a larger truck with a satellite dish on top.

Deputy Jones stood in front of a cruiser with a large copy of the diagram of the neighborhood spread on its hood. Drivers of the vehicles were gathered around him.

"You two are here and here," he pointed, and they nodded. He pointed at a third, "Your trucks go around back."

Grace sat in the station van, watching the orderly preparation with her cameraman, Steve Jankowski. The photographer sat in the driver's seat slowly sipping coffee, staring blankly at the proceedings. His stiff, graying hair was barely combed, and his eyes were red.

Grace had met Steve the night before, after her call from Eduardo Cruz.

"Get Jankowski," Vivian Ellis had told her. "He's fast, and he'll keep you out of harm's way."

"They tell me you're the best," Grace said when she introduced herself and shook the bear-like man's big paw. "Hope you don't mind an obscenely early start tomorrow."

Jankowski managed a half-grin. "I rise with the birds. But I'll warn you, I'm not very pleasant until my second cup of joe."

Grace laughed at his honesty. She liked him instantly.

They sat quietly in the Handy Homer lot, gazing blankly at the activity. It was just beginning to turn light. "It's my first drug raid. Should we go in with them?" Grace asked, knowing the slight tremor in her voice made her nervousness obvious to her colleague.

Steve turned his bleary eyes toward her. "Depends on what we see," he said in a husky voice. "Meth houses can be dangerous, not just from the action but from what's inside. I might go in—I'll play it by ear—but you stay behind me. I'll get some good shots, and you can wait for the story to unfold," he said emphatically.

Grace nodded, although she knew she would follow her own instincts. *Steve doesn't know how impulsive I can be when news is breaking,* she thought. She glanced back at the station truck. The driver was obscured by the glint of the rising sun off its windshield, but she knew he would tag right behind them, then quickly park and prepare for a live feed.

Suddenly, all the officers were into the vehicles. Two vans peeled out of the driveway, followed by several cruisers. It all happened so quickly Grace's senses were jarred alive.

Jankowski jammed the van into gear and bolted out of the parking lot, a half-block behind them.

"Remember, we're not supposed to be here," Grace reminded as they drove. "We would normally hear about this from a tip from the neighborhood, or, God forbid, another media outlet. So we have to give it enough time that we don't piss off my source. We'll still beat the competition by plenty."

Steve Jankowski turned and puckered his brow at her, then returned his attention to driving. Grace felt foolish. He was a veteran photographer, nearly twenty years with Big Six News Beat, Vivian had told her. He had covered hundreds of big stories, and she was probably insulting him. Still, she had to stay true to Eduardo's demand.

Within minutes, the house came into view. The vehicles ahead of them skidded to a halt, two in front and the rest at the side and rear of the corner lot. Jankowski stopped the van a hundred feet away where it could not be seen from the direction of the raid target.

Steve jumped out, ran to the back of the truck and pulled out his camera equipment. As Grace stepped down, she could hear boots on the ground, running, the heavy, violent, pounding thunder of a horse race.

She turned to meet Steve at the rear of the van and instantly realized he was scurrying to the scene. She scrambled after him, checking her watch. Five-fifty-nine. Before she could look back up, she heard Bam! Bam! Bam!

"Police! Open up," shouted a federal marshal nearest the door.

He stepped aside and a county cop swung a battering tool. Bang! The jamb of the front door made a cracking noise as it shattered.

Grace jerked up to see a line of officers and agents rushing through the front door of the house, shouting orders. Her breath caught as Steve piled through the door right behind them, stopping just inside the entry with his camera light illuminating the scene.

"Damn it, Steve," she swore aloud. But adrenaline propelled her forward, up the three steps to the run-down front porch.

Inside, the sound of pandemonium assailed the morning quiet. "Down on the floor!" a policeman yelled, his pistol ready.

"Down! Now!" another barked. Grace couldn't see past the officers swarming into the room, but she heard bodies hitting the floor and the sound of boots running through the house.

Jankowski backed out. "They're cuffing the guys in there," he yelled to her. "I'm going to hang around the door and shoot them coming out. You grab the first officer you can as they exit."

Everything turned eerily silent. ATF agents filed out with four men and two women in handcuffs. They were dressed in bedclothes, looking sleepy and frightened. A Gwinnett County officer emerged with a crying toddler in each arm.

Seeing an opening, Grace quickly approached one of the suspects an agent led by the arm.

"Sir. *Señor,*" she called out. "Why are you exposing children to this kind of danger?"

Jankowski caught up and started shooting. An ATF man frowned and stepped into Grace's path as the Latino turned his face away from the protruding camera lens.

"No interviews," the Gwinnett officer scolded. "This one can't speak English anyway."

Grace saw a policeman emerge from behind the house with a German Shepherd, muzzled and leashed, leading him toward a car. She briefly entertained following her instincts and chasing after him, but Sergeant Gil Batista, the designated spokesman, came out onto the porch.

"Steve, come on," she said urgently, charging up the steps with the photographer close behind. "Officer Batista," Grace called.

Steve immediately turned the camera on him over Grace's shoulder.

"Did you find what you were looking for?"

"There's all kinds of paraphernalia in there for making meth," Batista responded.

"How many arrests did you make?"

"We've taken four males and two females into custody. In addition, DFACS is on the way to pick up the two children we found in the house."

"The Department of Family and Children's Services," Grace illuminated.

"That's right."

"What kind of contraband did you recover?"

"The crews with their hazmat suits are searching the site now," the sergeant pointed toward agents moving in and out of the front door. "We'll know more in a few hours. But we observed large amounts of what appears to be crystal meth and the materials to produce it, plus cocaine, marijuana, a large cache of pistols and assault rifles, and very expensive automobiles and motorcycles parked in the rear."

**

The vehicles carrying the arrested drug dealers sped away. Task force members loaded their gear into the backs of their trucks while investigators swarmed across the premises gathering evidence.

"Tough morning," officer Cruz said to an Atlanta cop as they tossed their vests into the vehicle.

The officer grinned at the younger policeman. "Pretty routine, if you ask me. At least, no one got shot at." He thrust his hand toward Eduardo. "Doug McHughes, Atlanta PD."

"I'm Eduardo Cruz. I work out of Gwinnett County."

"Guess I've been doing this a little longer than you have. You go on enough of these, you appreciate the ones that don't end up in a shootout." They walked toward the front of the van. "You look like you work out."

"Some," Eduardo said.

"Thought so. I could tell by the grip."

"I have a little equipment in the house. The trouble is, I'd like to join a gym, but they're so damned expensive, know what I mean?"

McHughes nodded. "I've got just the deal for you. A bunch of us guys lift weights together at Impact Workouts up in Northwood. That's kind of halfway between the city and where you work."

"I can't afford it. My wife and I, we've got three kids and a pile of bills."

"That's why I'm telling you about this deal. Impact is owned by an ex-cop, a guy called Big Sam, and he gives us a huge discount. Come on over and check it out. I can get you a guest pass for a couple of visits. No pressure."

"Maybe I will," Eduardo said as they climbed into the van.
**

Back at the station, Grace quickly typed out the lead-in to the story and delivered it to Jackson Davis. But the anchorman, who would broadcast the noon news, was in a surly mood.

"This story is just another nickel and dime bust. It's a waste of my breath," he crowed, approaching her workstation with copy in hand.

"Thank you, Walter Cronkite," Grace retorted sarcastically. "What's the matter with it?"

"It's shit, that's all," Davis blustered.

"That's an accurate news story about a serious drug problem," Grace argued. She wondered if Jackson's complaint was genuine journalistic criticism or a misogynistic streak taking over. "If you don't like the way it's written, you do it."

"I will," he snorted and stomped off.

Grace busied herself with some research for her evening program. Only fifteen minutes passed before Davis returned and tossed several pages onto her desk. Annoyed, Grace picked them up and read them while the newsman hovered over her. She didn't look up at him as she perused the copy. She could feel his know-it-all glare burning into her.

"This is not right." She stood and shook the papers at him, pointing. "This is not accurate, here, and here. Use this if you want, but it's just wrong."

Jackson grabbed the pages. "I'm using this," he growled over his shoulder as he left again. Grace felt the anger rise from the pit of her stomach. At her last station, in Dallas, she had fought a grizzled old news director until he grudgingly acknowledged she had a brain.

Grace didn't want to fight that battle again.

She tried to return to her work, but the ire continued to build, flushing her face, rattling her senses.

Time to go cool off, she thought. She had discovered a corner of the front lobby, out of sight from the front doors, that provided a perfect place to relax, read, make a personal phone call. Or calm down.

She left her office and started past Jackson's when he emerged, almost colliding with her. Flustered, she turned away, but he stopped her.

"Grace."

She stared at him with contempt.

"I've changed my mind. Your copy's better. I guess I'll use it. The video you guys transmitted from the scene is great." He went back to his desk, leaving her flummoxed and elated. She had stood up to Jackson Davis' bluff and won. He wouldn't be a problem anymore.

    **

She sat in the lobby on a couch in the visitor's area and watched the newscast. No one else was there except Mrs. Nicholson, the receptionist. When Grace's story came on she scooted to the edge of the seat.

"Sergeant Martinez," she was concluding on the recorded interview at the meth lab scene, "what led you to this location?"

"We've had this house under watch for quite a while. But yesterday we had a new development. A guest at a hotel over on Jimmy Carter Boulevard reported someone broke into his room and took his computer and smart phone. We simply activated the finder app on the phone and it led us to the same address that had been under suspicion for drug production for months. We had probable cause and got a warrant to enter the premises."

"Thank you, sergeant," Grace nodded as he moved on. She

turned and looked into the camera. "Big Six News was the first on the scene as the suspects were cuffed inside and taken away to be booked." She motioned toward the street where the residents of the house were being helped into the back of police vans. "Even from the front porch you could smell the burning odor similar to cat urine permeating the air. Over there…" she gestured toward the side street as Steve followed her with his camera, "…you can see DFACS agents taking two small children to a waiting police car. We have obscured the children's faces to protect them. Meanwhile, investigators are swarming inside the house collecting evidence."

She paused and again looked directly into the camera. "Sometimes the simplest mistakes by careless criminals can work to law enforcement's advantage. Like the 'felony lane' at the bank. Criminals use the farthest teller drive-through lane when trying to cash stolen checks, hence the 'felony lane' in law enforcement parlance. By doing so, they establish a pattern of behavior. Alert bank employees and police understand this and can often nab members of the felony lane gang before they get away. But here we're not talking about mere stolen checks. We're referring to the stolen lives of those who get in the path of vicious and amoral cartel thugs. And the stolen futures of innocent children they prey upon with their poison. Watch my new addition to the Big Six newscast, 'Crime and Corruption.' I'll give you a more detailed look at this blight that's destroying entire neighborhoods. I'm Grace Gleason for the Big Six News Beat."

Grace continued to watch the monitor as Jackson Davis appeared on camera. "That was Big Six News Beat's newest reporter Grace Gleason on the scene. Watch for Grace to have more in-depth coverage of the Atlanta drug wars tomorrow evening at six o'clock."

She turned the volume down with the remote and sat back, happy that Davis had acknowledged her on air. It was her first big story, and tomorrow she could build on it.

Mrs. Nicholson smiled at her, then answered a ringing telephone.

Suddenly, a notion struck and energized Grace. Gwinnett County was the conduit for much of the trafficking out to other major Southern population centers. But the head of the snake was Mexico. She remembered going to Laredo once on a story when she was working in Dallas. Now the idea of going to that city and its mirror image across the border, Nuevo Laredo, made sense. It might be dangerous, but it would enable her to connect the dots.

She decided to pitch the idea to Vivian.

A chill went through her entire body, telling her she was onto something big!

5 TEXAS OR BUST

THE MORNING AFTER her meth bust story aired, Grace was running late. She had experimented with mass transit but still liked having her car at the station. Although rush hour traffic was a problem, she had figured out the least congested routes and times, so her commute was reasonable.

Unfortunately, on this day she had gotten a late start and was now creeping along with the masses. As Grace turned a curve on Piedmont Avenue and headed down Ponce De Leon, she was startled by a billboard directly in her line of sight. A giant photograph of her loomed with a headline promoting her news segment.

She knew the promotions department had some advertising planned, but seeing a larger than life version of herself staring down was uncomfortable. Yet like most anyone else, it gave her ego a boost—she was on her way to being a local celebrity.

At the stoplight, she activated her hands-free cell and speed dialed Eduardo.

"It's Grace Gleason, officer," she said. "I wanted to let you know I thought the drug raid story was great. Did everything work okay for you?"

"Perfect," Cruz answered. "I liked your report."

"Tune into my news segment tonight and let me know what you think."

"I wouldn't miss it," he said buoyantly.

Grace had enjoyed many successes in her Dallas reporting days, but nothing like this. She couldn't wait to get to the station and find out where this would take her.

She was nearly late. Tom grimaced when she crept in a moment before the morning meeting began.

Vivian Ellis, sitting in a side chair against the wall, held up a hand before Tom could speak. "Just a word. Let's all congratulate Grace Gleason for a rousing start to what should become a long-running news event at Big Six News Beat. Great first segment, Grace."

"Hear, hear," shouted the exuberant new reporter, Scott Matthews, leading the group's applause.

Grace felt her face flush, embarrassed but paradoxically enjoying the praise.

"Okay, getting started," Tom said, and he recited the list of stories. As he concluded, he said, "I've asked our esteemed newbie..." he nodded at Scott Matthews, grinning, "...to start us off this morning. He's been working his butt off churning out back-of-the-show stories, but he's developed several strong leads. Matthews, anything you want to toss out here?"

The young reporter hesitated, glancing around the room as if reluctant to take a shot. "This might be something," he stammered. "There's a trend going on out there that no one seems to have put together yet. Anyone notice how many convenience marts, liquor stores and bars have been robbed or burglarized in the last few weeks?"

No one responded.

Matthews waited.

"Store break-ins are commonplace in Atlanta." Tom seemed annoyed. "If they're significant, we report them."

"I know," Scott said in a firm voice as he grew more bold. "But there have been fifteen such crimes, most of them very similar, in a real brief span of time."

"I covered the latest one yesterday," Jackson Davis piped up.

"I saw your piece," Matthews retorted, sounding annoyed.

"But we're missing something. Every one of those jobs has happened the night before gross receipts were scheduled to be picked up the next morning, and when very few customers, if any, were in the place."

"What's your point?" Ellis asked.

"It's Al-Queda."

"What!" Tom exploded.

"Not actually the terrorist group," Scott responded with a sardonic tone. "I'm using a metaphor. But it's sort of like their operations—a coordinated effort, striking at exactly the time when the place is most vulnerable and seeming to know the operation backwards and forwards. I think they're all connected."

"You're saying a burglary ring," Vivian speculated.

"Right. Maybe a gang."

"What do you think, Grace? Possibly one of your drug-dealing outfits?" the news director asked.

"Could be," Grace replied, "but not likely. Some small offshoot of *Los Lagartos* might be pulling off these heists. But the big gangs are doing major drug transactions, not penny-ante burglaries and stick-ups. This rash of robberies and burglaries could be anybody. They are likely random and unconnected."

"A string of fifteen in a few weeks doesn't strike me as a two-bit deal," Davis challenged. "I think the kid's got something here."

"I do, too," Vivian agreed. "Grace, why don't you take this one."

"Wait," Scott Matthews protested. "I deserve a chance to work on this. It's my lead."

Vivian gave him a penetrating glare with the lethal effect of a rifle shot for a split second. She turned back to Grace. "Look into it, see if there are some common threads. If it does fit in with the cliques you've been investigating, you could tie a nice bow around your story."

Grace protested, feeling vulnerable. "I think I need to focus on my follow-up reports in Gwinnett County."

Vivian was silent for a moment, her laser-like gaze searing at Grace now. "I want you to look into this." Her voice was alarmingly firm.

Grace nodded in submission.

The assignment gnawed at Grace all day as she researched each heist and compiled the statistics. She picked up the phone to contact the Atlanta Police Department's information officer, but she hung up without placing the call.

It wasn't Grace's nature to push back at management. She had done it on rare occasions at the Dallas station, and it always made her uncomfortable. Only when her life had risen to a personal crisis—a career argument with her father, a marriage-ending conflict with her ex-husband, Jeff—did a rebellious streak kick in strongly enough to make her take a stand.

So when she went to her news director's office late that afternoon, she was uneasy.

"Got a minute, Ms. Ellis?" she knocked on the door.

Vivian looked up from her work. "Sure, Grace. Come in."

"It's about the assignment of those burglaries," she began, watching the news director's lips purse. "I'll do it if you say so. But I'm onto something important with the Gwinnett drug story. I want to go to Texas."

"Texas?"

"Atlanta, and specifically Gwinnett County, has become a major hub for the cartels' trafficking to the rest of the South. Even to other major markets in the Northeast and West. I think I should go to a border town and report from where it originates."

"Where?"

60

"Laredo. I'm familiar with that area, and it's a trafficking hot-bed. I can get help from my Dallas connections, interview dealers incarcerated there, get across into Nuevo Laredo and talk to the Mexican police. I'd be closing the loop for this story, tying the connection from there to here, then maybe go on out to one of the other target markets like New York or Las Vegas."

"We don't have the budget for that," Ellis protested.

"I can stay in San Antonio one night while I'm setting it up. I'll sleep at a roadside motel and eat beans and crackers."

Ellis laughed at the image, but as quickly, her expression sobered. She chewed at her lower lip, thinking, her gaze cast downward.

"No. It's too dangerous. I won't put you in that position."

"You hired me to do edgy journalism. Well, this is it. Exploring a story like the drug wars in depth is what I signed on for. And think about what it might do for ratings."

Vivian considered again, trying Grace's patience.

"Sorry," the news director repeated. "I can't expose you to that kind of jeopardy."

Grace heaved a massive sigh, desperate. "I have a very good friend, a retired detective. I know he'll go down there with me if I ask him. He's tough as concrete, and he won't let me get in harm's way. I know that from experience. Please."

Vivian pondered. "Your friend, this detective. He'll do it?"

"I know he will."

"You'll promise to put your safety in his hands?"

"I will."

Vivian rose and walked around to the side of her desk, leaning against the edge of it and looked down at Grace. "I'll give the theft story to Scott Matthews. Let him have your notes."

Grace rose, her heart pulsing.

"No unnecessary chances," Ellis warned. "No overnight across the border. No leaving the side of this ex-cop of yours. Have Mrs. Stephenson set up your reservations."

Grabbing the news director's hand, Grace shook it vigorously. "Thank you, Ms. Ellis." Grace was thrilled she had won her over.

She was going to Laredo. And if all went well, the center of narcotics hell, *Nuevo Laredo*, Mexico.

6 MEGAN

THE FORECAST was for a record high the last Saturday in June. Early in the morning, Grace already felt the oppressive humidity as she rang the apartment bell.

"Hi Mom," Megan said cheerfully as she swung the door open.

Nearly two months had passed since Grace had seen Megan except on their Internet video chats. They had phoned often, but now her daughter was finally here in Atlanta. Seeing and hearing Megan in person, rather than through a computer service or cell phone connection, restored order.

Grace wrapped her arms instantly around her daughter, feeling the softness of Megan's long, golden hair against her cheek.

Megan expelled a slight, amused giggle at the greeting. "Love you, Mom. Missed you."

The sound of Megan's voice soothed Grace. She pushed back and looked into her blue eyes. "You look tired, honey."

"I've been working my butt off to get this apartment ready. You're just in time to help me paint the kitchen. My last big job before my new roommates arrive. I still have to get back, close my old place and sort through my belongings."

Grace remained focused on Megan's Atlanta living arrangements. "Two men. Is that such a good idea? I liked it when you had women roommates in Dallas."

"Mom, don't be old-fashioned."

"Do you know these guys?"

Megan's musical laughter filled the room. "I've vetted them properly, madam reporter. Come on in and have some tea, Mom."

The space would be small for three people, Grace immediately noted as she looked around the living area and into the kitchenette. "At least you'll have your own space," she poked her head into the smallest of the three bedrooms.

"These guys are serious architecture students," Megan said as they sipped the fresh brew at the tiny cabaret-style kitchen table. "I've spoken to them both at length. Since they're third-year, they've already gone through the process that I understand thins out the feint of heart. And they can help me get accepted into the fraternity."

"Fraternity?"

"That's what it's like. A co-ed clan of fellow sufferers. They all work and play together, although there's not much time for fun."

The subject had been unspoken, but hovering like a zeppelin, so Grace asked the question. "Have you heard from your father?"

"Sporadically."

"It figures."

"He has a girlfriend," Megan offered, trying to sound casual. The words stabbed at Grace.

"Some bimbo in the movie business. Probably a porn star."

"Megan!" Grace admonished.

"I know, I didn't mean it. I think she makes commercials or something. It seems...I don't know, too early. You two never..."

"We said goodbye," Grace offered with finality. "That was two years ago."

"You're right. But I remember when we were all happy."

Grace sighed and sipped her tea. "So do I, honey."

Megan laid a hand on her mother's. "There's something else." Grace watched, waited. "The guy you were dating in Dallas, Matt? He got married."

Another stab. Matt Robertson had been her cameraman, and in a time of crisis they had bonded. Though all the warning signs had signaled he was too much younger and their backgrounds totally foreign, camaraderie had morphed into romance and then into intimacy.

That was when, uncertain, Grace had pulled away. The move to Atlanta had put an exclamation point on it.

"How do you know all of this?" Grace was astonished.

"I keep up. I'm looking out for your interests."

"Worrying about you is all the interests I need in my life right now."

Megan grasped Grace's hand harder. "If that's true, what about this Mexico thing?"

"I only have a couple of hours. Shall we cover up this ugly flowered wallpaper with something pleasing? I'll tell you all about Mexico while we work."

They bustled about, mixing the paints to the precise pale yellow hue Megan wanted. They taped the edges of the cabinets, then each took a wall and began to roll on the first coat. It would take two to eliminate the huge, garish red and green blossoms.

"Mexico," Megan repeated as they worked. "Why do you have to do it?"

"Part of the story. Part of the job," Grace shrugged.

"It scares me. That's a treacherous place, with all the killings and beheadings."

Grace didn't want to discuss this, but she had to. "I know how to be careful, Megan. And I'm getting Ned Moore to go with me."

"Detective Moore? From Dallas?"

"I'll be safe, I promise."

Megan laid down her roller and fixed her stark azure eyes on her mother. "You always have to do this. Go into these terrifying places and expose yourself to all kinds of risk. Why can't you be a normal mom?"

"Normal isn't what I do," Grace answered matter-of-factly. "I'm a newswoman. When we were in Dallas, I felt compelled to devote my time to stories I thought would help solve someone's problem. Root out injustice. Give people hope. With this new station, it has taken on a wonderful new dimension. I'm in a position to speak out for large numbers of people at one time. I take that responsibility very seriously, sweetie."

"I know you do, Mom. And I'm proud of you. But you take far too many chances. I don't want this to end up like last time, or worse."

Grace laid down her roller, pulled off her rubber glove and embraced Megan. "I promise to be careful."

The doorbell rang.

Megan answered it and returned with a young man in tow. "Mom, meet one of my new roommates, Bradley Carson."

Grace had been haunted by visions of some handsome play-boy sneaking into Megan's room at night, turning on the charm and corrupting her daughter. She almost laughed aloud at the thought now as she shook the young man's pale hand.

"Nice to meet you, Bradley," she said, almost hysterical with joy. He was tall and gangly. A scrawny attempt at a beard covered the point of his chin. His old-fashioned, horn-rimmed glasses added to his nerdy appearance. *Thank the Lord for geeks,* she told herself.

"Grab a brush," Megan said cheerfully. "You're in time to help us finish coat one."

As they worked, Bradley gave Megan what amounted to a primer for a new architecture student.

"You're lucky," he said in a deep voice that betrayed his meek appearance. "Since they've accepted most of your credit hours, you can launch right into the architecture curriculum and focus on it. You'll need to. They run you through a literal gauntlet at first. When you go in with your first project, the prof tears them apart, humiliates you. A lot of students drop out immediately. Don't give in. With each new iteration of the project, the instructor becomes increasingly supportive and helpful."

"Sounds like an awfully cynical environment," Megan frowned.

"It has a purpose. They only want serious students in the

class. And they're teaching that you won't get it right the first time. Eventually, they find merit in your work."

"Sounds tough," Grace shook her head.

"We lost over half of our students my first year. But those of us who stayed know we're in for a great ride. I'll always be thankful I hung in there."

Grace watched Megan soak it all in. *This will be good for her, having these guys give her advice,* she thought, casting out her earlier apprehension.

"Where is roommate number two?" Grace queried.

Bradley explained, "He'll get in next week. Has to travel from India. Raju Prakash," He grinned. "It's a common name over there. We call him Raj for short. Your daughter is fortunate to have a housemate with his talent. His father is one of the top architects in India. Good connection. Plus, there's another thing about him that makes us both fortunate."

"Oh?" Grace said inquisitively.

'The guy only weighs about one hundred sixty soaking wet. But he's an expert at MMA."

"What's that?"

"Mixed martial arts. The full contact combat sport. His uncle owns two karate schools. Raj started when he was a kid and progressed from there. He just achieved his brown belt."

"Does he compete?" Megan asked.

"He says the sport has changed. It used to be for hard-core competitors, but now there are training clubs. Raj has done a few exhibitions in his weight class, but mostly he works out and trains with other guys. Also does some instructing."

Grace clapped her hands together, ecstatic. "There you go, Megan. You can get him to walk you home from classes. There are disturbing stories about robberies and even rapes at nearly every university these days. Sometimes girls are too trusting."

Bradley smiled. "I'll see that he walks us both home."

They all laughed.

As Grace said goodbye, she was relieved and reassured. Megan would be fine.

"You won't see much of me for a while," her daughter warned as they walked to Grace's car. "I have six weeks to move my stuff, meet with advisers, go through class selection and shop for clothes and books and architecture supplies. Besides attending a whole round of orientations. When classes start, Bradley tells me they pull all-nighters, grab a few hours of sleep and do it all over again."

Grace turned back. "I understand. I love you."

"Watch your back in Mexico," Megan countered. "I love you, too."

7 INDEPENDENCE DAY

THE FOURTH OF JULY sprang from Grace's preoccupied schedule with little warning. She was at odds, in a strange city with no friends around her for a barbecue. Megan had returned to Dallas to spend one last hurrah with her high school and college cohorts and to scrape together the final load of her belongings.

When she stepped outside to get the newspaper, the dearth of traffic noise and human movement met Grace like some huge, silent wall, as if the world had gone to sleep. Back inside, the house an empty quiet, she watched the competition cover the annual Fourth of July parade. *We could do it better,* she thought.

She felt a sudden pang of loss. She and Jeff had established a tradition in Dallas. They would pack up Megan and go watch the marching bands and floats make their way down the tree-lined streets. Back home, Jeff would fix his famous ribs on the grill. She grinned, remembering he once nearly caught his shirt on fire when he squirted starter on the hot coals. *Sometimes that man scared me half to death with his silly antics,* she thought. *But when we weren't fighting, life with him was so much fun.*

She recalled one particularly blistering Fourth when they spent much of the day surviving the heat with red, white and blue rocket popsicles. Grace loved the photo she had of Megan and Jeff with that sticky mess all over their faces.

A wave of melancholy swept over her, and she turned the television off, staring into her coffee. She missed how close they had been as a family at the beginning. When and how did it all change? What had robbed her of the warmth she had felt with the man she had loved so deeply? Why couldn't Jeff have been willing to give just a little to keep her in his life?

She wondered if the happiness she had felt was an illusion. She shook her head, as if to discard unanswerable questions about the part of her life that seemed irrevocably unresolved, like the fireworks to be touched off tonight—a flash in the sky, and then gone.

It was Friday, but Grace had the day off. She had only a couple of hours to eat breakfast, shower and dress. Then she would gather the potato salad and wine she had stashed in the refrigerator and head for Shoreville and the home of police officer Eduardo Cruz.

His invitation had been totally unexpected. He had called her at the station on Wednesday afternoon.

"Grace, I want you and your daughter to come to my house. All my family will be there." He sounded ebullient. "We do a cookout every year, and I promise you'll have the time of your life."

"I couldn't possibly," Grace protested. "I can't intrude on your family gathering."

"You wouldn't be intruding," he laughed. "I don't even know half the people who come. My buddies and neighbors invite their friends, and my cousins bring their boyfriends and girlfriends. I can never keep track of all of them. I will challenge you to ping pong, but only after you've had at least two beers. I want you to meet my family. I've told them all about you."

The more Grace demurred, the harder Eduardo pressed his case. She was torn about it. Fraternizing with a story source was not something she would normally do. Even if she trusted her own instincts to stay at arms-length, the appearance of friendship could later lead to problems.

But finally, as he grew more insistent, she said yes. She promised herself she wouldn't stay all afternoon. An hour or so, tops.

Seconds after she had hung up, Christina Cruz appeared at her door, leaning against the Grace's entry, arms folded, smiling.

"My brother called you, right?" said the anchor. "Jackson told me you've met him. Eduardo said last night he was going to invite you. I didn't mean to eavesdrop, but I could hear you arguing with him."

Grace was surprised, wondering how much Christina knew about her pact with Eduardo. She decided to hedge. "I didn't know how to turn him down. I don't like to get too close to people I might have to interview sometime. Besides, it's such an imposition—to show up at your brother's with your entire family there."

Christina tilted her head back and laughed, her deep amber eyes twinkling against the olive tone of her face. "You don't know them, Grace. Half of Shoreville will come by before it's over, and Eduardo will be disappointed if they don't. I'm glad you're coming. We can get to know each other."

**

Traffic was light, and Grace arrived precisely at noon. True to Eduardo's billing, the throng of cars and trucks parked up and down the street indicated a huge turnout. She walked past the small, neatly mown lawn, following the clatter around the small one-story bungalow toward the back yard. She was surprised at how large the lot was, running deep toward an alley.

Smoke curled skyward from three grills on the deck. A dozen pre-teen children frolicked in an above-ground pool, splashing and giggling. Fifty or more adults milled around drinking beer and trading stories.

Eduardo looked up from one of the grills and grinned, walking to greet her in his chef's apron. "You came. *Como esta?*" he asked.

"*Muy bien, gracias,*" Grace smiled. She held out her salad

and wine, and a beautiful young woman gliding up behind Eduardo reached around him and took them, nodding.

"My wife, Adella," the officer beamed proudly. "Honey, this is Grace Gleason."

"I've heard much about you," Adella, a wisp of a woman, said with an accent that sounded more valley girl than Spanish. "Welcome to our home. Our children are..." she shrugged, looking around toward the pool "...somewhere over there. You will meet them later. Come with me to the kitchen."

Inside, the Cruz home was spotless. Christina and Jackson were there, taking turns stirring a pot of hotdog chili on the stovetop. Christina accepted Grace's outstretched hand warmly with both of hers. Jackson grunted, "Here's the golden girl," and Grace could tell from his indistinct speech and wobbly actions he had already been into the liquor cabinet.

Eduardo and Adella steered her around outside, introducing her in an obvious effort to make her feel comfortable. But as the food was served, buffet-style on a long table and the beer and wine flowed freely, they left her on her own. She was relieved; she didn't want to be an obligation. And she had never been one to shy from conversations with strangers.

Grace had been around the Latino culture ever since college at the University of Texas, and later during her career in Austin and Dallas. But she had not participated in it, close and personal, until today. As she watched their interactions, she noticed they had an easy way about them. Even their jabbing and joking at each other was respectful. And they were mindful of their elders' comfort, getting them plates of food, bringing them drinks, helping them walk and sit.

She had arrived before Eduardo's and Christina's parents and watched as they made their entrance. The mother, Juanita, belied her fleshy build with graceful movement, chatting in rapid Spanish with her children and friends who gathered around her. Raul walked laboriously with a cane. His thick glasses and insistence on holding Eduardo's arm until he was seated contentedly at a small table beneath an umbrella were signs of frail health.

Eduardo brought them each a drink and then left them to observe the activity. As Grace wandered around the grounds, chatting and watching the children play, she noticed several times that Raul was straining to observe her. She sensed he wanted to talk. She filled a plate and went to sit at the table with Eduardo's parents.

"You are not long in Atlanta?" Raul seemed to struggle with the language as she settled in a lawn chair beside him. "You like it here?"

"I like Atlanta very much," she answered.

"And *Los Bravos*—the Braves, do you watch them?"

"I went to one game," she watched his smile in response. "I don't have much time for sports."

"I have not been to see them," he said. "My eyes are not so good for TV, but I listen to every game on the radio. Some day maybe I will go."

"Yes, I think you should," she encouraged.

Raul took a long swallow of the rum and cola his son had delivered in a plastic cup. "You help Eduardo fight *los criminales*?"

The abrupt change of pace took her aback. "We are doing what we can. It's a huge problem."

"*Si*. Yes. We came here years ago, when Eduardo and his sister were children. It was not so much a problem in those days. There were drugs and bad guys, but not like now. Killing police and judges, killing each other. Leaving heads in the street like trash. And now they are coming to Georgia and ruining our county."

He shook his head and took another swig. "The executive from the cola factory, you know, *Señor* Fox, he went down there. He could not fix it. Calderon could not fix it. I don't know if anyone can..." His voice faded, and his gaze wandered off. Suddenly, he turned toward her. "And immigration. The undocumented. What do you think about all of that?"

Grace had grown uncomfortable with his probing questions. But she realized he was starved to talk the politics he had probably once discussed daily with his cronies. Now, she surmised confined to his living room with the radio, his eyesight failing, he had no such outlet.

"You are a citizen, you and your wife?" Grace asked. She looked at Juanita whose attention was on her grandchildren in the pool. She wondered if the woman even understood the conversation. Grace knew from stories she had covered the Latinos of Raul's and Juanita's generation reverted to their native tongue, regardless of their exposure to English.

"*Si,*" Raul responded. "Many years ago. But those who have come in, over the border, they don't have a choice. Running away for safety. Searching for work. President Bush, he was good—tried to get them citizenship. But the Congress wouldn't..." Raul's voice grew louder and more distressed.

Juanita, who had said nothing, scanned around nervously to determine who was listening. Her eyes caught Eduardo's as he hovered over a grill, and her look of concern brought the officer quickly to their table.

"Pop," Eduardo's strident voice startled Grace. "Let's go inside so you can rest." He laid a hand on his father's shoulder and smiled. "We're all going to the park for fireworks tonight."

"I wanted another drink," Raul complained, holding up the

cup with a shaky hand.

Grace half-rose and reached for it, but Eduardo shook his head no. She silently reached out, squeezed Raul's arm, nodded to Juanita and slipped out of her chair.

"I should go," she said to Cruz.

"Stay a while, Grace. The party's just getting started."

"I can't, really. I'll go say goodbye to everyone."

Grace watched Eduardo lead his parents into the house. Although they had achieved citizenship, it was obvious to Grace their memories and heart remained in Mexico.

The crowd was still growing. Mariachi music blared from outdoor speakers over a group of men pitching horseshoes and drinking beer. The children continued to frolic in the water.

Grace went into the kitchen where Adella and Christina were washing dishes. Jackson had perched on a stool at the counter nearby, drinking red wine, watching a network news program and making surly faces. "Those sons of bitches," he blurted.

Christina pursed her lips apologetically toward Grace, but said nothing.

"I have to leave," Grace announced to Adella.

"So soon?" Eduardo's wife asked. "You had a good time?"

"Very much," Grace said. "The time went so quickly. I'm sorry I didn't get to meet your children."

Eduardo came in and popped the top from a long-neck beer. "I'll go get them. They've been swimming long enough."

"No, don't," Grace said urgently. "Let them have their fun. I'll meet them another day."

Sorry about my father," Cruz said. "He gets excited."

"Not at all," she said. "He's an interesting man."

"Raul got the short end of the stick," Jackson said. "He made something out of a life of nothing and then the poor guy's payoff was getting diabetes and his eyesight going south. He brought his family up here for a better future, but then life did what it always fucking does—spit in his face."

"Your language," Christina scolded, peering nervously at Grace.

"I don't care," Davis raved on. "Life's not fair. Ever since the guy was diagnosed and had to go on insulin, he's been in and out of hospitals. Has sores on his feet and legs that won't heal. It's been hard on the family." He paused, weaving like a new colt trying to stand. "But he's a tough old bird. He hangs in there."

"Enough about Raul Cruz," Adella chirped. "Let's have a toast to our guest, Grace Gleason, before she leaves. May this be the first of many visits to our home."

"I say let's drink to the management of Channel Six, those incredible cowards," Jackson Davis crowed, draining his glass and becoming obviously more inebriated.

"Jackson!" his wife reprimanded. "You're being rude."

"Bullshit. Grace has been here long enough to see for herself. Vivian Ellis is like all the rest—she'll push her high-flown ideas for a short time and then that excuse for a manager Harvey Silver will crush her like a grape."

"You're getting plastered," Eduardo scolded.

"Probably so, officer. But damn it, you guys are out there on the line fighting that human trash every day and deserve better than what we give you. We chase ambulances and fire trucks, and the grunt work being done to repair the real ills of society goes unnoticed, unsupported, unsolved and underestimated."

"You're crazy, man," Eduardo retorted. "Look what Grace has

done in the short time she's been here."

Davis paced unsteadily around the group, more agitated. "Oh, this lady has come riding in on her white horse. All the way from her crowning success in Big D. She'll slay a small dragon or two at Channel Six." He stopped and faced Grace with a derisive look she saw in their first skirmish. "And the very first time she decides to stand up to the Silver and Ellis roadblock, they'll tell her the advertisers don't like it, or some politician who has them in his pocket will threaten them. They'll call her off, and she'll crumple like last week's discarded script. Or worse, she'll fight them and they'll can her sorry ass."

Grace stared with her mouth open, stung by Jackson's rant. Christina stepped in front of Jackson, turned and glanced Grace with an expression of horror. "Come on, Jackson. Time for us to gather our things and go home."

He continued to waver for a moment, then nodded. Christina organized their exit as if she had done it many times before. She looked at Grace with a plea for mercy in her eyes.

Grace returned a "no worries," reassuring shrug.

After Jackson and Christina said their goodbyes, Grace walked to her car with Eduardo. She was paradoxically upset by the anchor's tirade yet soothed by the comfort she felt from the family gathering she had just experienced.

"I've had a good time, despite your brother-in-law's bad manners," she summed up. "Thank you."

"Jackson is a complex personality. He can be a good guy, but he's a huge idiot when he gets loaded. You know, Grace, it is I who should be thanking you. You are doing our community and the Gwinnett force a great service. When do you leave for Laredo?"

"As soon as the arrangements are made. Two or three weeks."

"I wish I could go with you. For protection."

"It's fine. I'll be with a retired detective."

"Good. Besides, if I were there, I'd probably want to take out about two dozen of those guys on the street corners. Just stay safe down there."

"You sound like my daughter Megan. I've spent my entire life trying to protect her from danger. Lectured her, even fought for her. But now she's trying to turn the tables on me. She gives me a hard time about the life I've chosen."

"The child is father of the man…" Eduardo recited.

"What's that from?"

"It's Wordsworth." He reached out and touched her arm, his deep brown eyes burning with earnestness. "I mean it, Grace. Mexico is in the hands of Satan. Watch yourself in that God-forsaken place."

8 THE LONE STAR STATE

GRACE HAD NEVER met Hank Hamlin, Big Six's risk management attorney, although his negative bias toward the news department was legend around the station. Stories abounded about the feuds he had initiated with management over potential libel allegations, lawsuits, anti-competitive behavior and reporters going into harm's way.

"Hank should have worked for an insurance company," Christina Cruz once said in a morning meeting. "Their job, like his, is to say 'no'." Several of the staff around the table nodded agreement; few had avoided tangling with the obstinate lawyer at one time or another.

Grace was not surprised when he stopped by her space. Vivian had told her a visit from Hamlin was standard procedure when a reporter was leaving the country.

Unexpected, though, was what she saw when he popped his head into her cubicle. Grace had anticipated horns and a pitchfork. Instead, Hamlin looked solidly Midwestern, not exactly handsome, but well-groomed, hair smoothed back, clean-shaven, smiling.

"Got a minute?" He flashed pearly whites.

"Come in," she said, returning his smile.

"Hank Hamlin," he offered a firm handshake and sat without invitation. "Just take a few minutes of your time. I wouldn't normally be too concerned you're crossing the Southern border, but these days that's much riskier than it used to be."

"I won't be alone," Grace assured him. "An old friend from Dallas, a retired policeman, has agreed to go with me. He has the connections we need to have a safe stay in Nuevo Laredo. We won't be there more than a few hours, unless..." She hesitated.

"What?" the lawyer appeared concerned.

"Unless we get captured, tortured, dismembered and our body parts scattered around the state of Tamaulipas. Or suspended off a bridge over the Rio Grande."

She laughed at his astonishment, which lasted only a split second and immediately returned to the dazzling smile.

"Funny," he said. "But you do realize nothing down there can be taken for granted, right?"

"I know. I promise to behave."

"You're going to interview a cartel leader? How does that work?"

"His name is Guillermo Lopez Castillo. He was the big guy in the *Diablo* Cartel until the Mexican military caught and extradited him to the U.S. I'm told he has been doing time in a Houston prison but was recently transferred to Laredo where he's living under guard in some secret location cooperating with law enforcement."

"I'm sure he's a nice guy."

Grace ignored the caustic comment. "He supposedly speaks out now against the murder and mayhem that's tearing his country apart. Some think he's being paid by the ATF or DEA or somebody else in the government. The interview's not a sure thing."

Hamlin ran manicured fingernails through thick, dark blond hair. "Why would the cartel let him live? That doesn't make any sense."

"Good question. Maybe he's a double agent. I'll ask when I see him."

She watched the attorney's light brown eyes narrow as if trying to determine if he was hearing sarcasm.

"Look, counselor," she continued, "I'm told the authorities consider him a strong asset in their war against the narcotics trade. They keep him under such tight wraps that my man in Dallas had to pull some heavy strings to get me in to see him. It should be a huge coup for my news segment. And the station."

He stood, pulled his six-foot-three frame up and frowned at

her. She hadn't noticed earlier how tall he was.

"I really don't want you to go down there," he admonished.

"It's all arranged," she countered.

"I want you to be careful. Get in and out of there as quickly as possible. I'm sure you know how ruthless those guys can be. If they're willing to murder their local cops, politicians and judges, they don't give a rat's patootie about a Georgia news reporter."

She laughed aloud at his effort to bypass profanity. "I know, Hank. And I appreciate your concern. I'll be extra careful and give you a briefing when I return."

The shiny whites returned. "All right, Grace. Have a safe trip."

He was gone. A chill ran through her as her brain replayed his words. "*If they're willing to murder their local cops, politicians and judges, they don't give...*" She forced herself to stop the thought.

**

The flight to San Antonio was bumpy, nagged by late summer Texas winds. After the plane landed, Ned Moore was waiting for her in the baggage area.

She hadn't seen the detective in nearly two years, since his wife Martha's funeral. He looked a little older, more sad, she thought. Even so, his eyes lit up when he spied her approaching, and his muscular arms stretched out to engulf her in a fatherly hug.

"We have a lot of catching up to do," he said. "I've booked you at El Acapulco."

Her eyes widened. "On the Riverwalk? It's too expensive, Ned. My station won't agree to it. "

"Don't worry," the ex-detective smiled. "The manager is an old friend. He gave me a great rate. It should definitely accommodate your expense account."

He pulled her suitcase and found his car, the same old sedan he had driven when she worked in Dallas. Grace remembered he had told her the force gave it to him as a retirement gift.

"It's good to see you, Ned," she said.

As they drove toward downtown, she marveled at how unfamiliar the South Texas landscape had become in the relatively short time she had been away. It was rife with palms instead of pines, calla lilies instead of azaleas, moving traffic instead of jams.

Grace could see the HemisFair Tower growing closer as they cruised toward the river. "Jeff and I came down here right after he graduated law school. I remember it was the most captivating place I had ever visited."

"You two in touch?"

"Don't ask."

She watched his lined, tired face light up in a grin. "Then I won't," he promised as they pulled up in front of the once-elegant Acapulco, the first hotel built when the city beautified the river. Royalty and Hollywood celebrities had stayed there in its heyday.

"Here we are," Ned announced. "Go ahead and check in. I'll park and meet you in the lobby in an hour. We're having Tex Mex on the river tonight."

"Only if it's on me," she demanded. She knew he couldn't be earning much on a policeman's pension.

The evening flashed by on fast-forward. Moore updated Grace on many of the cops she had known. They reminisced about cases he had worked and she covered. She was relieved, though, that neither mentioned an explosive day when a murder suspect nearly killed her and Ned saved her life. *I might have broken down at such a traumatic memory,* she thought as they walked to the car.

Ned dropped her off at the hotel entrance just before midnight and headed for the parking garage. She was exhausted; as she unlocked her door, she knew she would have no problem dropping off to sleep tonight.

**

As Grace drifted off, it was nearly one a.m. in Atlanta. Scott

Matthews and Steve Jankowski were arriving at a crime scene thirty minutes after their nighttime assignment desk had received a citizen's call. Three squad cars were already there, parked randomly near a Korean-owned convenience store in an East-end suburb. Yellow tape had been strung around the front of the establishment. Despite the late hour, a small and curious crowd had gathered.

Cruiser lights still flashing illuminated the darkened storefront. Jankowski parked the truck as close as possible. Scott jumped out. "I know that guy," he told his photographer, pointing at a plainclothes cop who was chatting with one of the uniformed officers. "Hey, Detective Harrison."

The two newsmen approached the policeman and Steve fired up his lights.

"We just got here," the detective told Matthews. "My partner's inside gathering evidence. We won't have anything substantial for you tonight."

Scott signaled for Jankowski to turn off the camera. "Come on, Harrison," Matthews pled. "You know I won't blow your cover. Never have. Give me something to go on."

The detective half-smiled. "Okay, you've done me a favor or two. Witnesses say there were four of 'em. And, they got the safe."

"You're joking."

Harrison smiled. "Hauled it right through that plate glass window they're boarding up. But Matthews…" He drew closer to Scott. "…You didn't get that from me. You'll have to call downtown."

"The owner around?"

The policeman nodded toward an Asian man and woman talking excitedly to a cop who was taking their statement. Scott motioned to Jankowski, and they scrambled toward the owners.

The interview did not go well. The proprietors spoke poor English, and they were so keyed up, Scott couldn't get a straight answer out of them. They confirmed the place had just closed and they were on their way home. Apparently, Mathews surmised from their broken description of things, the security system had been disabled. That was it.

Driving back to the station, Scott grumbled to Steve, "Not much of a story."

"We'll make it look okay," the cameraman assured.

"But hey," Matthews added, "add another heist to the growing list."

**

They left early the next morning for Laredo. It was already hot. Ned pulled the car up in front of the hotel, Grace climbed in and within minutes they were on I-35 South. The drive would take two and one-half hours.

"That's for you," he muttered.

Grace sipped the coffee Ned had brought in a Styrofoam cup. "That food was fantastic last night," she said foggily, still waking up.

"I never get tired of coming down here and drinking the river water," Moore laughed. "And enjoying the freshest Mexican food in the world. My wife and I visited here once every few months, at least."

"That's so romantic," she said. "I know you miss her terribly."

"It's lonely, especially without any children."

Grace listened to the tenor of his voice carefully, recalling that his only child had died very young.

He went on unemotionally. "I meet up with my old cronies from the force once a week for coffee. I do a little security consulting. I'm in a bowling league," he added brightly, smiling over at her.

"When did you take that up?" she marveled.

"A couple of my fellow retirees got me started."

She chuckled at the thought of burly Ned trying to fit his chubby fingers into those holes and flinging the sixteen-pound ball down the lane as if it were made of feathers.

"We lived in Austin all that time and only got to San Antonio three, maybe four times," she said, adding a regretful postscript to her San Antonio memories.

"You and Jeff?" he threw a guarded glance her way, carefully but casually re-initiating the subject. "How is the old boy?"

She sighed heavily. "Getting rich in California." Her harsh answer signaled he should change the subject. He nodded and fell silent.

San Antonio grew ugly even before they had reached the southern ring of the perimeter highway. The dense foliage and palms of the Riverwalk area and the city skyline gave way to warehouses and lower income neighborhoods, then long stretches of undeveloped property. Only that morning she had read a column in the local paper about excruciatingly slow progress in this section due to poor planning and zoning restrictions.

Within minutes they were out of the city watching the scruffy-brush landscape of South Texas speed by. Except for a huge car plant, the area looked no different than Grace remembered from the times she and Jeff had driven down.

"The first time we went to Nuevo Laredo we were still in college," she reminisced. "We drove across the bridge into the heart of the city. We ate fresh enchiladas and drank *Carte Blanco* at a little bar called *El Lobo*." She laughed, enjoying the memory. "After we were married we returned a couple of times and bought hand-made furniture. But word started drifting up north about all the murders. And the ruthlessness of the cartels. We didn't dare take the chance after Megan came along."

"Damned shame what has happened there," Ned frowned. "Listen, Grace. You might not get to cross the border."

"What?" she shot back, straining forward against her seat belt.

"Nobody goes across anymore. You've heard about the human heads dumped in the streets, the bodies dangling from bridges."

"But just across the bridge. On foot."

"My contact Henry Barrera is an investigator on the Laredo force. We'll have to take his advice. I had hoped his chief could make an inquiry with the military on the other side, arrange an escort. But he didn't promise anything. I read in the paper this morning that they had a cartel shootout yesterday. Not far up the border, agents found a huge load of drugs in duffel bags on a Texas hunting lease."

"We've come all this way," she moaned. "What about the ex-cartel guy?"

"Don't know. We'll ask Henry. Grace, you'll get your story. But you might have to report it from good old U.S. of A. soil."

They drove in silence. Grace glanced at the sign for the Cotulla turnoff. *About halfway there,* she thought.

Then Ned played with the radio. The San Antonio stations were fading in and out as they grew farther away. His scanner kept pausing on Spanish-speaking stations. He growled and aggressively punched the "off" button.

Grace dozed for what seemed only a few minutes. But when she jerked awake and peered at her watch, she realized an hour had passed.

Springing from nowhere, a span of refinery tanks replaced the fields of clapweed and saddlebush and junco and bernardia. Then the magnificent World Bridge loomed ahead and within seconds hovered over them as they hurtled southward. A throng of trucks crowded the spaghetti-like tangle of bridge ramps, spilling out onto the chaotic interstate like an armada sailing off to war.

9 THE BORDER

LAREDO IS a small city of a quarter of a million people. But it gives the appearance of a vastly larger metropolis because of the international traffic passing through.

Grace's management had arranged for a cameraman from the local affiliate owned by Channel Six's broadcast company. She phoned their office as they reached the World Trade Bridge.

"Freddie is all set," the receptionist responded in a heavy Spanish accent. "He'll be in the parking lot."

They drove directly to the station. It was unimpressive—a stark white concrete structure surrounded by huge dishes and a tower. Its large, arch-shaped entrance was guarded by a ten-foot chain-link fence topped with several strands of barbed wire. The call letters, channel designation and network logo were prominently displayed over the arch.

The photographer was waiting. Grace jumped out to greet him. He was surprisingly young. She wondered warily if he was an intern.

"I'm Grace," she said. She cringed inwardly, questioning if he would be up to the task. She realized how spoiled she was, working with veterans like Steve Jankowski.

"Freddie Montsabais," he shook her outstretched hand with gusto, then quickly added, "I'm thirty-two." He bellowed at her aghast reaction. "I know. Everyone thinks I just got out of high school. I'll probably still get carded when I'm fifty. I've been shooting for Channel Nine for eight years. I won't disappoint you."

Grace flushed with embarrassment. She steered him to the driver's side. "Come around and meet detective Moore."

Ned stepped from the car and grasped the cameraman's

hand.

"Hello, detective. We'll take my truck, since I know my way around," the young cameraman told him. "I can bring you back to get your car."

Grace warmed quickly to this energetic young man.

They climbed into the vehicle and drove off. Freddie turned the van off the highway and drove down Saunders, a busy street with small businesses. It was a rag-tag area, yet bustled with commerce, dominated by used car lots and auto repair shops.

LPD headquarters was on the edge of this section, near the end of winding streets that curved around a private airfield. Grace was glad to have Freddie driving. It would have been easy to get lost.

As they parked, she noted the structure's widely windowed exterior. It was fronted by a large courtyard and a granite archway etched with "Laredo Police Department."

Officer Barrera met them in the lobby. "Hello, Ned."

The investigator shook Moore's hand briskly, grinning at his old friend, then turned to Grace. "And welcome."

As Grace started to gesture toward Freddie, Officer Barrera playfully slapped the photographer's shoulder. "No introduction needed. I know this young man very well. He helped us out when the network came down to shoot some segments of 'Border Battles.'"

"You worked on that show?" Ned asked Barrera.

"That was my baby. I coordinated it for the department."

Grace relaxed. These guys were veterans.

Henry escorted them upstairs to his office in the administrative wing. He brought them coffee and settled behind his desk. He was in his forties and wore a neat gray suit and pale blue necktie. His office was packed with awards and souvenirs from cases he had worked.

"Officer Barrera," Grace began, pulling a small notepad from her computer bag, "we've reported extensively on the narcotics trade that runs up to Metro Atlanta from Mexico. Tell me a little bit about your challenges in trying to stop them."

"It's a huge task. We've known for a long time the drug trade existed of course," he started. "But it was, for lack of a better term, more manageable. Then, about nine years ago, we experienced an alarming spike in homicides on this side. That's when it became obvious the narcotics business in Mexico was more rapidly becoming an enormous problem."

He took a sip of his coffee. "For several years we put most of our resources against what was coming at us from the south. But Laredo was increasingly dangerous. So now, much of our manpower is devoted to reducing crime in our city, and we're making progress."

"Can you quantify it for me?"

"Sure," the officer responded. "At the peak, homicides had jumped to around thirty a year. Now they're back down to ten or twelve, where they had been before the drugs escalated across the border. And vehicle thefts are way down, because we busted groups that were stealing them and selling them to the cartels."

The briefing continued for a half-hour or so. Grace wanted to get to the heart of the matter. "Investigator, you told Ned about the captured cartel leader..."

"Guillermo Lopez Castillo," he broke in, then stopped. In a moment of unconstrained decision, Officer Barrera ordered, "Let's go."

Startled, Grace bounced out of her chair and followed the investigator from his office. Freddie grabbed his camera, and he and Ned scurried to follow.

As the four stepped into the elevator, Grace's senses sprang alive, a geyser of adrenaline. Was she really being taken somewhere to interview one of the most dangerous villains in Mexican history? Her breath came in gasps as her brain raced to remember what she planned to ask him.

But her thoughts became engulfed in confusion. Barrera had pushed the "up" button, not "down." The car stopped on the top floor. He stepped out of the elevator and led them quickly through a corridor. The officer stopped abruptly and peeked through the small glass window of a door marked "interrogation."

"He's here?" Ned blurted out, dumbfounded.

Henry looked at Freddie's camera. "You can only film him from behind. Everyone knows what he looks like, but he wouldn't agree to his face being exposed." The photographer nodded okay, his expression fraught with anxiety.

As they entered the small, barren room, the prisoner was seated at a small wooden table. Two huge uniformed policemen sat on either side of him with their arms folded. Castillo was uncuffed. He was disheveled and unshaven, his prison clothes drab and wrinkled, his face haggard, firmly etched with deep lines. He lifted his tired eyes.

Officer Barrera pulled out a chair and motioned for Grace to sit. He gestured for Freddie to move around behind, and the cameraman aimed at Grace over Castillo's shoulder. Ned hung back against a wall with his Laredo *compadre*.

As Grace began to speak, a shudder rippled through her. The man across the table had killed brutally for a living. He had commanded an army of thugs who had ruthlessly slaughtered anyone who got in their way—judges, police, journalists, mayors, innocent citizens, rival gang members. She was having a conversation with a character more brutish than she could imagine, as if they were chatting over tea.

"*Señor* Castillo, until your arrest you led one of the most violent cartels in your country. Why were you involved in the illegal trafficking of drugs?"

The Mexican paused and cleared his throat. "When I started I was young. There was no work." His words came out in a rasp, the hollow echo of years of smoking, drinking and languishing in a musty jail cell. His English was thick with Spanish, halting but understand-able. "We told ourselves this was a way to feed our families and have a good life."

"And now?" she asked. "Looking back, do you regret the life?"

He considered for a moment. "I said at my trial I was re-morseful. I meant it. I expressed regret to my country, to *Los Estados Unidos*, and to my family."

"I read you had apologized, and you are now trying to make amends by working with law enforcement. But you left a wide path of killings, kidnappings and other gruesome atrocities. Your activities ru-ined countless lives through the sale of thousands of tons of cocaine. Why should we believe you are repentant, and not just trying to save your own hide?'

He emitted an angry scoffing sound. "Why should I lie to you? I will be in jail for the rest of my days."

"When you were arrested in Mexico, you continued to run the cartel from a jail cell before being extradited to the U.S.?"

"*Si.* It was not so difficult."

"What were your organization's worst crimes?"

"We did many evil things," he answered bluntly, "but recruit-ing and training American-born teenage boys, taking them to Mexican camps and teaching them to kill...that was unforgivable."

He motioned to one of the officers who produced a cigarette, gave it to Castillo and lit it for him. The prisoner took a long drag and continued, "And meanwhile, on our side of the river, we gave no hope for children except to grow up and work in our world. There might be one small school for a thousand children. Their future is to sell soda on the street corners."

"Soda—injectable cocaine?"

"*Si,* yes." He nodded. "They give in to the lure of big money and a flashy lifestyle. We had so much money and access to so many resources, it was..." he searched for a word, "...impossible for law enforcement to compete. Many of them joined us, at least those we didn't kill. It was a bad existence for them, and for their families. But it was a life."

Henry Barrera stepped forward, tapped Grace's shoulder and gestured with his head toward the door.

"One final question, *Señor* Castillo. If you had not gone into the life of drugs and crime, what would you have done?"

For the first and only time, the surly Mexican laughed, loudly. "*Quien sabe?* Who knows? Maybe a farmer."

**

Outside, in front of the LPD building, Grace delivered her report's conclusion. "The extradition and conviction of Guillermo Lopez Castillo is a shining example of how authorities in both countries worked together to put away a dangerous drug kingpin. Even though he provides valuable information about the cartels' inner workings, there are many more like him still free, committing murder and making the war on drugs an uphill battle." She relaxed, nodded to Montsabais and heaved a massive sigh. She didn't realize until that moment how tense she had been.

She turned toward Investigator Barrera. "I don't know how to thank you."

"Thank your friend Ned Moore," he grinned toward the detective standing next to them. "He did me a few favors back in the day."

"I know Ned told you we want to report from the other side," she offered sheepishly. "What do you think?"

"You just interviewed one of the most feared men in all of Mexico. You still want to go over there?"

"Yes."

"I can't get you across."

"But..." Grace began to stammer an objection.

"It's not possible."

Her shoulders sagged.

"However," Henry continued, "I am willing to take you down to the river and you can report from the Texas side if you want. It can still be a good conclusion to your story."

"Will you let me interview you there on camera?" she asked the investigator.

He hesitated for a long moment. "Let's go then."

**

The three climbed into Freddie's van. Barrera walked to a separate parking lot where his cruiser was parked. The officer pulled out of the driveway, and the van followed. The trip downtown took ten minutes—a hop onto the interstate and a jump off where it ended near the largest of the international bridges. Traffic swelled as the two vehicles emptied onto one of the surface streets packed with cars, SUVs and pickups jamming into the crossing lanes. The investigator wove his police car expertly through the turmoil and veered down a side street that ran parallel with the bridge. Freddie struggled to keep pace.

A customs official was waiting and motioned them to a gated area. The two officers spoke quietly for a moment, and the small group made its way on foot up to the pedestrian walkway that led across to Mexico.

Freddie aimed his camera, and Grace opened her report.

"I'm standing on the U.S. side of international bridge number one," she began, "the only span to Nuevo Laredo that allows pedestrian traffic."

She pointed, and Montsabais deftly followed her gesture with his lens.

"Over there you can see the eight-lane Juarez-Lincoln Bridge, also known as bridge number two. That one provides crossing only for non-commercial vehicles, which can back up for long periods. Part of the delay is from sheer volume. But make no mistake, much of it is due to searches for the tons of contraband that make their way through this area."

Grace turned toward the Laredo policeman. "With me is investigator Henry Barrera of the Laredo Police Department." She smoothly moved around so the camera was shooting over her shoulder, pointed toward Mexico and focused on Barrera. "Officer Barrera, why is it so hard to catch the narcotics coming across this border?"

"Nearly one-third of all U.S. international trade from Mexico takes this route. There are so many vehicles passing through, including the eighteen-wheelers going across the World Trade Bridge, it's impossible to uncover all the smuggled drugs. For every load you intercept, two or three might slip through."

"How are they hidden?"

"Every way possible, and the criminals are getting more creative each day. We find them stashed in every space imaginable in vehicles. They are cleverly concealed in products in the big trucks. One major cartel boss who was recently caught and convicted had a helicopter and was transporting cocaine to points as far away as Canada. You can see how so much contraband can make its way up the highways to cities such as Atlanta."

"Who takes the lead in this war against the cartels in your city?"

Henry responded, "The Laredo PD usually does, because an investigation normally begins with a local crime, such as a homicide. But we have learned our best efforts come from working with other agencies—the DEA, ATF, FBI. One of our most important sources of information about what's happening on the other side is the Joint Operations Intelligence Center."

"Do you get help from the local police in Nuevo Laredo?"

"There is essentially no police presence in the Mexican border towns anymore," he shook his head. "Many local law officials were drawn into the cartels because they didn't have a choice. If they tried to fight them, they died. There is only the national military. Some of them are corrupted, and the rest are limited in what they can do. But we do have an extradition agreement with Mexico. There have been a number of exchanges on the bridge. That's the jurisdiction of the State Department and the U.S. Marshals."

"Thank you, Officer Barrera."

Freddie pointed his camera at Grace as she delivered her wrap-up. "Large quantities of the narcotics that end up in Gwinnett County, Georgia, then fan out to markets all over the Southeast, come across this river," she said. "And when you talk to officers such as Henry Barrera, LPD, you can't help feeling they're doing everything possible." She paused for effect. "And that we're still losing the war."

Grace lowered her microphone and Freddie switched off the camera. Grace and Ned shook Officer Barrera's hand, and they walked the path to their vehicles. Freddie followed.

"I'm sorry you couldn't shoot the other side," the policeman said. "But it's not uncommon for United States citizens to get kidnapped or disappear."

"But if you were to go with us…" Grace tried weakly.

"Not on your life," Barrera interrupted, grinning as if he had heard a joke. "They kill their own cops. Why would they leave me alone?" He got into his car. "Call if you need anything else."

**

They watched Henry Barrera drive off. Freddie loaded his camera equipment into the truck and stood staring up at the massive old structure, his eyes tracing its span across the Rio Grande. "I haven't been over there in a long time."

Ned pulled the van door open and motioned for Grace to get in, but she hesitated, watching the photographer curiously. "What is it, Freddie?"

The young man turned toward her decisively. "Let's do it. Let's finish your story on the other side."

Ned continued to hold the door open, chuckling at the obvious joke.

"You're serious, aren't you?" Grace challenged in wonder.

"Sure am. Hell, we don't have to go far into the city. We can go a short distance from the end of the bridge, do your report, and then cross over to return northbound. You'd be telling your story from the battleground."

"No, Freddie. You're not doing it," Detective Moore protested vigorously.

The photographer reached into his pocket and pulled out a videocam the size of a cell phone. "I can shoot with this to keep from calling attention to what we're doing. They'll think we're tourists. The resolution might not be as good as what I shot earlier, but it's HD. Probably a lot better than some of the trash people shoot with their phones and we use that on the air. Your station probably does, too. You can tell your viewers you're at the source of the problem. It's credibility, Grace."

"I like this guy," Grace said, her heart rate at mach two.

"No way, Grace. I can't let you take that chance," the retired detective protested.

"I'm bilingual. I can keep us out of harm's way," Montsabais argued. "Come on," and in an instant he was hurrying back toward the bridge.

"You wait here, Ned," Grace said as she scampered to follow.

Moore stood flabbergasted, watching the two pick up speed toward the pedestrian crossing. There was genuine panic in his eyes as he decided what to do. He shook his head woefully, slammed the door shut and huff-puffed after them.

10 DANGEROUS CITY

THERE WAS LITTLE foot traffic going to the Mexican side. They were there within minutes. Freddie paid the tiny pedestrian toll for all of them and handed them each a temporary access card. They swiped them in the scanner and walked quickly through the huge convex entrance into Mexico. As they hurried toward the square, the sights and sounds surprised Grace. Not knowing what to expect, she had imagined a kind of ghost town. There were some boarded-up buildings here and there. Yet the place was bustling with taxis, street vendors, children mobbing them, asking for money or candy. Mexicans were streaming toward the other side, going to work or to shop in Laredo.

"It has changed a lot," Freddie lamented. "My wife and I used to cross over here on Saturday nights. We would drink tequila at the Camino Bar, have a nice steak and listen to music. You could hardly move through the streets. It's not the same. Except for these little beggars.

"*Vayase. Prisa,*" Freddie reprimanded. *Go away.*

The children remained, hands pushing toward them, pleading.

The trio moved quickly up the main drag, *Guerrero*. Grace felt a kind of uneasy fear creep in as she took in the scene. Except for abandoned buildings, it seemed merely an extension of the metro area across the river. Still, she knew what was happening there every day. The people couldn't possibly be oblivious to the crime and cartels that were scarring their lawless city. Yet they turned their heads. What else could they do?

About a block south of the bridge the taxis were lined up, but there was little business. Freddie stopped and positioned Grace where he could photograph the town in the background while she reported. "That first traffic light down there is Hidalgo," he explained. "We'll do it from here." He held up his tiny camera.

"We've crossed over the bridge into Nuevo Laredo," Grace said, feeling a little awkward reporting to a tiny handheld camera. "Over there," she pointed toward the northbound bridge, "where you see the line of vehicles, is the entry point for vast amounts of drugs that find their way north to Gwinnett County, Georgia. Down here in Mexico, warfare has claimed an estimated seventy thousand lives, from cartel members and politicians, to police and innocent citizens. Another twenty thousand plus have disappeared.

"Sources tell us that many of the tourist spots—shops, vendor kiosks, restaurants and bars—have dried up due to drug violence. But there is still a lot of activity, including children begging or selling trinkets they have made for whatever people will pay. For those who survive the constant threat of hostilities, life goes on."

In her periphery, as Grace spoke, she noticed two thugs, less than a block away, languishing in a shop doorway, openly displayed assault rifles. They glared at her, commenting to one another. A third, hanging back farther, lugged a rocket launcher. As Grace continued, with Montsabais shooting away, the three moved up the street toward them, serious and purposeful.

Her pulse quickened. She fought to keep her voice from breaking in panic.

Ned, who had stayed well apart from Grace and Freddie, now stepped in. His eyes reflected deep concern. He held up a meaty palm to block Freddie's camera lens. "Let's go," he said softly with a tone of gravity Grace had never before heard from the man. Ned had always been the strong one, the comfort in peril, the calming influence. Now his voice cracked as he took her elbow and guided her across the street with the photographer stumbling after them.

The three armed men picked up their pace, circling around them as if to head off their progress toward the northbound bridge.

"Que pasa?" one of the rifle-bearers growled at Freddie as

he quickened his step toward the Americans. He was tall, burly and unshaven, probably forty.

With reflexive urgency, Freddie turned and began to film the threatening Mexican.

"Who the hell are you?" the hoodlum asked in heavily accented English. "What's going on?"

Freddie stopped shooting and bravely faced him. *"Nada,"* he replied urgently. *"Somos touristas." We are tourists.*

By now the two men had reached them. *"Touristas? No, no lo creo,"* the smaller Latino responded. *No, I don't think so.* He was young and built squat like a wrestler, his shoulders and arms under his sleeveless tee shirt a wall of tattoos.

Freddie surprised Grace by stepping aggressively toward the two, intervening. He spoke to them in frantic Spanish. They responded, heatedly, gesturing toward Grace and Ned. Freddie's reply, in a low and confidential tone, became more rapid and frenetic. Grace strained to hear, knowing she wouldn't understand anyway.

She could see the third man, barely more than a teen, weaving his way with the rocket-launcher through the curious, gathering crowd. He moved closer and eyed them suspiciously. She glanced at Ned. He was peering at the entrance to the northbound bridge as if planning an escape.

Several in the growing throng of onlookers began to find their voice, speaking up excitedly as if rallying in support of the cartel gunslingers. Oddly, the scene felt to Grace like a television report of a planned mob in Iran. Thoughts of Mogadishu catapulted through her mind. A Benghazi raid. A U.S. marine chained to a Mexican prison bed.

Her mouth grew cottony dry. Perspiration soaked her neck and forehead.

The larger of the two armed men had a grip on Freddie's shoulder, shaking it methodically as they argued. Freddie pulled free and continued to squabble desperately in the man's native language.

The other Mexican stepped in closer, frowning. He slowly raised the barrel of his weapon toward Freddie. He lowered the rifle again, turned and grasped Grace's arm roughly. His eyes smoldered with menace. She panicked. Images of being kidnapped, dragged off to some hellhole of a jail, held as bait for ransom, or worse, flooded her mind.

Detective Moore stepped forward and reached toward the man's hand, his expression a ferocious scowl. Everything was happening with incredible speed.

Now, even more rapidly, the cavalry rode in without warning, a rescue from nowhere. The crowd buzzed and parted as one of the Mexican Army's new multi-role defense vehicles screeched to a halt within feet of the quarreling group.

Six soldiers, wearing camouflage and helmets, their faces obscured by ski masks, jumped from the SandCat with ready rifles. As quickly as they had appeared, the bad guys vanished into the crowd.

The squad leader motioned for them to follow him across to the northbound side of the bridge. "You need to hurry," he said to Freddie in Spanish.

Two of the soldiers, one in front and the other behind them, shepherded the three past the line of Mexicans waiting to go across into Texas. Grace, Ned and Freddie scampered to keep pace with the trotting soldiers, racing across the bridge on shaky legs.

"What did they say?" Grace yelled over her shoulder at Montsabais.

His voice rattled as he ran. "They got a black eye when they arrested the American marine. They don't want another incident."

Grace looked over the rail and down at the river. Three men were swimming toward Texas.

The soldier in front barked an order to the attendant who motioned them past the gate. As they moved through it, a familiar sight greeted them on the other side. Investigator Henry Barrera stood waiting, his gripping choler evident as he grimaced. Standing beside him was the customs agent who had helped them park earlier.

"I told you not to go," Officer Barrera fumed at Grace. Turning to Freddie, he growled, "You, you know better."

"Lo siento," Freddie cast his eyes at the ground, properly admonished. "Sorry."

"Fortunately, Officer Morales here kept track of you," Henry continued. "His brother lives in Nuevo Laredo and works on the other side. When they saw there was trouble they called the military." He scowled, leaning toward Ned. "They kill their own journalists, detective. And they kidnap Americans for money. Grace Gleason, you're very lucky."

"I get it, Henry," Ned said quietly, still gasping from the bridge dash. "We learned a lesson. We'll go home now."

"Good luck," the officer said. He walked down to the parking area, climbed into his cruiser and was gone.

**

Grace and Ned stayed at the station long enough to watch Freddie transmit her edited interviews to Big Six by satellite, then download the Mexico minicam video onto a computer and email it to Vivian Ellis.

It was growing dark when they got back on the road. Grace tried to fight off the weariness as they left Laredo. She wondered how Ned could even drive.

The tumultuous events of the past few hours cascaded through her mind. In a tortured way, the experience took her back in half-sleep to what her ex, Jeff, had once said about her work.

They had quarreled about her penchant for pursuing dangerous stories. One in particular, an unsolved murder, had driven a wedge between them because of her tenacious refusal to back down from covering a killer on the loose.

"I want you to stop chasing after that guy," Jeff complained one night at bedtime, referring to the prime suspect. Propped against a pillow on the bed, Jeff looked up from the legal briefs he was reviewing. "You're going to end up hurt. Or dead."

"Honey, I try to be careful. But it's my job," she defended, trying to look nonchalant as she applied lotion to her arms at the dresser. She attempted to fight off growing feelings of resentment. She believed Jeff's concerns came from love. But sometimes Grace wondered if his complaint stemmed from a driven wish to live their lives his way, uncompromised.

"You don't have to be that frigging station's go-to crime reporter," he grew more contentious. "I know you don't go looking for trouble, Grace. But somehow it always finds you."

On some level Grace knew her husband was right. The lengths to which she dogged killers and crooks put her in jeopardy. She truly didn't understand it herself. Maybe she was unconsciously trying to prove something to Jeff, to prevent being marginalized. Or perhaps she was simply so outraged by injustice she couldn't ignore the compulsion to go wherever it led her.

Whatever her motivation, this insatiable need to right wrongs had become an integral part of who she was. It had brought her to Mexico.

The unpleasant memory drifted away like ripples in a stream as Grace leaned back and tried to sleep. She was about to doze off when she felt the car slow down on the highway and shift suddenly to the right lane.

She opened her eyes to the sight of a huge German Shepherd, straining at its leash, trying to cross in front of them as Ned stopped the car. They had pulled into an inspection station. An officer yanked the dog back, and another waved them forward. He leaned in as Ned lowered his window. "Are you United States citizens?" the man asked. He had only a trace of Spanish accent.

"Yes," Ned replied. "Both of us."

"Go ahead," the officer said. "God bless you." The unexpected words sent a shiver down Grace's back and made her proud of her country. They went on in silence.

**

Ned met her for breakfast and then drove her to curbside at the San Antonio airport. All the while, as they bantered in their old familiar way and said their goodbyes, she had a nagging feeling she wouldn't ever see him again.

At the gate, she fished her cell phone from her purse and called Vivian.

"It's Grace. Did Freddie's footage get there okay?"

"It did, and it's fine," the news director said. "The cameraman emailed me about your confrontation at the bridge." She laughed. "It's kind of funny now. Not so much when I first read it."

"It will be a better story now," Grace told her. "It closes the loop from Mexico to Gwinnett County."

Ellis exclaimed, "At least we won't be reporting your capture. Or murder."

"Sorry, I have to go," Grace apologized. "Another call."

It was Ned. "I just heard from Henry," he sounded stressed. "You won't believe."

"What, quick? They're about to call my flight."

"They found Guillermo Lopez Castillo this morning."

"Found?"

"They got to him, Grace. His enemies kidnapped him out of that hideout somehow in the wee hours and hung his cold body from the Juarez-Lincoln Bridge."

"No!" she blurted out.

"They had cut out his tongue."

**

As she boarded the jet and settled into her seat, Grace relived the horror she had felt, the helplessness as those cartel members harassed them. They had escaped, but so many others—foreigners who disappeared and local Mexican citizens caught in the war—had paid a terrible price. Grace felt incredibly lucky the American officer had notified the authorities of their confrontation with the thugs. She had known when Freddie bolted for the bridge it would be dangerous. Yet she hadn't hesitated. Jeff was right. Her devotion to pursuing stories was so profound, danger drew her like a magnet. She always believed she would emerge unscathed.

And Castillo. Dead, mere hours after she had talked to him. She had conducted the last interview of his life! The network would want to run it.

She sat back and closed her eyes. It was clear to her this battle would never end. And her own closing words after the interview with Officer Barrera on the bridge haunted Grace. *"...you can't help feeling they're doing everything possible. And that we're still losing the war."*

She felt a hard, softball-sized knot in her stomach. Maybe she had been wrong, and Scott Matthews and Vivian Ellis were right. This drug story, as big as it was, had no beginning and no end. It was a bottomless pool of destruction she could report on forever, and the constant stream of madness would continue.

She recalled Scott had asked if the string of thefts might be gang-related. She had doubts, but if they were, and she could uncover it, at least she might serve the citizens of Atlanta. Maybe her focus was in the wrong place.

Yet she had come so far.

Eduardo was counting on her.

For the first time as a news reporter, Grace Gleason felt lost.

11 TEMPTATION

AS GRACE DOZED in her seat on the flight back to Atlanta, Eduardo Cruz arrived at Impact Workouts in Northwood carrying a gym bag. Officer Doug McHughes met him at the door, already dressed in shorts and a tank top.

"Cruz. Glad you could make it, man."

Eduardo scanned the state-of-the art equipment. "Hello, McHughes. This place looks like it has the best. Listen, I'll use the guest passes," Cruz said, "but I'm not promising I'll join."

"Sure. Go ahead, get dressed out right back there," Doug pointed out the locker room, "and come warm up on one of the cardio machines. I'll meet you at the free weights. We'll start you off pretty easy until we see what you can do. I'll spot you."

Fifteen minutes later, the young Gwinnett officer was breathing hard from a fast-paced, uphill run on the treadmill.

"You haven't been lifting?" the Atlanta officer asked as Eduardo joined him at the weight racks.

"Just some work on the stack machines down at the station house," Cruz answered. "For biceps and lats—that kind of stuff. Maybe once or twice a week. But I rarely go over a hundred pounds on any of them."

"That's a start," said the muscular McHughes. "But if you come in with us, several times a week, we'll have you lifting much more with free weights in no time. The key is not to compare yourself with anyone else. Go at your own pace. Think about working up to bench pressing your bodyweight and maybe squatting one-and-a-half times your weight. But gradually."

"If it'll give me guns like yours, I'm game."

For the next thirty minutes, he traded sets with McHughes.

The Atlanta policeman coached him, showing him the proper techniques. Doug used significantly more weight, and on his last lift he leg pressed two hundred fifty pounds.

"That's impressive," Eduardo said as McHughes finished the final set with seeming ease, merely grunting a bit.

"You can get there, Cruz," Eduardo's new friend promised as he toweled the sweat off his face and shoulders. "It took me a while to work up to that. Come on, I want you to meet some other guys." They walked to a nearby row of ab machines where a man had just completed a set and was examining his shirtless muscles in the mirrored wall.

"Meet Bret Larkin, a Riverwood deputy sheriff," Doug said. "And that's Carter Drake." A third man sat up from doing crunches and nodded.

Cruz shook each man's hand vigorously. "I saw you guys working out. Didn't realize you were cops, too."

"Well, I am, but Carter isn't," Larkin answered. "He got smart and left the force several years ago."

"Left the force?" Eduardo asked. "How come?"

"Why does anyone leave? It's a shit job for no pay," Drake grumbled. "I make more in one quarter as a security consultant than I used to in an entire year breaking up domestic fights and chasing gang bangers."

Eduardo gave him a wry smile. "I've got to get home or my wife will think I've got a girlfriend."

"I'll walk out with you," McHughes said.

The Atlanta officer and Cruz walked to the parking lot. Doug reached into his bag and pulled out some papers. "Here's the stuff Sam gave me on a membership—application, rules and regs, all that shit. Just in case you decide to join."

Eduardo glanced through the material and whistled. "Man, that's a great price he gives you guys."

"You should take advantage of it."

"I'll consider it. First I'll need to talk to Adella. We don't make any monthly commitments without putting it in our family budget."

"Smart." Doug grasped Eduardo's hand in a friendly, firm handshake. "Hard to put two quarters together these days, the way gas and everything else has gone up."

"Trust in the Lord with all your heart and lean not on your own understanding," Eduardo smiled. "Proverbs three, verse five."

McHughes straightened up and peered at the Gwinnett officer. "You one of them religious freaks, Cruz?"

"Religious, yes. Freak, no," Eduardo answered. "We simply trust that if we do the right thing, God will provide."

"Maybe the big fellow is looking out for you after all. There's another way to get the membership free."

"Oh? That sounds even better."

"Not a free membership, actually. But a way to offset it. You've got a rep for hating these drug gangs, right?"

"You said it. They're ruining my home county."

"Some of us guys—you met a couple of them tonight—have figured out a way to bleed the drug money out of those assholes. We weaken them and help ourselves at the same time. Hard to maintain gym memberships and pay all the bills on what we make, right?"

The younger officer looked askance, not answering.

"We target the bad guys and take away their means of support. I figure we're doing the community a favor. The more we take away their bread, the less they have to butter."

"Doesn't sound legal to me," Eduardo said slowly.

"And what those bastards are doing to your hometown is lawful? Get smart, man. Think about it. We can use a savvy young guy like you who knows all the gang action. Especially in Gwinnett County."

"I don't know. I'll think about it," Eduardo promised.

"Think hard. Your bill-paying worries will be over, and you'll be able to afford to come to Impact Workouts at police rates, no sweat. Meanwhile, no one gets hurt but those *Los Lagartos* losers."

Doug climbed into his new over-sized SUV and squealed away. Eduardo stood staring at his six-year-old compact sedan, shaking his head weakly.

12 HOME AGAIN

IT'S UNIVERSAL, the satisfying appeal of returning from a vacation or business trip or distant crisis. Every time she travelled, Grace experienced a sense of relief and comfort.

She was home. It had only been hers for months, yet when she opened the door, her heart flooded with a kind of soothing familiarity of smells and sounds and sanctity.

Yesterday she had been knee-deep in the South Texas imbroglio of narcotics and murder. Now, as she dropped her bags in the foyer, the trip seemed ages ago and continents away.

She went into the kitchen to look for a snack and noticed her message light flashing. Suddenly she realized she had never turned her cell phone back on after deplaning. Megan would be furious. In the car, Grace had intended to call right away, as she always demanded when her daughter returned from a trip. But her fatigue, the banter with the taxi driver, and a brief review of the notes from her experiences had distracted her.

She punched up the first message, fully expecting Megan's anxious reprimand. Instead, it was Charlie, the night assignment editor. *"Grace, I understand you're due back today. I've been trying to reach you for an hour."*

She stretched and glanced at her watch. Her muscles ached and her head hurt from lack of sleep. "It's midnight, Charlie. Please don't," she uttered aloud, exhausted.

His message continued. *"There has been a turn of events in*

that string of robberies. The Handy Homer home improvement mon-
strosity up in Gwinnett County was hit tonight after closing time. Vivian wants you to take it. The manager won't be available 'til six, and
Steve is going up. Let him know if you'll ride with him or meet him
there. I know you just got back today, but we need you, Grace."

She called and got the assignment editor's voicemail. "Charlie, it's Grace. Tell Jankowski I'll be there in the morning and ride with
him."

She decided against the snack. Bone-deep tired, she trudged
to the bedroom. She undressed and fell into bed. Five hours of sleep,
a quick shower and she would be back in the saddle.

**

Jankowski was waiting in the truck in the station parking lot.

"Welcome back," his eyes twinkled knowing she didn't want
to be there. "Here." he handed her a large coffee.

"Thanks," she murmured, still groggy. "Where's that twerp
Scott Matthews? He's supposed to be covering these robberies."

"Out of town," Steve said. "Grandfather died."

"Oh, sorry."

There was hardly any traffic. Drivers who were heading south
to the airport for an early flight or going toward the city and their workplace before the crush, pushed the speed limit on I-85. In two hours,
this same freeway would be packed with frustrated commuters crawl-
ing at ten miles an hour.

The cameraman pulled the van into the Handy Homer driveway after a high-speed twenty-minute drive. "Seems like we've been
here before," he chuckled, recalling their coverage of the meth lab

raid.

There were several police cars parked near the front entrance. Jankowski parked next to the news car of their FM sister station. "Radio's already here," he noted.

As they approached the store, the other reporter greeted them. "Grace, hi, Rick Dent, ninety-eight point seven radio." He was short, rotund, early fifties, with thinning brown hair. He impressed her as a jittery sort.

She smiled and shook his hand. He had a sound pack slung over his shoulder and was carrying a microphone. "I just got here. The manager's going to come out since that's still a crime scene in there. The detectives came back out to question him a second time. That says to me they think it could be an inside job."

"Or he was too sleepy to be coherent last night," Grace laughed. She introduced the radio newsman to Steve Jankowski and they waited.

"I like your new segment," Dent said brightly. "Maybe we can collaborate on something sometime."

She smiled cordially, having no idea what they might possibly work on together. The news business isn't totally accidental, but the disordered nature of it doesn't lend itself well to partnerships. Except for a reporter and her trusted cameraman. She glanced at Steve setting up his equipment, happy to have such a professional on her side.

Grace was pleased that none of the other outlets had yet arrived. What could have been pandemonium promised to be a controlled exercise, with her at the helm.

"I'm going to see if I can get to the manager," she told Steve as they walked toward the doors cordoned off with yellow crime scene tape. She glanced over her shoulder to see Dent hanging back, watching.

Peering through the front doors, she could see a man talking animatedly to one of the investigating officers. Several other cops moved toward the back of the store. When the investigator turned to join his fellow police, Grace motioned frantically to the manager.

He opened the door and gazed out at them. "Hi. Johnny James," he said. "I'm the manager."

Grace almost laughed, recalling an old joke about not trusting a man with two first names. Johnny was medium height, thin and surprisingly young. His Adam's apple bobbed as he spoke in a deep, droning tone.

"The detectives are in here poking around."

"Grace Gleason, Channel Six," she said. "Can you come out and talk to me for a minute?"

Johnny swung the door open and held it, not emerging. Grace was positioned so that Steve's shot over her shoulder would capture the manager. Rick Dent got his mic close enough to pick up the sound. Grace appreciated him staying out of the shot.

It was still semi-dark outside. Grace held a sheet of white paper near Johnny James' face for Steve to get a white balance. Steve signaled "okay," and Grace turned abruptly to face the manager who shifted nervously back and forth.

"Mr. James, describe what happened here," Grace began.

"Well, ah," he stumbled, his eyes wide in the camera lights, "I don't think the police want me to talk to you."

"Just, in general terms," she persisted. "For example, what time did the burglary occur?"

"Sometime overnight. There were no employees here at the time. The burglars somehow got in without tripping the alarm and seemed to know where the safe was located."

"Are you saying it might have been an inside job?"

He hesitated. "I don't kno...maybe," James continued to stammer. "All I can say is they hit us on the biggest sales day of the week. Kind of spooky."

"How much did they steal?" she asked bluntly.

"...I don't know if I can say."

Grace moved the microphone a bit closer to his face. "You don't need to be specific. Just in round numbers, about how much?"

His eyes darted toward the camera and back to Grace, reflecting the pressure he was feeling. "Well, uh...it could have been thousands, maybe."

"Thousands of dollars," Grace repeated for emphasis.

The young manager edged to Grace's side, trying to turn his back to the camera. Steve maneuvered to keep Johnny's face in the frame. "You know, Miss Gleason," James mumbled toward Grace's ear, uneasy at being on record, "I probably shouldn't have said that. About the money, I mean. I could get fired."

"Don't worry, Johnny," she assured. "We'll confirm it with the police."

James nodded half-heartedly, his eyes shifting from the microphone to the camera and back again. The store door popped open, and the detective reappeared and grabbed Johnny's shoulder.

"No press," he told the manager gruffly, pulling him back inside the store.

Grace lowered the mic. "Thanks, Johnny." He closed the door and went back inside. She grinned like a casino winner at Steve. "That will do nicely."

"I didn't get my chance," complained Rick.

"You got everything I did," Grace answered. "You can insert your own questions on the track and cut me out."

As Steve packed his gear into the truck, Rick followed Grace to the passenger side, reached out and touched her elbow. Not realizing he was there, she jumped. His approach might have creeped her out if he weren't such a comical little guy. Instead, she smiled.

"Sorry," he apologized for startling her. "Listen, I meant what I said earlier. I like what you've done since coming to Atlanta. If you want to pursue this string of property crimes, I'd be up for working on it with you. We could share information."

"This is a one-time thing for me," she told him, watching the disappointment wash across his face. He squinted through his thick glasses, as if waiting for an explanation. "The guy who's investigating all of these robberies for us got called out of town," she added.

"All the same, listen to my news reports and keep it in mind," he insisted. "It would be great to help each other out. I'd make an appearance on 'Crime and Corruption' if you wanted."

"We'll see," she dismissed, puzzled by his overture.

As she climbed into the van, the Channel Two truck pulled into the lot. She smiled widely and waved at them as the Big Six News vehicle pulled out.

Riding back, Grace turned toward Steve and asked, "I can't figure out what Dent's angle is. Do you think it's about getting to the bottom of a series of crimes or trying to piggyback on our hard work?"

"Not the latter," Jankowski answered matter-of-factly. "Dent's been around for centuries, and he's a real news guy, one of the good ones. You could do worse than keeping him in your speed dial list."

"Let me out at my car," Grace requested as they approached the station.

"Not going in?"

"I'm beat. Had a long trip, five hours of sleep and then this. I'll call Ellis and tell her if I don't get some rest, I'll be sub-par all week. Plus, I would have had breakfast with my daughter to catch up. The least I can do is take her to lunch."

"She must be quite the young woman, architecture and all," he smiled.

"Pretty and smart. Nothing like her mom," Grace chuckled and jumped from the truck.

Before Steve pulled away, she held the door open. "Don't tell Vivian where I'm going, okay? She doesn't need to know."

Jankowski cocked his head and pursed his lips, as if to say, "Whom do you think you're talking to?"

She felt immediately foolish. Of course Jankowski knew that managers don't expect their news staff to have families or take time away from the business. Photographers and reporters talk family all the time, but they don't reveal much to their demanding managers.

"Right," she responded to his reprimanding expression and closed the door.

Her cell phone chimed as she crossed the parking lot.

"It's Rick Dent. I did some digging. The Handy Homer jackpot was fifty thousand."

"How did you get that so fast? And why tell me?" She was flabbergasted.

"Grace, I have good sources. It's like I said, we can help each other out."

As she hung up and started her car, fighting fatigue, she considered the unusual overture from Dent. What could that radio guy possibly be up to?

13 BUDDING ARCHITECT

WEEKS PASSED between Grace's reunion with her daughter after the Texas trip and the next time she saw her.

"You have to meet me for lunch," she had scolded on the phone. "I know that Tech program is demanding, and I'm happy you keep me posted by phone. But honey, I simply refuse to go this long without seeing you."

Ever since Megan was a teenager, Grace had hovered over her. She and Jeff both had busy careers, and he essentially abdicated their daughter's supervision to his wife. Despite deadlines and frantic calls from assignment desks, Grace managed to keep methodical track of her daughter's whereabouts, ensuring she was always with adult supervision. Grace had not had her mother's care as a girl, and she was determined Megan would always be her highest priority. After the divorce, even with Megan in college, sharing an apartment in a Dallas suburb, Grace stopped by frequently to check up. She insisted Megan make time for her, as she did now.

Properly chastised, Megan agreed to meet at The Goalpost, a local hamburger hangout near the campus.

She slid into the booth where Megan was waiting. "I don't have much time, Mom," her daughter lamented. "My first project is due..."

Grace interrupted, reaching out and taking her daughter's hand. "Its okay, honey. I'm just glad you could break away for a bit. I missed you."

"Decide what you want and I'll go up and order," Megan said. "They don't wait tables here. Everyone jokes about this place. They say they come to get an oil change or a lube job. But these are the most yummy chilidogs and hamburgers east of the Mississippi. And the onion rings..." She let Grace's imagination finish the sentence. As

117

she stood, Grace handed her a twenty.

Megan brought the food back on a tray and gave her mother change.

They dug in. Grace used their brief time to catch up. "Tell me about school," she said.

Her daughter chomped down eagerly on an onion ring and rolled her eyes, half-smirking as she chewed. "You should ask my roommates. Their experience has been a lot different than mine, but I've given them an earful."

Grace asked, "What does that mean?"

"I'm a woman."

"So?"

Megan swallowed her food and took another bite of hot dog, chewing energetically. "So I'm one of several hundred women in a class of over a thousand. A lot of the instructors are male and some are skeptical about females being in the profession."

"In this day and age?" Grace challenged, incredulous.

"They say it's much better than it used to be. Far fewer in-structors are prejudiced than in the old days, apparently. And even the misogynists are more subtle now, from what I hear. But there's still a rotten banana or two. If I'm unfortunate enough to get their class, I can sleep with them to get good grades or work fanatically hard and develop a thick skin. Since my mama didn't raise me to find the former option acceptable, I've had to choose the latter."

"I can't believe there's still sexual harassment in the class-room," Grace was astounded.

"Mom, I have a British instructor who called me a 'piece of skirt' in the middle of class. I calmly stood up and told him we had an appointment with the dean. I was shocked when he actually followed me into the hall, so I dragged his ass down to Dean Dunwoody's office. Fortunately for me, the dean knows Raj is my roommate, and his dad is tight with most of the faculty. Mr. Prakash has given a small fortune to this institution."

"Is that guy the exception?" Grace asked, concerned.

"It is," Megan responded, "but the truth is a couple of my female classmates picked the first option which makes it hard on the rest of us."

"My God," Grace shrieked in horror. "Let's get you out of that awful place."

"Emeritus Dean Wainwright has kind of taken me under his wing. Dean Dunwoody must have talked to him. Wainwright teaches landscape architecture, and that's what I'm going to focus on starting next year. We had a long talk. He told me they have been working to weed out the prejudiced ones. He also said I could do anything I put my mind to. You've kind of drummed that into me for a few years, too. I'll be all right," she reassured.

"'Piece of skirt,'" Grace repeated the insult. "I feel like going over there and giving that Brit a piece of my mind."

Megan shook her head. "I've handled it." She hesitated. "Mom, I hate to bring this up…"

"Oh, oh. Sounds like money."

"Dad was supposed to send me a check at the first of the month. I didn't get it. I left him two messages but still no check. He has no idea how much supplies cost for architecture classes."

Grace frowned, reached into her purse and extracted her checkbook. "How much do you need?"

"Mom, can't you just call Dad and make him send the money?"

"You need it right away, yes?"

Her daughter nodded.

"So, how much?"

"Four hundred should do it for now. Thanks, Mom."

"Don't worry, I'll call your father. I'll get it out of him."

Megan's eyes teased. "Sure you aren't looking for an excuse to talk to him?"

"Don't you wish," Grace reacted caustically.

"Actually, sometimes I do," Megan laughed.

"It's not going to happen." Grace closed the subject.

**

Later, at home, Grace called Jeff using her internet video service.

He looked older, more tired to her. "Megan needs money," Grace told him pointedly.

"Give her some," Jeff answered tersely, his voice hoarse and weary.

"I don't need a smart-ass answer, Jeff," she said, exasperated. "You promised to pay for her project materials. She has asked you twice, and still there's no check.

"You're right," he apologized, his tone softening. "I got really busy. Look, will you please give her what she needs, and I promise to send you a check tonight."

"I gave her four hundred. But Jeff, she has assignments every week, and the materials cost a fortune."

He sighed, rubbing his eyes. "I'll make it for a grand. That should last a while."

"Thanks," she said, ready to hang up.

"Grace," he stopped her, "I'm thinking of coming out for Christmas to see Megan. I have meetings in Washington, D.C., and I can pop in on the way."

"Jeff, why can't you come to see her when you're not just…" She stopped herself, realizing her castigation would fall on deaf ears.

"Not just what?" he asked.

"Nothing. I'm sure she'll be thrilled to see you."

"What about you?"

"Not a chance." She abruptly ended the conversation. "I've got to go to work."

14 NICK PONTELLIS

THE OWNER of the Silver Rush Showbar had grown up a military brat and went to high school in Valparaiso, Florida, where his father was assigned to a desk job at Eglin Air Force Base. His parents urged him to pursue the military, but he resisted.

"They say I'll break a family tradition—you know, my father, his father, et cetera," Nick complained to a buddy one day at the shooting range. They had gone there for target practice, one part of military life Pontellis said intrigued him.

"Why not try it," his buddy suggested. "The service is a pretty good life, if you ask me. Good pay. Great benefits."

"I never saw the value in being one of a million guys taking orders. I want to be the guy calling the shots. I figure I can get there faster in civilian life than trying to climb the damned rank ladder. My old man's been in for nineteen years and never got above staff sergeant."

He donned ear protection and squeezed off five shots, hitting the target's head with all of them.

Pontellis took a job working in a warehouse, making decent wages while trying to figure out his future. Meanwhile, his boss's wife introduced him to her niece, and within six months Nick married Jasmine Martelli.

Finances were difficult at first. Nick was making enough to cover the bills, and Jasmine helped with her job as a hairdresser. But they both liked nice things they couldn't afford—clothes, dining, cars.

"I'm tired of driving a six-year-old compact that looks like some teenager's transportation," Jasmine told him one Sunday as they drove to mass.

"Fine," he said. "Get a better job."

"You get a better job," she retorted. "What about the new furniture you promised me, and a bigger house?" She pouted all the way to the church while Nick fumed.

"I know she's right, though," he related the story to three of his work buddies the following week. They had stopped at an exotic dance club, The Velvet Vixen, after work to have a drink and take advantage of free happy hour *hors d'oeuvres*. "I just can't figure out what I want to do. All I know is I want to make a lot of money."

A dancer who had been romancing the pole peeled off her bra and sauntered over to their section of the bar. Wearing only a G-string, she kneeled down and shimmied, trying her best to seem seductive while not appearing bored. One of Nick's friends slipped some dollar bills into her garter. She gave an entreating stare to the other three, but they continued talking and ignored her. She shrugged and moved to another section of the club.

"This is it," Nick's dollar bill-dispensing friend chimed triumphantly.

"What is it?" Pontellis asked, chomping on a chicken wing.

"This," his buddy motioned around the room. "There is where you can make a lot of money."

Nick's eyes opened wide. "Oh, I get it. Man, would I ever like that, getting into this business. Some people think these places are seedy and degrading, but I like them. Look around at these guys. They're all laughing, drinking, having a blast. Dropping big bucks on booze and private dances in the back."

"So?" his friend smiled.

Pontellis shook his head no, vigorously. "Jasmine would never go for it. She doesn't trust me as it is."

"Believe me, she'd start trusting you when you came home with a new Mercedes or a mink coat."

"Maybe. But these places must be pretty tight. I wouldn't even know how to get in the door."

"Nothing ventured," the co-worker remarked as he finished his drink and stood to go. "Time to get home."

As it turned out, Nick had an easy time getting his foot into the door of the exotic dance industry. He spent six weeks dropping in on different clubs when Jasmine was at work or playing cards with the girls. He asked questions of bouncers, strippers, waitresses and door greeters. And he heard about a club that needed a night manager.

Jasmine was opposed.

"You're not going to work in that nasty place," she moaned when he broached the subject over breakfast. It was the perfect time to tell her. Jasmine was only half awake in the early morning, and if an argument ensued, he broke it off to go to work.

"I don't want you around all those naked whores," she lamented.

"First of all, a lot of them are lesbians," Nick argued, watching her arch her eyebrows skeptically. "That's a fact. Second of all, even if I wanted to make it with any of them, which I don't, I would be absolutely stupid to fish off the company pier. That's inviting trouble. Honey, we can make a mountain of dough and furnish this place—no, our new, bigger place—with the finest things money can conjure up."

He paused, reached across the breakfast table and took her hand. "And you, my gorgeous wife, can get rid of that ugly ride you're driving every day."

"We'd never see each other. You'd be working nights and me

days."

"So, you can start working at night. Or hell, quit. We can hit the sack late and wake up whenever we please. Have strawberries and cream in bed, plus roll around in the hay 'til lunchtime. It'll be a great life. And I haven't told you the best part."

"Which is?"

"I've got big plans, baby. As soon as I've learned the business and scraped up enough cash, I'll buy a place." He stopped and looked at his watch. "Time for work."

Jasmine acquiesced.

**

It took Nick five years to put together enough cash reserve to start looking for a club to purchase. He knew from being in the business Atlanta was a Mecca for strip joints. Most of them featured totally nude dancers who catered to the booming tourist trade.

He heard about a rundown place in foreclosure called Dancer Dollies that was available in his price range.

"Perfect," he told the realtor who was trying to move it. Nick had made his first trip to Atlanta, and already he liked the city. There was a can-do buzz around the business community, and he could tell after stopping by two of the most popular dance emporiums there was an enthusiasm for nightlife. When the agent took him to Dollies, Nick recognized how close it was to the iconic Buckhead where social life thrived and cash flowed.

"I can take that place and make something high-class out of it."

The agent chuckled cynically. Nick ignored him. He pushed hard to close on the place before someone else snapped it up.

**

Pontellis owned the Silver Rush less than a year when he was robbed the first time as he exited his car in his own garage. The Atlanta media went into feeding frenzy. A strip club owner had been targeted. Carrying a briefcase stuffed with cash skimmed from the gross receipts of nearly a week at his club, he put up no resistance as three ski-masked hijackers accosted him at gunpoint.

"You assholess will get yours," he shouted defiantly as one relieved him of the case. "I'll find out who you are, and you're dead men."

With the barrel of a .38 caliber pistol waving, one of the robbers motioned Pontellis toward the kitchen door. As it opened, Pontellis' wife Jasmine poked her head out, obviously curious about the commotion. She screamed when the gun was pointed toward her.

"Get inside," commanded the nervous club owner, pushing his wife back into the room. He scrambled to follow her.

Two intruders sprinted to exit the open garage as the third, clinging to Pontellis' briefcase, pushed the button on the wall and dashed to duck beneath the door as it rattled shut.

The three hurtled down the long driveway, up Riverwood Drive and around the corner where a black Cadillac Escalade sat waiting. Four minutes after grabbing their loot at gunpoint, they were speeding out of Riverwood Heights.

Safely inside the kitchen, Pontellis wrapped his arms around his wife as she shook and sobbed.

"Calm down, Jasmine. Those sons of bitches," he proclaimed. "I'll find them."

"You could have been killed," she wailed, mascara streaming down her cheeks.

"I'm too damned ornery to die. You know that, sweetie-pie,"

he laughed, and she laughed with him through her tearful sobs.

Nick pulled a cell phone from his pocket and dialed. Not the police. It was Bret Larkin, the Riverwood cop who moonlighted security at the Silver Rush.

"Larkin? I've been robbed…In my own God-damned garage, that's where…No, I'm okay. But they got away with all that cash… Blue jeans, dark shirts, ski masks. Nothing much to go on, but get the word out that we're looking for those guys, okay? There's a reward. I'll see you tomorrow morning and we'll figure out how to nail the bastards."

**

At Channel Six, the relationship between station manager Harvey Silver and his news director, Vivian Ellis, was tense. Despite the fact that Silver had hired her, he berated Vivian when a rival station scooped them, or when he didn't think coverage of a news event was dynamic enough. Compliments were not his strong suit.

Early on the morning of the Pontellis robbery, he had asked to see her. It was seven-thirty a.m., about the time they each arrived on the job each day. Vivian approached his office cautiously, as always, never knowing what hammer he might be ready to drop on this particular occasion. After all, he had offered her the job on the condition that she could improve ratings.

"Our numbers were up last week," he opened the conversation brightly.

"I know," she answered, waiting for however.

But it didn't come. "The Gleason report you set up seems to be working," he said, coming as close to praise as she had heard in months. "I've been getting some pretty good anecdotal feedback. But…" he paused, as if searching for a rebuttal.

126

"What?" she persisted.

"It's too damned one-dimensional. It's crime. Yet you call it crime and corruption."

"So?" she waited, obviously missing the point.

"Where in hell is the corruption? This show won't live past yearend if we don't dig deeper. Probe into city politics. Find a white-collar crook or two."

"We can do that," she said eagerly.

"But hear me out. It's a delicate balance. We have friends at city hall and in the governor's office, so you need to pick and choose carefully. Still, if there's a scandal brewing in the legislature, or one of the county commissions or a city hall, let's get her to dive into it."

The meeting lasted less than five minutes, and Ellis appeared relieved to escape without a tongue-lashing. Now, she had a mission and a challenge for her new star reporter.

**

Word of the Pontellis robbery reached Channel Six an hour later that morning. The club owner had delayed calling the police, using a hysterical wife as an excuse.

Scott Matthews had already been out to the scene and interviewed investigating officers when Grace got a call from Ellis. "Come over to my office," It was an order, not a request.

Vivian's workspace was small and efficient. No memorabilia, plaques or awards. Just several television monitors, a computer, printer, stacks of story files and local newspapers—tools to get the job done.

"You wanted to see me?"

"Come on in, Grace." She smiled warmly. "The owner of an exotic club was robbed last night at his home."

"I heard," Grace said.

"What do you know about him?"

"Not a lot. He came up here from Florida recently. Bought the old Dancer Dollies Club over in Buckhead. He spent at least a million dollars renovating it. Rumor is he's linked to the mob, but no one has proven the connection. It's all speculation."

"Grace, I've been looking for a good angle on the fight going on between the local neighborhoods and the club owners. The home-owners associations want totally nude dancing shut down. The Holly Hills subdivision has fought Pontellis tooth and nail because they believe his place will bring drugs, prostitution and crime into their pristine community. Meanwhile, the city is sympathetic, but zoning ordinances aren't in place to keep it out."

Grace chimed in, "Their hands are tied until someone changes the law."

Ellis nodded. "There's talk that the state legislature will trot out a new bill in the next session, limiting alcohol sales to clubs that are just topless."

"That's been tried before," Grace said.

"I know. The courts overrule them every time, but it doesn't keep them from rewriting and trying again. Grace, I need you on this story. Interview Pontellis about the robbery. Don't broach the neighborhood squabble right off the bat. Segue into it. Let's see what he has to say about the residents' fears, because up to now only his lawyers would talk publicly about it. You could score a coup here."

Grace took a deep breath before responding. "You know I don't want to stray off path. This is not my story."

Vivian surprised Grace as she narrowed her eyes and delivered a harsh response. "It is now. I'm telling you I want you on this."

She waited as Grace tightened her jaw and sat silently.

"We like your reporting so far. But we have to focus on ratings to stay competitive with other programs in the time slot."

Grace nodded, thinking Vivian must be getting positive feedback. Management must believe her work was making a difference. "All right," she agreed. "You've got it."

**

Pontellis seemed pleased when he told his security head Bret Larkin he was about to be interviewed by a new reporter for Channel Six.

"I thought you hated the news media, boss," Larkin said.

"I do. Hate them like the flu," Nick scowled. "But this Grace Gleason gal is kind of new in town and has a hard-hitting style that might be useful to us. If she starts digging around on this robbery, she could come up with some information we can use to find these guys. Those idiots over at the Atlanta PD haven't made any progress."

"Here she comes," Larkin said. He pointed toward the front door and disappeared behind the bar as Pontellis moved to greet her.

Although it was early fall, the heat outside was still oppressive, and Grace was perspiring as she entered the club. She stopped suddenly inside the door and pulled her sunglasses off, struggling to adjust her eyes to the darkness. She took the owner's outstretched hand.

"Nick Pontellis," he shouted.

Loud, pulsating music accompanied two female dancers who rotated their semi-nude bodies around poles on the stage as a handful of customers watched.

"You're Grace Gleason."

"Yes, I am." She glanced down at his fancy cowboy boots, then up at his solid face. He was handsome, about six feet tall, too corporate-looking to be running an exotic bar, Grace thought.

He held an outstretched hand out in a sweeping gesture. "What do you think of the décor?"

Grace looked around. The walls were painted carnation pink, and a huge mirror covered the area behind the bar. The curtains on the stage were deep maroon velvet, reminding her of an old-time theater, and the entire club was carpeted with a black confetti pattern.

"I'd be surprised if anyone pays much attention," she quipped.

"Let's go to my office where it's quieter," he said, leading her backstage and down a hallway past the dancers' dressing room. Nick's office was unremarkable, only large enough for a desk, several chairs and a "casting couch."

"You'd be surprised how many of my customers say this club looks much better than the old one," he sounded hurt she didn't heap praises on his interior design skills.

Grace set a recorder on his desk and turned it on.

He appeared unfazed.

"Just to be sure I don't forget anything," she explained.

He nodded.

"Mr. Pontellis, you got hit for a lot of money last night. How much was it?"

"Sorry, Grace, but we don't discuss the finances of the club. As you know, it's privately owned."

"Any progress with the police?"

"There were three guys in masks and gloves. Not much to go on."

"You have no idea who might have done this? Do you have

any enemies?"

"There are lots of people who'd like to see me go away," he said.

"Such as?"

"We're in the Bible belt. I run a night club."

"Strip club," she interjected.

"My dancers are not nude. Grace, this place is high class."

"Really?"

"More like a Vegas bar."

Grace scoffed, "How upscale can it be if women are pulling off their clothes for money?"

Pontellis scowled. "It's not just women taking their knickers off. We provide entertainment and a great night out for our patrons. My dancers only take off their tops and dance with G-strings on."

"You can't compete in this town if you take that approach. Your competition all feature completely nude girls, and that's what the conventioneers want, not to mention the pro athletes and entertainers who frequent your clubs. Many people in the community think places like this are fronts for prostitution and other criminal activity. What is your response to that?"

The club owner was matter-of-fact. "Grace, this is a respectable establishment."

"The Holly Hills association wants you out," Grace countered.

"I'm going to change their minds. This business will be good for the neighborhood. The homeowners will come around when they realize Silver Rush is like any other successful, tax-paying operation." He stood up, signaling the interview had come to an end.

Grace wrapped up without fully revealing what she actually thought about this man's interview responses. Was he truly naïve? Or as sneaky as a copperhead? He had failed to convince her he was running a legitimate nightclub unlike the sleazy nude bars in other parts of town. She suspected Nick Pontellis was part showman, part con artist. Rumors about VIP rooms where high roller clientele engaged strippers doubling as prostitutes were simply too prevalent to ignore.

As she left the club into the blinding daylight, a realization hit her. Vivian might have been right—she could fight the drug war until she was blue in the gills, and she might not make a dent. But there could be a fight right here she could win.

She vowed to keep a watchful eye on the smooth Mr. Pontellis and his "high-class" nightclub.

15 LITTLE FOX

OFFICER CRUZ was waiting for Grace at their usual table, at the corner outside the coffee shop. She became nostalgic, remembering her periodic meetings with Detective Ned Moore at a little diner when she worked in Dallas.

Eduardo stood, but his sparkly smile was absent. "I went ahead and ordered you some sweet tea. I don't have much time today."

"Why so glum?" she asked.

He started to answer, but stopped when the waitress brought Grace's drink.

"Leave the check," he said curtly. She left. He stared into Grace's eyes. "I'm very concerned."

"About what?"

"I don't feel like you're pursuing this story hard enough. I haven't heard from you in a week, and you're doing those pieces on that bar owner, less than a pillar in the community, I might add."

"That's the point of my news reports, Cruz. I can't do a one-story segment."

He clinched his teeth. "You have to push harder," his intensity startled her. "You're taking your eye off the ball."

Grace felt her neck stiffen. "Whoa, officer. Since when did you become my news director?"

Eduardo sat back and slumped slightly, gazing into his coffee and then back at her. "I'm sorry. I just hate what's going on here. We're being out-maneuvered by these drug dealers every day. I didn't mean to take it out on you."

"I want to finish what I started," she assured him. "I feel like I'm getting so close to the heart of the story. But my management feels it's getting stale. I'm going to lose my audience before I even get it built up."

"Stale?" he retorted, confusion in his face. "How is that possible?"

"We're not getting anywhere. Your department's fighting it with a rifle shot, not a bazooka. And my viewer responses haven't been as passionate as I want. Even your own brother-in-law is balking about tying his newscast stories to my segment."

Eduardo shrugged. "Jackson's a jackass."

She shrugged noncommittally. "Maybe, but he knows the news. He understands what will get us ratings."

Cruz thrust his arms into the air. "Ratings? Is that all you guys care about? How about the kids who are victimized by these gangs? How about the businesses that have to close down or move elsewhere or pay the gangs for protection because of this reign of fear around here?'

"I'm on your side. But ratings sell advertising, and I have to produce them or I won't stay on the air."

They both sat in silence for a minute. "I might have something for you," Cruz finally said.

She leaned forward, interested.

"Little Fox Martinez," he continued. "He's a gang-banger who got all shot up by a rival gang three years ago. He's in real bad shape now, and he's come over to our side. Says he wants to help the kids he once recruited into the business."

"Isn't that dangerous for him?"

Eduardo shrugged. "He's cooperating with us, ratting out some of the guys who were his friends. Someone's protecting him. I don't know who—maybe his uncles and cousins who still live the life. But I talked to him, Grace. He'll let you interview him. I can set it up."

"Then, I want to do it."

The countless apartment complexes dotting Gwinnett County were all similar to the one in which Eduardo Cruz had grown up, before his father made enough money to buy a house and move the family. Years of neglect and creeping poverty had ravaged these developments until they were ugly scars on the county landscape.

They had become havens for drug dealers who stationed lookouts at the only entrances to warn of approaching police or rival groups.

Marco "Little Fox" Martinez had lived in one of these buildings all his life. When he was only nine he had been recruited into the local clique, *Los Legartos*, that was part of the larger network of six gangs called *El Grupo Leal*.

Martinez passed muster with the group's leaders first by pulling off purse snatchings and small robberies. Then as he grew older and more brazen, he triggered rival gang members during drive-bys.

He rarely went anywhere alone. "I ain't making myself no easy target," he told a buddy one night as they walked to another apartment complex to visit some girls. "Homes, we should travel together. You know, don't take no chances."

But a few days later, he was victimized by an enemy group's assault as he was walking alone from buying cigarettes at a nearby convenience store. He let his guard down that night and paid the price. Little Fox spent months in a hospital after being struck five times by bullets. When he was released, the brain damage he had suffered made walking and speaking a chore, which would dog him for the rest of his life.

**

It was still early in the evening when Grace interviewed him, but the days were rapidly getting shorter. Steve's camera light was the only illumination in front of the apartment building except for a few lamps in windows. Streetlights in the neighborhood were shot out as quickly as the power company replaced them.

"This evening I'm talking to Marco Martinez, who was ambushed by a gang three years ago. He lived a life of gangs and crime. Now he struggles with daily life after nearly being killed."

Grace turned and leaned in toward Little Fox, straining to understand his stunted speech. "You've left the life of crime?"

Martinez nodded. "When you're a kid," he labored to say, "you get caught up in the excitement. You see these guys driving nice cars, diamond studs in their ears, and you say 'that's for me.'"

"But you paid a huge price," Grace interjected.

"Maybe, maybe not," he answered. "They shot me up, and I got out. But I might not be talking to you right now if I had stayed in the life."

**

By the time she wrapped up the interview and Steve dropped her off at her car, Grace was worried about being late. Megan rarely had openings in her schedule Grace could fit into, and she didn't want to miss a chance for dinner with her.

She rushed to Lu Chow's and then to her daughter's apartment. She half-ran to the door lugging a large order of food.

"Chinese!" Megan said brightly. "I haven't eaten all day. I'm famished."

"Same here." Grace entered the room, set down the bags on the kitchen table and slipped off her jacket. The days weren't that much cooler yet, but she had worn it to look better on camera.

Megan's roommates, Bradley and Raj, emerged from their rooms and greeted her.

"You two look like you could use a meal," Grace laughed.

Raj rubbed his bleary eyes. "We've been working around the clock on our assignments," he said in a heavy Indian accent. "We work right through to completion and sometimes forget to eat."

Bradley cut in, "Or just don't have time to go find something, since we're always on deadline."

"Well, I worry about all three of you, working these long hours and not getting any nourishment. I brought enough for everyone."

Bradley rubbed his hands together. "Looks like we won't starve after all."

Megan retrieved dishes and flatware, and they filled their plates from the cartons with rice, beef broccoli, cashew chicken and moo goo gai pan. They carried their plates to the living room and sat, chatting while they ate.

"Megan told me about the harassment women receive from some of the faculty," Grace said.

"It's not the norm, but it happens," Bradley seemed eager to corroborate Megan's story. "Like last year, I was working on a project with my team, and we hit a wall. One of my team members said, 'Let's go over and talk to Professor Hegendorf.' We thought he was crazy, but he said he went there and hung out all the time—Hegendorf was fine with it. When we arrived, the professor answered the door in a robe. The kicker is that I could see one of the women in our class scurrying out of the room...shall we say, scantily clad. Professor Hegendorf thought it was hilarious."

"Megan won't tell us which prof she hauled into the dean's office," Raj said. "When I find out, I'll kick his ass."

They laughed heartily and dug into more food.

"I'll say one thing," Megan added, "I'm so glad I got this apartment with these guys. One of my classmates joined a sorority, and the strain of keeping up with the social side of Greek life and making good grades are driving her crazy."

"We predict she'll drop out by next term," Bradley said.

"That's sad." Grace frowned. She sat back, sipped some tea and thanked her stars for the good decisions her daughter was making. Finishing the program would be tough, but she had the make-up to do it, and supportive roommates.

She glanced at her watch. "Mind if I turn on the news?" Grace asked. "It's time for my broadcast."

"One of my favorite things," Megan said.

Grace pressed power on the remote. Her segment had already started. Grace was in the middle of the Little Fox interview.

She didn't always watch her newscasts, since she could review them at the station. But sometimes, seeing her work with the perspective of a regular viewer, she could become more objective about what worked and what didn't. Some of her best ideas for follow-up had come this way.

"So help me understand, why would you endanger yourself now by talking to me, dissing the gang life this way?" she asked.

The station had added subtitles to some of Martinez's response, when his impaired speech might be hard to understand. Marco labored to get the words out. *"I'm no longer a danger to them,"* he responded slowly. *"I paid my price, and my homeys here know that speaking out against gang life won't affect their recruiting one way or another. I'm nothing but a has-been around here. But I'm alive. And I'm still their friend. We grew up together."*

Grace faced the camera for her final cut-away. *"And so Little Fox Martinez goes through life watching the nine-year-olds in his hood get recruited into* Los Lagartos, *robbing, selling narcotics and eventually being challenged to kill. Martinez is out of that gang now, but he carries a lifetime of scars. Meanwhile, the cycle goes on, and Gwinnett County remains a drug hub under the grips of seemingly unstoppable narcotics activity. I'm Grace Gleason. Tomorrow night watch my special, 'Crime and Corruption,' where you'll see the entire interview. Plus, I'll have much more on the rash of property crimes plaguing Atlanta. Are they an integral part of this gang culture? Tune in to find out."*

"Awesome, Mrs. Gleason," Bradley chimed enthusiastically.

"Good grief, Bradley. Call me Grace. I'm not that old, am I?"

"Okay, Grace," Bradley repeated, making it come out awkwardly. "But seriously, you're doing a great community service with those gang reports."

"I don't know," she answered. "I took this job because I thought I'd have an opportunity to affect large numbers of people's attitudes and understandings, not just keep the news in front of them."

"But you are," Raj assured.

"How can I be sure? We know how many eyes are on us. But it's really hard to determine if we're making any progress against the headwinds. We know they surely aren't south of the border."

Megan bounced up off of the couch. "I think you are. I'm proud of you, Mom. But now we've got to study. There's something called finals before the term ends."

Grace rose and hugged her daughter. "Of course, Megan. Thanks for letting me park here for a little while."

"Anytime, Grace," Bradley said, proud of his new, first-name basis friend with celebrity. He followed Grace and Megan to the door. "At least, anytime we don't have projects due or tests coming up," he added, chuckling.

"That means never," Grace joked, hugging Megan again and disappearing out the door.

At her car, she was startled by a sudden cool gust and stirring of leaves falling to the street. The energetic puff of air reminded that summer had ended. Soon she would be buying candy for kids trick-or-treating. Atlanta was much like Dallas, where she had marveled at how instantly the new seasons could sneak up on you. She shivered at the thought of winter coming in less than two months.

Driving home, Grace felt good about her brief dinner with Megan and "the boys," as her daughter referred to the roommates. She also felt positive about the segment they had watched. Little Fox was a breakthrough interview, and she had Eduardo Cruz to thank for that.

Maybe she was making progress in the battle to expose this scourge. But there was a nagging in the back of her mind about another brand of lawlessness that had bared its ugly face in Atlanta; the string of crimes against all of those businesses was something she now felt she couldn't ignore.

She wondered if the drug war stories she had been pursuing were somehow connected, if the increased thefts were symptoms of the noose of terror the gangs were tightening around the city and turning its neighborhoods into battlegrounds. Grace wished she had asked Little Fox that question.

Then she had an idea. Very soon she would pay a visit to the Atlanta Police Department, apply pressure to learn if they were withholding information about the robberies. She would have to approach them with a news angle, or they wouldn't talk to her. She wanted to know why they appeared so clueless.

If these thefts were being pulled off by *Los Lagartos* and their associated groups, she would have an inside track on reporting it.

16 APD BLOWBACK

OVER THE NEXT few weeks, the heists of local businesses escalated. On October 14, two masked gunmen robbed a clerk at Larry's Package Store on Piedmont in Midtown just before closing time. On October 19, the security system at Ned's Auto Body in Norwood was breached in the wee morning hours, and the thieves confiscated a small safe.

On Halloween night, at the popular Tommy's Bar in Gwinnett County, patrons and wait staff were forced to lie face down while two bartenders had to turn over the day's receipts to four thieves wearing ski masks and baseball caps.

At their morning meeting the next day, the Big Six news staff discussed the latest addition to the crime string. Tensions ran high.

"We need to connect the dots on these crimes," Scott Matthews harangued. "Does anyone but me think what's happening is an epidemic? We should be going after the APD for allowing this to go on."

Eyes turned toward Vivian Ellis. "Tom?" she asked. "What do you think? Is it a story, or a collection of random crimes?"

Grace grinned to herself. She knew what was coming. The assignment editor was accustomed to running the meetings, but he rarely took a stand. "Well," he hedged, "let's see what Jackson and Grace have to say."

Davis sat up a little taller, his chin lifted in illusory importance. He cleared his throat loudly. "There's no common M.O. That's what worries me. Some while the places are open, some in off-hours. Maybe it's several different groups of perpetrators. I don't think we should go out on a limb. If we're wrong, we'll damage our reputation."

Grace saw Scott Matthews' "help me" glance of desperation.

"It seems to me we're missing something here," she offered. "Jackson is right. There's no pattern to the crimes per se. But there is a common denominator. In every one of them, the guys who did it seemed to have inside knowledge."

"What do you mean?" Vivian pressed.

"Go back through each one. Whoever committed the crime knew what day to hit the particular business. They knew what hour would be best, when the places wouldn't be crowded. How to bypass security if the place was closed. Where the safe was located, and in some cases how to get it out of the building.

"These are sophisticated operations by people who have a plan, who know what they are doing."

Matthews seemed to bubble with excitement. "Do you think the drug gangs might be involved?" he asked. "Their revenue sources had to suffer when their umbrella organization EGL was eliminated. They might need cash to support their operation."

"Maybe, but I doubt it," Grace commented. "These jobs have characteristics that don't seem to fit. The gang-bangers I've been covering are young and reckless, unsophisticated. Not very smart, really, just brazen. Unless they have someone masterminding the operation who's a lot sharper than most of them, I'm not sure they could pull this off."

"There's something else," Scott said. "One of the victims, a Korean store owner, said two of the robbers spoke Spanish to each other."

"What?" Ellis exclaimed.

"You didn't report that?" Grace asked, astonished.

"Hold on," the young reporter said. "Those people were hard

to understand. And they appeared very confused. I think that's what they were saying."

"You think!" Vivian challenged.

Everyone sat silently.

Tom drummed his pencil on the table, looking annoyed.

"Here's what I suggest," Grace said thoughtfully. "We need to go on the offensive. We all agree this story is growing, regardless of who's committing the crimes. And if we concur there's enough of a pattern to be concerned, let's go after the police department for not having a handle on it by now."

Jackson held a hand up defensively. "Wait a minute, Grace. We need a lot more facts than we have now to take on the APD. One press conference and they'd cremate us."

"How about it, Scott?" she enthused, ignoring Davis. "You want to put together an analysis of all the heists—types of hits, amounts stolen, various methods used?"

"Sure," Matthews burst in. "Already got most of it."

MaryAnne spoke up for the first time, suddenly excited. "We'll put Scott on 'Crime and Corruption' and you two can do a tag team."

Ellis broke in. "All right. Just be sure you're correct on everything you report. You're getting ready to bring down the wrath of Atlanta Police Chief Omoro Stone upon our heads."

They smiled and nodded with her. All but Jackson Davis, who sat silently glowering as he always did when his views were disregarded.

    **

It took Matthews two days to pull together the facts of the story. Grace sat with him and MaryAnne as they edited copy and screened hours of B-roll footage the station photographers had shot in the aftermath of some of the offenses.

Finally, they were ready. It was a Wednesday evening. Grace knew as they prepared to go on the air hell would break out at city police headquarters no later than first thing Thursday morning.

She sat on her stool facing the camera. "Turning from the gang-related drug stories I've been covering, 'Crime and Corruption' takes a look at a different sort of crime beginning to plague Atlanta," she opened. Behind her, the huge screen depicted a late-night scene of police car headlights illuminating a storefront with detectives questioning potential witnesses. Meanwhile, uniformed officers strung crime scene tape around the establishment.

Grace continued, "Big Six News Beat reporter Scott Matthews has been following the recent spate of blatant burglaries and robberies that seem to have Atlanta's police department stumped. Scott?" Matthews walked into the set and perched on the stool across from Grace. "Tell us what you've found."

Various crime scenes continued to flash on and off the screen behind them as the young reporter began his report. "Grace, dozens of businesses have been either burglarized after-hours or robbed at gunpoint in a few months. That compares with just half the number of such crimes the same period last year. Something is causing a dramatic uptick."

"An increase in property thefts is disturbing. But it's not that unusual, is it?" Grace noted. "Atlanta is growing, the economy is worse. Don't those elements invite more crime?"

"It's a trend, and it's exponential," Matthews answered. "Last year in that timeframe, less than ninety thousand dollars was stolen. More than three hundred thousand dollars have been taken in the most recent outbreak, not to mention half a dozen safes hauled right out of the establishments. That's a new wrinkle over previous years."

"Sort of like the smash and grab raids that went on for a

144

while?"

"Yes, except much more sophisticated and obviously calculated."

"How so?" she asked.

"In nearly all of these recent burglaries, the bad guys seemed to have some knowledge of the location—the alarm systems, for instance. In every case, the masked intruders appeared to know how the business operated, what hours they would have the most cash on hand, when customer activity would be light. The way they ordered clerks and other workers around, it was as if they worked there."

"Inside jobs?"

"Possibly."

Grace reached for the screen and swept away the last video of a robbery scene, reached for another icon and tapped it. A full-screen image of Police Chief Stone appeared, in a huddled conference with several of his division heads.

"You spoke with the Police Chief about this growing problem?" she questioned Scott.

"I tried," he answered. "When I called the APD, I could only get as far as the head of their public affairs division, Aretha Herrington."

"And what was her response?"

"She said she thought we were on a witch hunt."

"One last question." Grace hesitated for effect. "We've been reporting extensively on the extent of gangs in the metro area, especially as they relate to drug trafficking. Could the two be connected? Burglaries and robberies to support other gang activities?"

"There's no evidence to support it," Scott said. "But of course, it's always a possibility. Where there are gangs, there is crime."

"Thank you, Scott Matthews. We'll look forward to your updates on this story." He nodded, and the camera pulled in on Grace.

"Join us Friday evening when we'll have the latest on the Gwinnett County drug scene and on this troubling wave of property crime gripping Atlanta. I'm Grace Gleason, and you've been watching 'Crime and Corruption.'"

**

Scott was waiting at her desk as she returned. He was ebullient, his blue eyes ablaze. "That was fantastic! What a rush," he burst out.

"Good job," Grace said, a hand on his shoulder. "But let's not get too excited. We're not way out in front of this story. It's ahead of us."

"But we've launched it, Grace. I'll chase down everything I can find between now and Friday."

She settled into her chair, tired, trying to mirror his enthusiasm but failing. "Do that, Scott. I appreciate how hard you're working on this. We will feel heat from city hall soon that you haven't experienced yet. Put on your flame-retardant suit, because boy, you're going to need it."

"Hell, I'm ready," he laughed and retreated to his cubicle with a bouncy gait.

"I wish I were," Grace murmured in his general direction. "It's about to get very dicey."

Her prediction couldn't have been more accurate. A call came at seven-thirty the next morning as she sipped coffee and scanned the morning paper at her workstation.

"It's Aretha Herrington, director of public affairs for the APD. I caught your program last night. You guys are really stirring the speculation pot, aren't you? It's not enough to beat up on Gwinnett County? Now you want to bring down the Atlanta police force as well?"

"I don't want to bring anyone down, Officer Herrington..."

"Not officer," Aretha interrupted.

"Pardon me?"

"I'm not a sworn police officer. I'm a civilian employed by the department."

"As I was about to say, it's not my intention to play gotcha with you guys over at the APD," Grace said. "The only people I want to 'bring down,' as you put it, are those guys your department can't seem to catch."

"Don't you think we're working on this?"

"No one over there seems to think these crimes are related, and the chief won't talk to our reporter about it. The public has a right to know what's going on."

"That's the trouble with you media types. Show me in the Constitution—or the city charter for that matter—where there is a right to know."

"I can't believe I'm hearing this. Who do you think pays your salary?"

There was an embarrassed silence. Then, "Gleason, we've got every available detective sifting through witness statements, clues, analyzing M.O.s, the whole bit. But you jumping on the air and getting the public all stirred up is only going to get in our way."

"Sorry," Grace said, actually meaning it. "I know you have a hard task. But I have a job to do, too. And when we don't think the APD is moving fast enough, or taking an obvious problem as seriously as they should, we're going to report it."

"The chief is really, really pissed. That's off the record."

"Good," Grace said. "I hope he stays that way until something gets done." She paused, then, "And Aretha?"

"Yes?"

"Nothing is off the record."

The resounding click on the other end of the line informed Grace the conversation was over.

"And goodbye to you, too," she said cheerily to the dead phone line.

Except that she didn't feel jovial. Grace imagined it wasn't the last angry call she would get from the police department's public affairs department.

17 JEFF, AGAIN

THE COURT MAY say it is. But a divorce is never final. Like a persistent summer cold, the unstoppable gamut of unfinished business lives on, interfering with closure. Memories both fond and bitter, unresolved issues, grudges, wishes, regrets. And the eternal loose ends—the children. All of these lingering factors conspire to make a marriage live far beyond its tenure, revive emotions, force contact, replay old scenes of what-if and what-might-have-been. And, sometimes, revive old passions.

"Daddy's coming through on Christmas," Megan managed to sound nonchalant, even over the phone.

"Well, that would be just like him," Grace knee-jerked.

"Mom."

"I know, I know. I'm sorry. I promised you—and me—I wouldn't do any of that sniping anymore. I am over it, honey. The old emotional responses just come flooding back sometimes. Your dad told me when I called about your school money that he would be stopping in Atlanta."

"I'm glad he'll be here. I really want to see him. It's been over a year, and I can't wait to show him my new place."

"Let me know the schedule when you have it then, so you and I can plan our activities."

"What about you? Will you be seeing him?"

"Not sure," she answered, knowing she had no intention of spending any time with her ex. But why burden Megan with her lingering bitterness?

**

Jeff arrived three days before Christmas. He had sent her a bury-the-hatchet email, cordial and seemingly caring, asking her to have dinner. Although deep down she dreaded it, she unaccountably said yes.

Grace met him at Staton's Grill, next to his hotel. She was surprised at how nervous she was. Getting ready, she had changed her clothes three times and shoes five, not fully understanding why.

It was not yet seven, so the restaurant wasn't crowded. Jeff greeted her inside the entrance, smiling widely, a wrapped package in his hand. He felt familiar, comfortable, not dated like an outfit that had hung in the closet for a long time without being worn.

"Merry Christmas," he said cheerfully, air-kissing her cheek.

She accepted the gift tentatively. "I...I don't have anything for you. I thought..."

He stopped her, holding his hand up. "It's all right, Grace. I didn't expect anything. It's just a special bottle of wine from a vineyard a client of mine owns up in Napa Valley. I just thought you might like it."

They were in uncharted waters. It was the first time since their domestic hostilities and paper-signing ceremony they had sat down together to be sociable. Every conversation to that point had been discussions about Megan, payment of college expenses, the sort of things that added stress to an already strained relationship. Tonight, what began as a stiff and awkward moment quickly settled into relaxed and easy chitchat. It reminded her of their earlier years, in college and then as a young couple. Grace was surprised at how readily and easily the awkwardness melted away, replaced by reminders of what had once brought them together.

She passed the wine list to him, deferring. "Order something white and crisp for me," Grace said, as she had requested countless times in the past.

She watched Jeff as he perused the list. His rugged, athletic face had softened, a bit puffy, more lined. Darkness had invaded the areas around his eyes, and his short-cropped, corporate hair was rapidly turning gray.

"The lady will have the Pinot Grigio," he told the waiter. "For me, a Martini, extra dry, three olives."

Grace leaned back in surprise. "Jeff, a Martini? You've been a beer and wine drinker for as long as I can remember."

"Client cocktail parties have converted me," he responded to her curious gaze.

It only took a few minutes of small talk to turn to their daughter. "Megan and I had a great afternoon together. She has really grown up," Jeff said.

"She has."

"You've done a terrific job with her."

"It wasn't just me, Jeff. You were right there until—well, you know."

"We did okay, didn't we?"

And so the night passed with surprising ease, the two slipping effortlessly into their couple mode, talking of their work, their respective cities, world news. After two glasses of wine and dessert, Grace began to feel as if they had never been apart.

"Come up for a nightcap," he entreated as they finished their coffee. "It's too early to turn in, and there's an unbelievable view of the skyline from my suite."

**

Whatever qualms she might have had about overkill disappeared as they entered the breathtaking room overlooking the illumination of the city. Atlanta had long ago topped many of its tallest buildings with unique lighting features. She had been awe-struck by the sight many times as she drove from point to point, but she rarely got to view it from this angle. She soaked up the spectacle as Jeff poured them each a glass of wine. As he joined her to watch, his arm slipped automatically, naturally, around her.

He drew her gently to him, touching his lips to hers. His kiss

151

was the same, startling her even more than her willingness to return it.

"We shouldn't," she said, pulling away.

"Why not? We were married over twenty years."

"You've probably had a dozen women since me," she said.

"Not that many. And you?"

"None," she answered, seeing no point in delving into the one relationship she had experienced. Opening that door, the romance with a cameraman in Dallas, would require a world of explanations. Who was the guy? What had happened? She felt totally unprepared to answer any of those questions.

He kissed her again, stirring lust inside her that she had pretended not to miss. He grinned his Texas frat boy grin and led her to the bedroom. And although she knew she should leave and ignore the instinct telling her there was still love between them, rather found herself unbuttoning his shirt as their bodies fell in unison onto the huge bed.

Nothing had changed. His soft touch on her breasts, the comical grunting sounds he made as their bodies merged, the wild rush she felt as she rolled on top, leaning back with her eyes closed, as they had done hundreds of times.

**

Afterward, she stared at the ceiling for several minutes, silent, breathing heavily, confused.

"I can't believe we just did that," she said.

"We might be divorced, but we never really stopped being a couple," he said.

"But we did. We signed papers."

"Come on, honey," he intoned with his customary charm. "They're just documents. You're still the mother of my daughter. You're still the girl I met in college."

"We'll always have Austin," she laughed, and he chuckled,

too, at the paraphrased Hemingway line she had used so many times describing their life together.

"It wasn't all bad," he said, massaging her shoulder.

"Just at the end. When you decided you couldn't live without California."

He nodded. "Looks as if I'll have to now."

She sat up, pulling the sheet over her naked body. "What do you mean?"

"I'm moving to Washington, D.C. My firm wants me back there to lobby the government agencies for our clients. We're moving heavily into the White House's green agenda."

"D.C. No wonder you've switched to Martinis. You'll be on the hardcore party circuit."

Jeff paused, seeming to mull something over. He pulled his shorts on. "You could come with me."

He sounded detached for such a revolutionary statement, and she knew his approach was by design. She searched his face for a smile, but it remained serious, purposeful.

"You're joking!" she exclaimed. "Why in hell would I go to D.C. with you?"

"Because of..." he paused, sweeping his arm across the bed, "...this. We had a great life together."

He reached out to take her hand, but she pulled back.

"Grace, darlin', the only thing that drove us apart was your refusal to follow me to the job of my dreams. I want you with me. I miss you, Grace. You could work in the nation's capitol. No problem getting a job there with your track record."

Grace climbed out of bed and started dressing, the sensation of *deja vous* overwhelming. "I can't believe this," she said, incredulity gushing out. "I am building something here. The very thing that split us up was your refusal to accept my career as equal. Now you're rubbing it in my face one more time?"

"Jesus Christ, calm down," Jeff's voice rose with rancor. "I'm not refusing to acknowledge anything. I thought you'd feel flattered. I'm saying you could be successful in the hottest news market in the country. Come on. What's so callow about that?"

"Not callow. I call it selfish. It's all about you and what you want, Jeff. Just as it always has been. You…" she hesitated, fighting back tears.

He slid from the bed and took a step toward her. He started to speak, and she held up a hand and continued dressing. "And what about all the little chippies you've been with out there in la-la land? Am I just supposed to forget about them?"

Jeff stood awkwardly in his shorts, looking dumbfounded. "None of them means anything, Grace. Just people to pass the time with. I moved, damn it, but I didn't die."

She was fully dressed, staring at him, tears welling up. "It hurts. Again. I should have known this would turn out badly," she said. "Have a nice trip back."

"Grace," he implored as she walked to the door.

She slammed the door behind her.

In the corridor, waiting for the elevator, she sobbed slowly and then built to a crescendo. The bell rang. As she stepped into the car, Grace thanked God no one was there to see her. The elevator door slammed, firmly closing this chapter in her life. Grace could not be with a man who belittled her accomplishments. She was off on a great start to an exciting opportunity. She was not going to let Jeff or anyone take that away.

18 OFFICER DOWN

DEMANDS OF THE news business sometimes interfered with Grace's rarefied status of having her own news segment and some freedom to choose stories. Despite her management's efforts to protect her from the mundane, order could turn to chaos. It was the nature of the business, and she knew it.

All it took was a frantic call to pull her down from her lofty perch.

She had signed off the air, completed some notes in preparation for the next day, and driven home. The Atlanta winter was spitting half-frozen mist, and just watching it pelt her windshield made her shiver.

Safely inside, Grace turned on the gas fireplace and took off her shoes. She poured a glass of Merlot and slid a Corbin Labeau CD into the stereo. She was too tired to eat, so she sat sipping wearily.

Her spirit sagged even more at the sound of her ringtone. She glanced at her watch. Eleven-fifteen. She contemplated leaving the phone in her bag, but she knew she would regret it if it were Megan.

She dug her cell out and checked the screen. The assignment desk.

"Grace, we had a call that a cop has been shot in the Edgewood Heights housing project," Charlie said.

"That's Gwinnett County."

"Right. I can't get another reporter out there for several hours. I need you to take it, okay?"

"Charlie, no."

"Sorry Grace. You're it. Jankowski's already out there to get video, so you'll have to take a cab. Don't drive into that neighborhood. Steve can take you back."

"Charlie! I just got home," she continued to protest.

"Can't be helped. It's your turn for on call. And Gwinnett County has been your beat for weeks, anyway," he laughed.

Grace sighed. "I'm on my way."

She called for a taxi, changed tops and ran downstairs.

The car was there within minutes.

"Where to?" the driver asked. He was sixty, portly, a two-day scruff of grayish beard covering his broad face. When she told him her destination, he turned, his eyes narrow. "I can't drop you off there alone, lady."

"It's okay," Grace reassured. "I'm a news reporter, and my cameraman is already there."

She could sense his reluctance, a fatherly concern. Yet as they approached the scene, it became obvious she would be safe. A gaggle of police, ambulance workers and gawkers had converged on the entrance to the ramshackle apartment building. The Channel Six news truck with the satellite dish on top satisfied the driver.

As they pulled to a stop, she watched one of the ambulances race out of the neighborhood, red lights flashing and siren wailing like a humpback whale's mournful call.

Grace paid the driver and stepped out into the chaotic setting.

Yellow crime scene tape had already been stretched around an area near a huge green dumpster. Lights from the television cameras brightly illuminated the victim's pool of blood. A police nightstick lay in the crimson puddle.

As she approached her photographer and the police officers combing the area, Grace could hear the crescendo of chatter from bystanders. The hostility coming through the din worried her.

"Hey," Steve said as she approached. "A real nightmare." He

turned his camera toward the police officers searching the site. Two of them approached the crowd hanging around, mostly Hispanic but a mix of whites and blacks as well. Some of them turned their backs, whispering together in hushed tones.

Grace pulled out her notepad and flagged down a passing policewoman. "Grace Gleason, Channel Six, officer, what can you tell me about the victim?" she asked. Jankowski's lights flooded the officer's face.

"We're not releasing his ID yet," the woman answered. "He's still alive, but it doesn't look good."

"Was he city or county? Do you have a shooter?"

The woman squirmed, her eyes glancing at the camera lens. "They're looking for his family. We can't release anything about him right now. When it's time, we'll have an announcement."

She seemed relieved to turn and walk back to her duties.

"This could get ugly," Grace mumbled to Steve, surveying the crowd. "Cops are a close-knit bunch, and when one of their own goes down they can get rough if anyone holds out information. Let's stay alert for any signs that things might turn combative."

"You got it," Steve nodded and moved back toward the dumpster to continue shooting the crime scene.

Grace edged toward the officers who had approached the crowd. They were methodically culling individuals and asking questions.

"Were you here when it happened?" she heard a cop ask an elderly man, who shook his head no, then turned and slowly walked away.

"Do you know who did this?" a detective queried two teenaged girls who hugged each other in fright.

"We just got here," one answered meekly.

None of the onlookers offered information.

Grace noticed a young boy, about ten, hanging around the edge of the group, his eyes wide. She slowly inched toward him. She pulled a stick of gum from her purse and held it out to him. He took it, threw the wrapper on the ground and stuffed it into his mouth.

"Did you see what happened?" Grace asked.

He shook his head no.

"Did you see the officer before the ambulance took him away?"

A nod yes.

"Did you know the policeman?"

The boy said something so softly she couldn't discern it.

"What?" she asked, crouching down to his level. In her peripheral view, she could see Steve's camera move in closer toward the child.

"He was nice. He gave us money."

She held her microphone close to capture his small voice.

"Gave you and the other kids money?"

The boy nodded. "He said it was okay. Money he took from drug dealers."

An elderly Hispanic woman emerged from the crowd and grabbed the boy by the hand. She shook him and led him away from Grace.

"No hablar con extraños," she chastised in her old, scratchy voice. Grace knew the phrase from her Texas days. *Don't talk to strangers.*

**

She arrived at the station early the next morning, eager to follow up with Gwinnett County authorities and write her story for the initial newscast. Jackson Davis was waiting for her.

"They haven't released the officer's name yet," he said. "There's a press conference in two hours."

158

She nodded.

"I know who it is."

The pronouncement startled her. She stood and peered over the cubicle compartment at Christina Cruz's empty space, then turned to him, eyes wide, mouth agape.

He nodded solemnly. "Christina's at the regional medical center now. He's in a coma."

"No!" Grace uttered.

"We can't give it out until they announce it. Write the story without it, and we'll plug it in when we can."

Her stomach was churning almost as furiously as her mind was spinning. *Not Eduardo.*

"Jackson, I interviewed a young boy last night. He said the cop who was shot gives him and his friends cash confiscated from crack dealers. We've got video of the interview."

"Okay."

"Okay? It's wrong," she said impatiently. "He was violating policy. It's way beyond breaking the chain of evidence. It's a crime."

Davis made a dismissive hissing sound with his lips. "Damn it, Gleason, it's some little kid. You can't rely on what he said. Even if he's right, we're talking about drug money. Eduardo grew up around that illegal crap and hates it." His eyes burned into her. "I won't use it."

"He was defying police policy, and worse," she repeated, exasperation in her voice. "If Eduardo would ignore that regulation, who knows what else he might wink at? You're trying to protect him because he's your brother-in-law."

Jackson scowled. "Hell, he's your friend, or at least I thought so. Grow up, Gleason. Be real. You know Eduardo. He's one of the good guys."

"I know, but..." she stammered.

"Get over it," the anchor shot back at her. "Write the story without the kid. I'm warning you, if you try to use it, it'll never get on the air. I promise. Pray for your friend's recovery. I'm going to the hospital to be with Christina. Have the copy on my desk when I get back." He stood steaming for seconds, then spun around and was gone.

She felt conflicted, distraught. It was Eduardo, and he was in a coma. He might be dying. How could she be concerned about anything else?

"Please, dear God," she whispered under her breath. "Let him live."

19 SHOOTOUT

TWO DAYS PASSED. Grace had gone into the station early to learn if there was any change in Eduardo's condition.

Christina looked haggard. There was despair in her voice. "I spent all night there," the officer's sister said. "It's frustrating when I can't do anything for him."

"You are," Grace said softly. "Holding his hand, speaking to him. He must know you're with him."

She returned to her workspace and prepared for the morning meeting. It wasn't scheduled until nine, but already Grace was dreading that daily blood-letting. Then her excuse to miss it dropped in on her cubicle, gift-wrapped in the form of Steve Jankowski. He was lugging his camera in from outside, trying to catch his breath.

"Just got back from the scene of a shooting. Big mess. Got some good video."

"Oh?" Grace said, feigning interest only for her friend's sake. "Is anyone going out there to cover it?"

Jankowski turned up a big grin. "I think you'll want to cover this one. The victim is your buddy, Nick Pontellis."

Grace half-rose from her chair. "Pontellis?" she exclaimed. "Is he..."

"Dead," Steve finished it for her.

**

The Pontellis garage was ringed by crime scene tape. Several uniformed officers and two plain-clothes detectives milled around talking, pointing at potential evidence, discussing theories. Grace recognized a detective she had met earlier on a story—a stout, friendly black man named Truman Brown. She hurried to him.

"Detective Brown. Grace Gleason, Channel Six."

His greeting was friendly. "Hey, Grace. I remember you."

"What happened here?"

"I've got to be off the record, Gleason."

"Sure," she promised.

"Nick Pontellis. Owns a strip bar over in Buckhead. Gunned down as he was getting out of his car."

"I saw the video our photographer shot," she said. "His car door was still open, and there was a lot of blood beside it on the floor. Was he ambushed?"

"Could be."

"Look at the hole smashed through the panel of the garage door that's still closed," she continued her probe. "He must have suspected he was going to get hit. It looks to me like he phoned the police and shut the robbers in there with him."

"You're a regular Perry Mason." The officer shook his head.

She ignored his sarcasm. "By the time the cruisers got here, the perpetrators had punched their way out and headed for the woods."

"What makes you think so?"

Grace walked around the yellow tape toward the edge of the driveway, the officer following her a few steps. "See those dark brownish spots running out onto the lawn?" Grace pointed. "I don't think that's from an oil leak. That's blood, detective."

"Maybe," he remained noncommittal.

On a roll, Grace continued her speculation. "Pontellis still had his pistol in his grip, right?"

"It's at the lab," was all officer Brown would admit.

"I'll bet you ten dollars the blood type won't match his. Detective Brown, he shot that guy."

"Not sure yet," he continued to stonewall.

"And judging from all of the spent shells scattered around, there must have been more than one," she persisted. "Pontellis was hit nine times, I heard."

"Who you been talking to?" Brown scowled.

"We have sources," Grace said. "You know, I interviewed Pontellis after he was held up the first time. He impressed me as a man who stuck to routines. It seems to me they wouldn't have gone to all that trouble unless they knew he'd be carrying a lot of cash that night."

The detective walked back toward the garage. "We might learn more when we interview his wife. Officers are in the house calming her down. Gotta go."

"Detective Brown, think it could have been an inside job? Someone who worked at his club?" she asked.

"Too soon to tell," he responded.

"I think I'll go poke around at his place of business," she said.

Brown half-turned back. "Good luck with that. Getting anything out of that bunch will be like back-to-back root canals." He laughed and disappeared into the garage.

＊＊

Rick Dent was waiting in a booth at the Peachtree Diner. It was a noisy, bustling place on Piedmont Avenue, at the edge of Midtown where the business district melted into a semi-seedy neighborhood once considered a desirable address.

"Thanks for coming," she said. "Heard you were out at Pontellis' place before I got there."

"I ran a story on our early news," he answered. "That was one hell of a war they had out there."

Dent already had a hamburger and cup of coffee.

The waitress came. "Tuna salad and cola," Grace smiled up at her. She nodded and bustled away.

"I just can't put it together," she told the radio reporter. "He gets home, gets ambushed I guess, and locks the guy or guys in with him. That's like suicide."

"You met him, right?" Rick asked. "He was cocky. People like Pontellis think they can fight any battle and no one can take them down. Someone emptied nine rounds into the guy's back. Meaning..."

She finished it for him, "...meaning he was in retreat." Her eyebrows went up in recognition. "There had to be more than one of them. Otherwise..."

Dent interrupted, "...otherwise he would have stood his ground and shot it out."

She sat back as the food came, drinking in the comment. She liked the way they finished each others' sentences. It meant they thought alike analyzing news events. Maybe Rick's previous proposal about working together wasn't so far-fetched after all.

"I can't decide how much I want to get involved in this," Grace confessed.

"Why?"

"My stories have been mostly focused on the drug trade. The Gwinnett County gangs. I feel I'm on an important trail and don't want to get distracted."

"I hate narcotics and gangs as much as you do," he said. "But something doesn't smell right about these robberies going on around town. You heard the Handy Homer manager. The guys who held him up seemed to know about the store's operation—what night to hit them, where the safe was. Pontellis got hit on two separate nights when he had boxcar loads of cash on him."

Rick paused, his squinty eyes searching her face through his dense glasses, as if hoping to see a light bulb illuminate over her head.

"And the string of so-called smaller robberies at all those convenience and liquor stores? The safes disappeared in a third of them."

She sat taller, astonished. "How do you know that?"

His pudgy face drew up in a happy smile, his eyes squinting behind the thick spectacles. "I told you, Gleason, I do my homework. You need to work with me. I'll even go on your news segment if I get something really solid."

She returned his smile. "Maybe sometime, but don't hold your breath," she replied. "We'll see if it makes sense."

"Who knows, if these crimes are all connected, the trail might lead back to those gangs and the drug wars you report on."

**

Grace was unprepared for the brouhaha her broadcast the next evening stirred up. For the first half of the fifteen-minute segment, she waded through more heart-breaking stories of the gang conflicts in Gwinnett County.

"*Los Lagartos* and all of its permutations continue to stay one step ahead of the authorities," she said as she punched up a map on the big screen showing where the various criminal elements wielded their power.

She tapped icons on the screen and a montage of suspected cartel leaders filled the screen. "Guillermo 'Bomber' Morales, Jaime Cueller, Gilberto 'The Madman' Gomez—the list goes on and on. We're losing the drug war due to the drug business's inherent disdain for human life."

She paused for effect. She took a deep breath and touched the screen. A video of Atlanta police chief Omoro Stone appeared from his press conference that morning.

Grace considered Chief Stone a formidable obstacle in covering this story. She had paid rapt attention to the man and understood he ran a tight, guarded operation.

"That guy knows who he is and where he came from, " Rick Dent had told her the day they talked at the diner.

"What does that mean?" she asked.

"Officers tell me he speaks proudly of his slave ancestry. He has been a success at everything he has done. Stone's the epitome of self-assurance."

Such a deep knowledge of self, wrapped around an ego three miles wide and penchant for confidentiality, had probably accounted for his maintaining the position as top cop for more than a decade.

A towering figure, six feet four, Stone was considered by his colleagues and the citizens of Atlanta to be a larger-than-life figure. That presence, and his innate leadership skills, helped him rise through the ranks in law enforcement rapidly during his early years—faster than others with equal opportunities for advancement.

He was born George Stone in the tiny south Georgia town of Maxwell. His parents, Moby and Winnie, named him for his paternal grandfather. It was his grandfather's death that led to a research of his roots and an eventual name change.

He was close to his grandmother, Mary, and instinctively—especially for a teenager—made efforts to comfort the lonely widow. She had moved into their house after her husband's passing, and young George spent hours sitting with her in the kitchen after school while she shelled peas or sewed quilts and he did his homework.

"Grandma, where did my name George come from?" he asked one afternoon as she stirred a pot of beans. " I read at school that African-Americans gave up their names during slavery."

Eighty and frail, Mary drew in a breath. "Colored slaves took on the names of their owners. That's where Stone came from," she said. "George was given to your grandfather by his father, because it was a name passed down through his family."

"So Grandpa and I weren't the first George Stones?"

She smiled. "No. You're the fifth I know of."

The conversation, more than any of the others he had with her, seemed to affect the young man. He began to spend time in the school library reading African-American histories and searching through the personal accounts of slaves.

The next time he spoke to his grandmother on the subject, several weeks later, he was full of facts and figures about the slave trade. And of historical references to individual families.

His grandmother had been snapping beans in a large pot, but when he asked again about his ancestry she stopped, sat back and took off her glasses. She looked tired, and her eyes were slightly bloodshot as she fixed them on the inquisitive teenager.

"Your father was descended from a Mandinka tribesman named Omoro," she began. "He was brought to America from Gambia, West Africa on the slave ship Lord Ligonier in the mid-1700s. That's about all I know."

"How do you know that much?" he pressed.

"Some black families who want to know their roots have to do a lot of research. I ain't got an inkling about mine, we never studied it. But your grandpa was lucky. The story got passed down by his family, one generation to another."

George thought for a moment. "If Grandpa knew our story, why didn't he tell my parents?"

"I reckon he did, some time or other."

He looked aghast. "Then why didn't they tell me?"

The elderly woman reached out a bony hand and placed it firmly on top of her grandson's across the table. "Now don't you go getting cross with your mama and daddy just 'cause they haven't dug up your slave past for you. Some things are painful and best left alone. You got a big future ahead of you, George, and that's all they care about where you're concerned."

But George didn't let it go. When he went to college at Albany State, pursuing a degree in criminal justice, he took a black studies course. By the time he was a sophomore he had decided to change his first name to Omoro, in honor of his slave ancestor, who had had no voice in changing his name to George.

He told his parents without hesitation one day when he was home for semester break. Enjoying a long-awaited home-cooked meal of his mother's black-eyed peas, collard greens and cornbread, he informed them of his newly acquired name as matter-of-factly as he might have told them he had tried out for the band.

"Why would you want to do such a thing?' his astounded mother asked.

"I want to honor my predecessors," he answered proudly, then turned to eye his father squarely and added, "and yours. And to call attention to the plight of African-Americans who suffered under slavery."

His father didn't respond. But the young collegian Omoro Stone stole a glance at his grandmother, seated with them at the table. She smiled softly at him and winked.

Stone joined the APD upon graduation. After serving as a beat officer and then investigator in the robbery unit, he was promoted to sergeant where he worked in Internal Affairs. He attained the rank of lieutenant and was made evening watch commander.

After being promoted to major, he served as chief of staff to the Chief of Police. When Stone's superior resigned and moved to Detroit, Mayor Raymond Walker named Omoro interim chief. Less than a year later, after interviewing a raft of candidates for the permanent position, Walker eliminated the "interim" tag and made Omoro Stone the Atlanta Chief of Police.

The announcement in the daily paper was accompanied by a front page review of Stone's career under the headline, "Nobody Saw That Coming."

Stone was popular within the ranks, for he fiercely defended his troops. In a speech to his sworn officers a few months after his appointment, he said, "Once you are on this police force, we are all brothers, and your blood will forever run blue." He repeated this mantra in various forums many times after that.

The chief's actions supported his words. Often, when a complaint came in naming an officer, he dismissed it immediately, claiming it was a misunderstanding and not an officer mistake. This paternalistic attitude made it difficult for the citizens to file paperwork against a policeman or get any satisfaction from a grievance.

But Omoro was no fool. Over the years, he had learned how politics work. He did most of his advocating for his rank and file behind the scenes, so no one really knew how much influence he wielded. It became common knowledge around the force that Stone's support of his officers elicited intense loyalty, and few would dare undermine him.

One noteworthy instance occurred when Chief Stone pushed for a reorganization of the department. It involved flattening the ranks and eliminating an entire level of command. He wanted fewer layers between himself and his troops, and he worked behind closed doors to secure the support of Mayor Walker.

A captain openly campaigned within the union to fight the

change, which would have eliminated his position. The renegade en-listed, and received, support from subordinates in his division. Omoro Stone never forgot. Quietly, without fanfare, he saw to it the rebellious captain's officers found themselves working at the airport or some other undesirable shift. And the complainant? The chief found ways to make his life so miserable he transferred to the Gwinnett County force at reduced pay.

Chief Stone wasn't all vitriol and spite. He had a charming side, at times even engaging with the media. He used reporters to disseminate information he wanted the public to have, skillfully ma-nipulating the most seasoned journalists. When reporters bellied up to the bar and traded stories, they were all the same.

"Omoro has a knack for making you think he was sharing ex-clusive information," Christina Cruz told Grace one rare evening when Grace joined the anchor and several others for happy hour. "Then he'll leave you with another worthless sound bite revealing absolutely nothing."

The chief was shrewd. He kept his cool even under the most intense media spotlight. And he had his guard up at all times, most notably around open mikes and hot cameras.

Just as surely as Chief Stone valued loyalty from his employ-ees, he equally distrusted the media. He did his best to use reporters' interest when it suited his purpose, but otherwise he was unfriendly. Grace knew that. She had been warned by other correspondents.

**

Grace took a quick glimpse toward MaryAnne, directing traf-fic at the console, and wondered if she were about to start a war with the fractious and ambitious head of Atlanta's Police Department.

She gave an earnest gaze into camera one as best she could. "You may have seen the Atlanta police chief's appearance this morning after a shootout in the garage of nightclub owner Nick Pontellis last night. Let's listen."

"Last night a fatal shooting took place at the private residence of an Atlanta businessman," Chief Stone said. He looked darkly serious and official, dressed in full uniform, including hat. "We have put our top homicide detectives on the case and won't rest until we identify the perpetrators."

Grace reached up and paused the video, reduced it to half the screen and pulled up another. It was the murder scene—Steve's footage of police gathering evidence in the garage, then his astute close-ups of the blood trail into the woods.

"Atlanta's finest have not acknowledged there was more than one shooter, at least not at Chief Stone's news conference," she said. "Nor will Detective Brown admit for the record the trail of blood into the woods means there are wounded killers running loose out there."

Grace moved to her stool, perched on it and peered into the camera purposefully. "So let's take a look at what has happened in Atlanta for months."

She summed up the large number of robberies, played a snippet of her interview with the Handy Homer manager, and reviewed her interview with Pontellis after his first robbery.

Then, "We must ask the obvious question: Where is the Atlanta Police Department? Is there a connection between all of these unsolved crimes, these burglaries and hold-ups that have our city paralyzed and citizens deeply concerned?"

**

As Grace launched her verbal assault on the Atlanta Police Department, News Director Vivian Ellis sat fidgeting in her office desk chair. "Crime and Corruption" was on her monitor, and station manager Harvey Silver leaned against the edge of Vivian's desk watching it with her.

"This is exactly what I've been talking about," Silver said, his cheeks growing slightly rosy. "I've told you she's going to have to tone it down or we'll lose advertisers."

Ellis cut her eyes at Silver, annoyed.

His gaze remained pasted on the monitor. "It's one thing to demonize Gwinnett County drug gangs," Harvey continued. "Hell, everyone agrees with that. But City Hall holds a lot of sway with people who can make or break this station."

Vivian lowered the volume with the remote. "What are you saying, Harvey? Tell her to drop the story?" the news director asked in a harsh tone.

"No, damn it Vivian. I'm not saying to drop the story. I'm saying focus on the facts of the cases and stop speculating about the APD being incompetent."

"Harvey, she's got our numbers up."

Silver stood up and frowned down at her. "I want ratings, but not at the expense of our ad revenues. And I sure as hell don't want the city police making our life difficult. Let's go in there."

Vivian rose, and they walked together down the corridor toward the newsroom studio.

Grace peered intently into camera two. "Way back in the late seventies and early eighties, Atlanta went through the trauma of a series of murders of children and young men. Wayne Williams is still serving consecutive life terms for two of those killings."

She touched the screen and a larger-than-life photo of the convicted murderer appeared. The camera pulled back and the image showed his press conference on his parent's lawn. "Prior to his arrest, Williams proclaimed his innocence. But on June 21, 1981 he was arrested and charged with two murders, and eventually for many of the twenty-nine child homicides. At that time, Atlanta's citizens, particularly the black community, were frightened and exasperated by the lack of action from police and city hall. Mothers of some victims formed a committee and began to pressure the Atlanta PD. It took a year for police to admit publicly the crimes might be related."

. She paused for a beat, glancing toward the newsroom entrance where Vivian Ellis had appeared with Station Manager Harvey Silver at her side. Grace took a step in their direction as a camera followed her. "I can imagine the frustration of a community needing answers. Do we have another stonewall on our hands, courtesy of the Atlanta police? I tried to ask Chief Stone what they have learned about a possible connection between these crimes. Let's watch."

Grace tapped the screen, and footage of the chief's press conference came up. Steve had shot a great over-the-shoulder angle of Grace thrusting the microphone toward Chief Stone.

"Chief, in decades past, the APD has been slow to connect related crimes," Grace stated on the video, "such as the notorious child murders that haunted the city. Because there's such a raft of possibly connected burglaries and robberies in succession, do you think Atlanta might have a crime epidemic of another form on its hands?"

Omoro Stone's broad mouth morphed into a scowl. "I won't dignify that question with an answer. You've got some nerve, insinuating that we're not investigating these crimes thoroughly." He turned and pointed to another reporter.

The video went to black, and the Big Six logo filled the screen.

Grace turned to camera one. "A string of serious crimes in a short period of time, one resulting in a murder. And the Atlanta PD knows nothing, sees nothing, hears nothing. You can be sure I'll follow up. I'm Grace Gleason, and this has been 'Crime and Corruption.'"

"And out," producer McWherter said.

Grace relaxed for a moment, then glanced toward the news-room doorway. Silver and Ellis were both watching with alarm written all over their faces.

Grace's stomach did a backflip as she wondered how long she could persist before management timidly pulled the plug.

20 MESSY BUSINESS

GRACE DIDN'T HAVE TIME to worry over her fate at Big Six News. Three days after her on-air implied indictment of the city's police department, chaos struck the heartbeat of the city.

"I need you." Vivian's voice sounded strident and desperate as she peered over Grace's cubicle wall.

"Sure. What's up?' She noticed Cassandra Barrett, a station photographer, was with the news director.

"We just got a report that a shooting has gone down in Buckhead. Some guy went berserk at a stockbroker's office. Need you and Cassandra to jump in a truck and go cover it. She has the location."

"Where's..." Grace started.

Barrett, a young woman in her twenties, cut her off. "Steve's out on assignment," she reported curtly. "You and I have never worked together. I know you prefer Jankowski, but you use him too much as it is, and damn it, I'm just as good."

Grace felt herself flush from the confrontation. She realized she had trod on this woman's toes, and she hadn't even seen her shoot frame one. She hadn't meant to play favorites, and now she could rectify the fault by giving Cassandra a chance. "I know. Sorry," she offered softly. "Let's get going."

The Piedmont Office Court near the confluence of Piedmont and Roswell Roads was complete pandemonium. Cassandra deftly steered through the mess of vehicle and pedestrian traffic. A uniformed officer motioned the Big Six van to pull over near some barricades. Grace saw several other news crews already at the scene.

"What's going on?" she asked the officer as she jumped out.

"Some day trader shot up his office," the policemen replied, pointing toward the offices. "Guy took off and is being chased on foot."

Suddenly, shots rang out from the direction of the office plaza. As if signaled by the director of a Hollywood movie, the gathered crowd scattered and ducked. Simultaneously, another large group of police officers, reporters and bystanders instantly scurried en masse toward the racket.

Grace was rushing to keep up with Cassandra who, fifteen years younger, was sprinting through the plaza and shooting footage at a lightning pace.

Several cops had formed a human barrier, arms outstretched. "Stay back," one yelled.

Two ambulances, lights flashing and sirens blaring, jumped the curb behind them and parted the crowd like the Red Sea. Grace and Cassandra followed them toward the office building where police officers and fire department paramedics were rushing in and out of doorways.

Cassandra nodded as Grace pointed toward the first gurneys being lifted from the ambulances and pulled inside. They approached as closely as they could while Cassandra filmed, but the emergency vehicles, hordes of on-lookers and uniformed first responders created obstacles.

"Look!" Grace shouted at Cassandra, hurtling around the vehicles. She sped toward a second building.

"Where the hell are you going?" Cassandra's shrill voice split the air.

"Follow me," Grace urged.

They hurried toward the structure where frightened workers were spilling out of exits. As she ran, Grace could see SWAT team members, heavily armored, chasing toward the far end of the plaza and out toward Piedmont Avenue.

"Get footage of this building too," she shouted. "I think the guy shot up both places."

"Already got it," the photographer snarled back, sounding peeved.

Just as Cassandra approached the entrance of the second building, she was restrained by the outstretched arms of several policemen and security guards. She aimed her camera lens past them as paramedics from a fire truck parked on the other end of Piedmont raced in the front doors with life-saving equipment.

"Officer, Grace Gleason, Channel Six," Grace approached a policewoman urgently. "Where did the shooter go?"

The woman's eyes darted toward the sprinting SWAT team members disappearing around the corner. "One of them said he got into a van," she answered as Cassandra captured her response on camera. "Looks like there's going to be a chase."

"Come on!" Grace called out, "Let's get back to the truck."

They were both gasping for air as they crawled into the van. Grace's cell phone chirped.

"Where are you?" Rick Dent asked.

"Just got back in our vehicle," she responded frantically. "You?"

"Chasing the SWAT team vans. The guy got away and

they're on his trail. But the traffic is shit. I can't get through."

"Keep me posted," Grace advised. "I'll do the same. We'll hook up later at the diner."

Cassandra tried, but she couldn't get the Big Six van onto Piedmont Avenue. Police barricades, civilian vehicles and swarms of people on foot were causing havoc.

They pulled over and Grace yanked out her laptop, pounding out the story as she knew it so far. Meanwhile, Barrett was editing digital images to be fed back to the station.

As she finished her report and transmitted it, Grace felt the vibration of her cell. The text from Vivian read, *"News briefing. First office building."*

"We're going back," Grace reported to her camerawoman.

They arrived at the conference site just in time. Lieutenant Hondo Henderson was holding court in front of the building, with the APD's public relations officer Aretha Herrington at his side. The ambulances had already left. The shooting scene was surrounded by yellow tape as investigators arrived. Scores of people who had spilled out of adjacent buildings or driven to the area after hearing reports, milled aimlessly around the brick plaza area.

"Here's what we know so far," Officer Henderson told them. "A man entered his place of employment, Tulane Investments, and opened fire on his co-workers. He then proceeded to that building over there."

He pointed as cameras turned from him and toward the second shooting scene.

"Investigators are interviewing witnesses at this time. We cannot discuss the identity of the suspect, as he is still at large. Our first estimate is that nine people were shot in the two buildings, but we cannot at this time reveal their condition or the number of possible fatalities. That's all we have for you right now."

The shouting began.

"Where'd the guy go?" a female newspaper reporter called out. "Did he say anything?"

Henderson frowned. "No details on that yet. SWAT is trying to track him down."

"Why'd he do it?" Grace recognized the veteran reporter from Channel Twelve.

The lieutenant furrowed his brow and held up both hands. "That's all I've got right now. We'll give you an update when we have it."

Cassandra stopped shooting and tugged Grace away from the other reporters. "Just got a text from Tom at the assignment desk," she said secretively. "Police have traced the van to a gas station at Woodville."

"That's way up north in Cherokee County," Grace gasped. "Does he want us up there?"

"No. Scott Matthews and Steve Jankowski are on their way right now."

"Then let's get me on camera and go live with what we know," Grace said.

She delivered the report, closing with, "The pandemonium we experienced here minutes ago has subsided. But the assailant remains at large. Meanwhile, first responders are transporting the victims to area hospitals as investigators comb the area to piece together exactly what happened."

As Barrett packed her camera gear into the van, Grace got a text from Rick. "Drop me off on your way back," Grace requested, climbing into the vehicle. "I'm meeting Dent."

**

He was waiting, his droll mouth upturned in a half-smile as Grace entered the diner and slid into the booth, feeling all the springs in her body unwind.

."Some day, huh? Did you lose them?" he asked, his voice raspy.

"No," she answered, her brain still swimming. "The station told me after the briefing Matthews was headed for the gas station."

Responding to the ding-ding of his cell phone's text tone, Rick fished it from his pocket. "They caught the guy," he said. "Cornered him, and he shot himself."

Everything in the place seemed to go silent. Grace sagged, her outstretched palms flat against the cool surface of the tile tabletop. "My God."

"Some folks are crazy," he said matter-of-factly.

Grace had always taken pride in her tough exterior. A hard-nosed attitude had seen her through trying times in her personal life and helped make her a fearless crime reporter. Yet at times like this, she felt the stone façade fracture a bit. Her watery eyes searched his. "All of those innocent people."

"I know," he commiserated.

The waitress brought them tea. Grace drew in a long breath and sat up straight. "Such a frenzied day. And a distraction from what we're trying to accomplish with this robbery business."

Rick squinted his eyes behind the goggles, looking a little

fatherly. "Relax," he reproved. "The news is a messy business. You can't pre-plan everything. You should know that by now."

"I really do," she sighed heavily. "But sometimes I wish…"

He interrupted, "Don't wish. It won't do any good, and you'll just get frustrated." He pointed across the street. "See that building? That charming little boutique hotel?"

She nodded.

"Do you know its history?"

"Not really."

The radio reporter took a drink of his tea. "It used to be the Weinkoff. Five years after Pearl Harbor, the place caught fire. The hotel was full of teenagers attending a youth conference, holiday shoppers, tourists in town. One hundred nineteen people died, still the deadliest hotel fire ever in the United States."

"That's awful. But what's your point?"

"The news is random. And we're in that business. The back stories sometimes are the most fascinating."

"Such as?" she asked, her curiosity peaked.

"For one thing, a kid from Georgia Tech took a photo of a woman jumping from a window of the building and won a Pulitzer."

"No! Was she killed?"

"Almost. She broke all kinds of bones, had a bunch of surgeries, lost a leg. But that woman worked until retirement and lived to the ripe old age of eighty-six. Meanwhile, the fire was a catalyst for updating building codes all over the country."

She sipped her tea and quietly snickered as he gulped his, making a slurping sound. Grace mused that Rick never did anything in a dainty way.

So you're making a point," she returned thoughtfully to his Weinkoff tale. "We report all of this chaos and chase it around until it exasperates us. But our real value is in finding the good that emerges out of the other end of it."

He leaned back and smiled, not needing to respond.

21 HARVEY SILVER

STATION MANAGER SILVER was at Big Six for five years before Grace arrived. Ambitious to a fault, the tall, dark, well-dressed former small radio station owner had eschewed the business end of a microphone or camera for a management position at the station. How he had arrived at that decision was deeply rooted in his formative years.

The Silvers were one of only three Jewish families in Macon, Missouri. Harvey's father, Sol, owned a menswear store that did less sales volume-wise than the two larger department stores. But Sol Silver had two precious gifts. One was the ability to make people like him despite their religious and cultural differences; the other was an incredibly detailed knowledge of good values in custom-tailored menswear.

The richest men in town—bankers, business leaders, the mayor, the owner of the town's only country club—quietly came around to Silver's Clothing to get fitted for their suits, carefully hand-made at off-the-rack prices.

Sol Silver couldn't join the country club, but he mixed and mingled with the city's elite at charity events and non-social gatherings. He and his wife, Willa, owned one of the most magnificent homes in Macon, a two-story, colonial-style mansion at the top of a hill on the edge of town.

Harvey's father paid him minimum wage to work in the store after school; Sol told his son repeatedly he expected him one day to take over the business.

At school, Harvey made decent grades though he had an aversion to studying. Where he made his reputation was in extra-curricular activities. Despite working part-time in the store, Harvey found spare hours to participate in the radio/television club, and he single-handedly organized a student-run bank. It not only operated as a true concern but also taught Macon High School students how to save and deposit their money, balance a checkbook and earn interest.

The two club experiences foretold Harvey's future. When he enrolled in the University of Missouri, he argued with his father that he wanted to declare journalism as his major.

"I'll go along with it, but only if you have a double major—journalism and business," Sol said in August before Harvey returned for his sophomore year. Harvey had worked all summer in the menswear store. Sol told every customer who came in his son would return after graduation, eventually take over the business and let him retire to Florida.

Harvey couldn't have known how critical his father's stubbornness was to molding his future. Agreeing to the business major was a way to get what he wanted—an education in radio and television and an understanding about how such businesses worked from both the reportorial and financial sides.

Every time he returned home during breaks, the young man told his father he wanted nothing more to do with the clothing business.

Sol was visibly heartbroken when his son moved to St. Louis after graduation, accepting dual roles of assistant manager and on-air newsman at a small FM radio station.

"That's it. You're on your own," Sol erupted on the Saturday morning that Harvey broke the news he was leaving. "Don't ever come to me for money."

His father watched helplessly as Harvey defiantly loaded his car to drive across the state. "Don't expect to get any of the money when I sell the store," Sol put a final point on it. He pivoted and stomped back to the front door.

"That's fine, Pop," Harvey retorted unemotionally, watching his father enter the house. "I don't want to end up in the suit business and dry up in a little midwestern town."

A slamming door was his father's final communication with Harvey.

Within two years, the young go-getter landed an assistant station manager job at the number three television outlet in the gateway city. There, he also befriended a co-worker, Marvin Baker, who always seemed to have some kind of deal in the works.

"I have an opportunity for you," Marvin told him one day at lunch. They were sitting in a booth at Two Bucks Simple, a funky little deli that made the best pastrami sandwiches Harvey had ever sunk his molars into.

"What now?" Harvey teased sarcastically. "Import zebras and cross them with donkeys?"

"Land, my good man," Baker replied, ignoring the sarcasm. "They aren't making any more of it, you know. I found two hundred acres for sale down in the Ozark foothills, an easy drive from the city. It's hilly, wooded and has a stream running through the center of the property. Man, it's beautiful."

He held up his hands as Harvey frowned.

"Hear me out. Right now this place is owned by a rich old farmer who has built half of the town nearby—Huzzah Circle. Harvey, the price is right. Between both of us, we can scrape together enough cash to buy it, subdivide it into five-acre lots and sell it as retirement property. I have a friend who's a builder, and he's willing to package low-cost houses with the deals."

Harvey finished off his sandwich and took a swig of soda. "Hell, I don't want to get into real estate," he exclaimed. "I want to stay in the broadcasting business."

Marvin grinned with self-satisfaction. His friend had bitten the apple.

"That's just the thing. This old guy not only wants to sell the farm, but he wants to package it with the town's only radio station."

"What? That's nuts."

"Listen to me," Baker insisted. "This is the smaller of two farms he owns. Meanwhile, he has also built three tract-house subdivisions and the town's only radio station. Now his wife is making him give up one of the farms, and he doesn't want to keep the station. Damn, Harvey, it's a chance for us to make some incredible loot on a land deal, and do what we've both talked about—own a broadcast outlet."

**

After four months of haggling back and forth with the owner, Harvey and Marvin closed the purchase. But the pipe dream of a retirement community, it turned out, was much more difficult than they had imagined. The legal processes of subdividing the property, negotiating construction deals with the builder and finding buyers for the lots became a nightmare. When a wealthy doctor offered to buy the entire acreage for a one hundred dollar per acre profit, they jumped at it.

The young entrepreneurs also discovered two owners of a small-town radio station was one too many. Splitting the profits of the tiny operation wasn't much of a living. Harvey wanted out. Marvin had married a local girl and decided to stay there and raise a family. It didn't take long for the friends to negotiate a buy-out they both could live with.

"What will you do?" Baker asked Harvey as they celebrated closing the deal over a beer at the local saloon.

"Go back to the things I love."

"Which are?"

"Big city life. Man, this town is like the one I grew up in. I don't want to end up here. I know you like it, but I need more access, more nightlife. More women to meet."

"That's it?"

"No. Television. I miss it, Marv. There's an assistant station manager job open down in Atlanta and I'm in the running."

Marvin raised his glass. "Then I hope you get it. We'll always be friends, right?"

Harvey tapped his friend's glass with his. "For all time."

**

At Channel Six in Atlanta, Silver wore his ambition like a badge of honor. He made it no secret he wanted to move on up to the networks. Meanwhile, he used his business knowledge and personal charm to ingratiate himself with the two most important people in his career path—the chief executive officer and the president of the parent company, Compass Communications.

The Big Six station manager's job was hanging by a string due to fading ratings and dwindling advertisers. Silver took advantage of encounters with the two bosses to excite them about his ideas for returning the station to glory. That he had not shared the plans with his direct supervisor was lost on them. Unceremoniously, they fired the station manager and replaced him with this up-and-comer who had fresh strategic arrows in his quiver.

In essence, Harvey Silver had run off his predecessor without a confrontation. And without giving the man the support he deserved from his assistant.

Silver engaged Vivian Ellis to run his news shop because he believed she would shake things up, diversify the newsroom, move some of the dead wood out. She would, he promised, produce programming that would make them proud and boost their numbers.

"You have a year," he told Vivian when he offered the position. "Our ratings are pretty good, but Channel Nine has been eating into our lead. It's time to re-establish our relevance."

"What happens in a year?" Ellis asked.

"I'll re-evaluate. If you restore our preeminence in the market, you stay. Unless…"

"Unless what?" she asked, eyebrows raised in curiosity.

"Unless you want to follow me."

"What do you mean?"

"Atlanta's a great market, but it's not where I belong. I'm eventually headed for a New York position, and after that, who knows? Network, probably, or cable news."

Ellis rocked back in her chair, amazed. "You're sure of yourself, aren't you?"

"Hell, yes, I am," he smiled. "How about it? Are you in?"

An enthusiastic grin lit up her almond face. "I'm in."

It had taken Harvey nearly five years of waiting patiently for this opportunity. He was the station manager now, with no time to waste. He had hired an ambitious news director and challenged her to be creative.

"I have lots of ideas," Vivian told him.

"Such as?"

She grinned mischievously. "I'm not going to tell you everything. But here's a start. I know about a hard-nosed crime reporter in Dallas I want to bring up here, a tenacious woman named Gleason. I'm confident she can help us build ratings. I'm going after her."

Silver nodded supportively.

22 VIVIAN ELLIS

THE MORNING AFTER Grace's on-air attack of the city police department, Vivian Ellis called her. It was early, and Grace had just started on her first cup of coffee.

"Come and see me. We need to talk before the morning meeting starts," Ellis' tone was terse over the phone.

"Sure. What's it about?" Grace tried to hide her annoyance.

"Aretha Herrington is here."

It was obvious to Grace the APD's public affairs flack wasn't making a social visit. As she trudged toward the news director's office, Grace dreaded what promised to be an unpleasant encounter. Further, she wondered whether or not she could count on Vivian Ellis to back her. Grace had not yet learned to read her boss. At times, Ellis was positive and supportive. Yet there was an unpredictable streak in her that often manifested itself in pointed barbs and unexpected criticism.

The world through Vivian Ellis' eyes was one big news story. After all, life-changing events happened right outside her door everyday as a child growing up in the Joyland neighborhood in Southeast Atlanta. The name—Joyland—was a cruel irony. It might have conjured up positive marketing vibes when the developer first named it, but it had quickly become anything but a Garden of Eden.

Her small, wood frame childhood home was bordered by the downtown connector to the west and in the shadow of Carver Homes Housing Project to the east. The sound of gunfire erupting outside was almost a nightly occurrence.

Vivian was the youngest of six children. Her oldest brother, Quentin, was killed in a gun battle between gangs when she was only seven. Her mother, Nora, rode the bus to Buckhead every day but

Sunday to clean houses. It was a meager living, but she was able to keep the lights on and the rent paid.

Nora Ellis rarely spoke of Vivian's father. When Vivian was thirteen, she asked about him. Nora said he left before she was born and was "out there somewhere." That was all her mother would say, nodding her head in a way that told the young girl "no more questions."

The pastor of the Oak Street Baptist Church, the Reverend Dr. P. James Alvin reached out to Nora Ellis as she struggled to raise her family. Vivian was a bright girl; Reverend Alvin took notice and kept her grounded, looking forward to escaping the streets for a better life.

"You study hard, Vivian," he said one day after Sunday School. "Don't let nobody take away your God-given right to something better'n that neighborhood."

The advice resonated with the bright little girl, first at Slaton Elementary and later at Prince Middle School. At Carver High School, Vivian Ellis graduated at the top of the class. A Hope Scholarship and admission to the Grady School of Journalism at the University of Georgia in Athens opened the door out of Joyland. She never looked back.

After Vivian graduated, Georgia State Senator Arthur Langford from the old neighborhood made some calls and helped her get an internship at Channel Twelve, the number three station in the Metro Atlanta market. The gritty newsroom was a perfect fit for her. She knew the neighborhoods and language of the inner city streets, so she didn't spend much time as a gofer. The news manager, Tom Ritchie, quickly put her on the path to becoming a writer and producer.

One day, barely a year after she had started there, Ritchie called her into his office. She had covered a touchy story involving a mistaken police shooting of an elderly Joyland resident, scooping the top two stations.

"You did a real professional job on that story," he said.

"My mother knew that woman," she told him. "She used to give me candy when I was a little girl. I guess I was pretty motivated to give it my best."

He smiled broadly. "You always do, Vivian. That's why I'm making you the lead producer of the morning shows.

Vivian was a hard-driving force in the newsroom, always pushing reporters to fight fiercely and dig deeper. She had an inexplicable presence when she walked into a room that made writers and reporters sit up straight and pay attention.

Ellis' scraping and struggling seemed to be over. She had a modest apartment near the station, and now she had money for extras such as manicures and pedicures.

Yet every time she made her weekly drive back to Joyland to help her mom with expenses, she returned to the office depressed and peevish for a day or so.

One afternoon, stopping with fellow producer Myrna Westin for happy hour at The Tenth Street Tavern, her friend mentioned it.

"You don't seem real happy. Something wrong?" Myrna asked carefully.

Vivian heaved a sigh of relief, apparently happy to have the subject broached. She laid it out over a margarita. "I'm bummed all weekend after I go over there," she said, feeling the light buzz from the tequila. "It takes until Wednesday for me to feel normal again. It's a kind of emptiness. Maybe I get depressed from watching my mother struggle and scour for every morsel of food on her table. Or it's possible that I feel guilty because my sisters and brothers wrestle with their own demons and I can't pull them up from the grip of poverty."

Her friend looked her hard in the eye. "Listen Vivian, you've rescued yourself from that life. Do what you can for them, but you're not going to be able to save the whole damned world. Be thankful you've crawled out of that oppressive place."

**

When the executive producer position for the six o'clock news opened up, Vivian saw a chance at a great career opportunity. Station management saw a golden opportunity for their rising star. Vivian made significant changes to the show's format, and the ratings "...went through the roof," Ritchie announced in morning meeting after the quarterly sweeps were published.

Leading the newscast with coverage of local crime and corruption paid off in a big way, and Ellis proved she was skilled at showcasing reporter talent, the more theatrical the better. It seemed as if things couldn't get any better for Vivian Ellis. She was living the dream.

Yet in those happy hour get-togethers, one-on-one with Myrna Westin, she continued to confess her life felt incomplete.

"I know I should be happy," she said. "But I want my climb to success to mean more. I need for it to have a point."

The next day, like a lightning strike, a phone call from Harvey Silver, station manager at Big Six, changed everything.

When Silver offered her the job, director of the city's top news operation, saying yes was easy. But the conditions he put on the job would bring her even greater pressure to achieve beyond her own expectations.

**

The negative dynamics were obvious to Grace the moment she entered the news director's office. Vivian sat erect at her desk. Across from her, in one of two side chairs, Aretha Herrington leaned forward, gesturing forcefully as she spoke to Ellis. Herrington was black, slim and attractive, with cornrows in her hair. She wore a conservative navy blue suit.

The room fell eerily silent when they saw Grace come in.

"You know Aretha Herrington." Ellis motioned toward the public affairs officer.

Grace extended her hand, which Aretha reached out and shook stiffly.

"We haven't met, but we've talked on the phone," Grace answered. Aretha shot her a haughty frown.

"Ms. Herrington came by to talk about your report on the police chief's press conference," Vivian's voice had a hard edge. "She feels that..."

The public affairs woman interjected, "...that you weren't being fair. You know we can't go running out there making public statements about ongoing investigations. Grace, this sensationalism is only going to hinder out ability to solve these crimes."

"Oh? How so, Aretha?"

"Be reasonable. When you go on the air making accusations, the public gets riled, and we spend our time fending them off and answering complaints instead of doing police work."

"I sincerely doubt that one little newscast will prevent you from solving a whole string of crimes, much less the Pontellis killing."

Herrington turned to the news director, a plea in her expression. "Vivian?"

"We'll talk about it in our staff meeting," Ellis assured. "We're in the ratings business, but we don't want to stand in the way of the APD getting bad guys. We're on your side."

Herrington rose from her chair. "Why didn't you come to me?" she asked. Herrington's mouth turned up in more of a scoff than a smile.

Grace shrugged. "I don't know. Would it have done any good?"

After Aretha left Vivian's office, Ellis frowned. "I'm not real happy we had to have that dialogue," she said sharply.

Grace took half a step back, surprised. "We didn't have to," she said to her boss. "You don't want me to fold up and not report, do you?"

Ellis took a deep breath. "I want you to do your job without my needing to deflect visits from city authorities."

Grace's hands went to her hips. "I agree with you. Have other city authorities come to see you about my reports?"

The news director shook her head in dismissal. "Let's get ready for the morning meeting, okay?"

Grace retreated to the newsroom, knowing it was the prudent thing to do before she got her back up too high and told her boss what she had been tempted to say.

She had only seen traces of this enigmatic woman's cantankerous side. Now it was bursting into full bloom like next summer's garden. Grace had to figure out how to strike a balance between chasing down miscreants and keeping management at bay.

23 INTERNAL AFFAIRS

IMPACT WORKOUT'S OWNER Big Sam didn't spend much time among his customers. But he kept tabs on them, especially the cops. He checked the computer several times a week to see who was coming and going, and often emerged from his office to conduct a visual scan of the customers.

The huge man walked into the gym and surveyed the sparse crowd. He spotted Bret Larkin doing presses with light weights on a flat bench. Nearby, Carter Drake was sweating profusely on an elliptical machine.

"What happened to you, Larkin?" Big Sam pointed to the protective wrap on the Riverwood officer's leg.

"Slight fracture," Bret answered quickly. "Had a nasty fall chasing this two-bit perp. I can't run on the treadmill for a while. Meantime, gotta keep lifting to stay in shape."

"I heard Cruz got shot."

Larkin said, "He's in real bad shape."

"Sorry to hear it." Sam waited a beat. "You know, I haven't seen Doug McHughes in a while."

The policeman grunted as he lifted. "Doug's got the flu. Been damn sick for a couple of weeks."

Big Sam spotted Larkin on his final lift and helped him ease the weight back into place on the rack. "Man, you guys are the walking wounded." He gave a half-wave to Drake as he disappeared down the hallway to his office.

Bret Larkin sat up on the bench and cast a wary look at Carter Drake, who shrugged and increased the speed on the machine.

**

Across town, Rick was waiting at their usual lunch booth. "I got you sweet tea," he said.

"You always read my mind. What a morning," Grace said.

The waitress brought water. "What'll you have?' she asked.

"House salad," Grace ordered.

"Same," Rick nodded. "Add some chicken." The server jotted it down and left.

"You sounded like a volcano on the phone," Dent said. "That meeting with Herrington must have been some dust-up."

Grace squinted. "I can't understand why everyone's so jumpy about my coverage."

Dent nodded. "That's easy. The public is getting antsy about the city's inability to solve this thing. You're stepping on some toes that are already very tender."

"Well, they all seem hyper-defensive."

The radio newsman started to speak, then stopped, started again, stopped again. Grace watched him, curious what was on his mind.

Finally, he said, "I've given this a lot of thought. We've got a slew of robberies and burglaries that all look like inside jobs, right? A high-profile burglary at Handy Homer where the perps appeared to know everything about their operation. A strip joint owner murdered carrying tons of cash, by guys who obviously knew his routines. We're both skeptical about them being Latino gang-related. I'm starting to wonder…" He stopped short.

Grace raised her eyebrows in understanding. "You don't think…"

"It's possible," he interrupted.

She gasped. "I don't think so, Rick. It's too huge. Everyone would be buzzing by now. I've seen brazen cops, but never so nervy as to pull off something that covers this much ground."

His puffy mouth pulled up into a caustic smile. "But wait; there's more."

"You sound like an infomercial." She couldn't help laughing.

"I know. But there really is. I haven't told you everything." He watched her interest build. "I was doing some snooping over at the Seventh Precinct. You know, where Pontellis' bar is located. There's a cop there who is mysteriously on medical leave."

"And?" Grace shrugged.

"Talked to his partner. She doesn't know what's wrong with the guy, and says no one else does either. He just sort of disappeared several weeks ago. Might be the flu. But that's not all, either," Dent enthused, replicating his mock infomercial performance. "Before he went on leave, he reported his handgun missing. It was a nine millimeter semiautomatic."

"Same caliber Pontellis was killed with but not that unusual." She stirred her tea, deep in thought. When she finally looked up at Rick his stare was locked into her eyes.

"Want to go sniff around Internal Affairs?" he asked.

She nodded. "Sure. But let's take a camera. I'll call Steve Jankowski."

Atlanta's Department of Public Safety headquarters was only a few years old, built for ninety million dollars to house both the APD and the Atlanta Fire Department. The five-story, glass-and-brick building was small by some critics' standards, wedged sideways between two busy streets on the edge of downtown. The department had previously resided in a humongous building abandoned by a major corporation.

But proponents for the new edifice had argued it would be specifically designed for use by law enforcement, not force-fit into an old warehouse and distribution center that also housed parks and recreation, motor transport, city records and even an art gallery. It was so large no more than one-third of the massive structure's space was occupied.

The Office of Professional Standards made its home perched

197

on the top floor of the new building. Major J.D. Woods had command-ed the unit for eighteen years, having worked his way up from a beat officer and more recently a precinct commander after achieving the rank of lieutenant.

Major Woods made a practice of never talking to the media and kept a low profile internally. It was common knowledge around the department that seasoned officers didn't fear an OPS investiga-tion, because they knew how to elude it. Supervisors understood the procedures almost as well as those of their own unit.

Most public complaints amounted to the officer's word versus the citizen's, and the cop usually won. Major Woods would make sure any complaint had the proper paperwork, but once that was complet-ed, his job was done.

On this day, however, he was in for a surprise. Dent had learned the major often kept his car parked in a section normally re-served for SWAT team trucks. He had no idea a news crew was wait-ing to ambush him as he came out of the building and walked toward the unmarked cruiser.

"Major Woods, what's going on with Officer Doug McHughes?" Grace blurted out, rushing toward the officer. Jankowski was right be-hind her, and Rick Dent followed with his recorder microphone.

Major Woods was tall and wiry. His pasty skin and sunken cheekbones made his ever-serious mien almost eerie. He took a step back in obvious surprise, and his usually grave expression changed to a flash of confusion.

But only for an instant.

"You don't belong here," he barked, gathering his composure and drawing up to his full six-foot-two.

"Can you answer my question?" Grace persisted. "What do you know about McHughes' service revolver and his possible connec-tion to the Pontellis murder?"

The major half-turned and motioned her away. "Miss Gleason, I am on my way to the grand opening of a new police precinct to better serve our citizens here in the city. This is not the time or place to shoot questions at me." He stopped for a moment, pensive.

"Why don't you and your camera follow me to the opening of the precinct on Fifth Street, and after the event I will talk to you." He climbed into the car and started to pull the door shut.

Grace threw a quick glance toward Dent. "Fair enough," she answered. "Thanks."

Grace and Steve turned and hurried to their news truck.

Dent scrambled behind them. "You really want to go to this photo op?" Rick asked as Steve pulled out of the parking spot and fell in behind Woods' police car.

"Not really," she laughed. "But I hate being stone-walled by these guys. Maybe if we stick with him long enough, he'll slip up. Let's take the camera to the precinct, play along, see what happens."
     **

The new Fifth Street police precinct was four miles from headquarters, and they were there in minutes.   Steve pulled into the precinct parking lot. Major Woods was already in place with all the brass in the department, the mayor and several city council members lined up near a wide satin ribbon just in front of the precinct's glass and steel front door. A handful of men and women had drifted out of nearby office buildings to watch the event. Several panhandlers and cart vendors warily observed the goings-on, hanging back a farther distance.

The onlookers were nearly outnumbered by a small gaggle of reporters and public relations representatives from the police department and the mayor's office.

Mayor Ronald Walker was fidgeting, waiting for things to settle down so he could proceed. He rested his huge double chin down on his chest, peering over reading glasses at notes an aide gave him, his other hand in his pocket jingling change, indicating he wanted to get this over with.

Finally he spoke above the din and the crowd hushed. "We are pleased to welcome this Fifth Street police precinct to the Haven-brook neighborhood," he said in his deep-baritone, authoritarian tone over a portable sound system. "This precinct will be the new home to dozens of sworn officers. I couldn't be more proud of our men and women in blue who will be serving and protecting this community."

After that brief opening statement, he stuffed the notes into his breast pocket and moved in front of the ribbon. A staff intern handed him a giant pair of scissors, and he cut the sash with an exaggerated gesture. A round of scattered applause, similar to that heard at a golf tournament, ran through the group.

Mayor Walker spent a few minutes of handshakes as the sound system was broken down. The small crowd dispersed, and the head of Atlanta's Office of Professional Standards walked toward the parking lot. The Channel Six crew followed.

"Major Woods, you said you would talk to me about McHughes," Grace exclaimed, following him to his car.

Woods turned. "I'll talk to you," he said, clearly agitated by Grace's probing. "Is your camera rolling?"

Grace glanced at Jankowski and nodded yes to the officer. Dent's radio microphone's green light was on, and he seconded her go-ahead.

"We are looking into all aspects of the Pontellis murder," Woods said. "I'm sure you understand our policy is that all information to the media must come from the public affairs officer. So I have nothing else to add to your story."

Grace's eyes opened wide at his arrogance. "You're the head of Internal Affairs. We're about to do a story implying a possible connection between one of your officers and a murder. And you have nothing to say?"

"You do your job and I'll do mine," the major barked.

200

"Yeah, but you're not doing it," Dent said sarcastically.

"You media types always think you have the answers," the officer fumed. "Well, we don't have the luxury of sitting back and second-guessing. We have to have the facts, and we need to adhere to protocol."

Grace responded caustically. "But none of that explains why you've got a policeman who suspiciously went on leave right after a strip club owner was shot to pieces."

"And that same cop reported his service pistol AWOL right afterward," Rick Dent chimed in. "Any of that add up for you? Because it sure doesn't for me."

Major Woods clinched his jaw. "This is serious police business. As I told you, we are looking into all aspects of the Pontellis murder. Period. End of story. Would you like to do a cutaway?"

Woods flashed a quick, condescending smile, seemingly proud to show he knew the media drill of the cameraman taking a picture of the reporters talking to the police.

Grace motioned for Jankowski to shut down the audio and take video from a distance of the two interacting.

The IA man stood silently steaming, glaring at Grace and Rick. He took a deep breath. "I don't give one big crap if anything adds up for you people. I'm dealing with a tall stack of internal problems with this force you can't begin to imagine. Now, I'm going to work, and I suggest you mind your own business." He paused, narrowed his eyes, looking more sinister than usual. "You know, Miss Gleason, everyone makes mistakes. I'm sure if I ran your social security numbers through DMV and NCIS I could find something you or Dent might have done to sully your wonderful reputations."

"Are you threatening me, Major Woods?" Grace shot back, fuming at the veiled warning.

"We're through here," the IA man curtly ended the exchange. He climbed into his cruiser and zipped away.

"You might be through, but we aren't," shouted Rick comically toward the disappearing car. He turned and chortled toward Grace, "I guess I told him."

Grace laughed. "Did you detect a certain tone of denial in that man's voice?" she asked, almost giddy.

"Denial and frustration," Rick said. "Let's go do our own investigation. Do you think Officer McHughes would be happy to see us?"

24 MCHUGHES

ATLANTA POLICE OFFICER Douglas McHughes owned a small ranch-style house in an older section of the city inside the perimeter highway. Several nearby neighborhoods had gone upscale, having been bought out by builders who leveled the residences and constructed half-million-dollar cluster homes in their place. McHughes' block had remained untouched, although several of the houses had "for sale by owner" signs, clear invitations for offers from developers.

The policeman's house needed paint, and the yard was not as neatly mown as some of the neighbors' were. Rick and Grace parked near the corner, and Steve parked the news van behind them. They walked to McHughes' home.

After ringing the bell, Grace was surprised when the officer yanked the door open and peered out. He wore faded blue jeans and a tee shirt. Nearly half of his face was behind the door, but she could see the edge of a white bandage that covered the hidden part from nose to ear.

"Yeah?" McHughes greeted them brusquely.

"Grace Gleason, Channel Six," she announced. "Are you Doug McHughes?"

"Yeah," he confirmed.

"This is Rick Dent. He's with our radio affiliate. We're here to find out why you're on leave from the Atlanta PD."

"I've been sick," Doug said.

"What about that?" Grace indicated the bandage. McHughes swung the door open more fully to reveal the extent of the gauze and tape. Jankowski moved in closer with his camera.

"I had an accident," he responded.

Dent stepped forward, his recording device running. "We

heard you lost your service pistol."

McHughes frowned. "I didn't lose it. It was stolen."

"When was that?" Dent persisted.

"Look, I don't feel good. I need to go lay down."

"Sorry to hear that, but what about the pistol?" Grace continued.

"Someone took it right before I went on leave. I don't know who got it."

Dent pressed on. "Officer McHughes, you must have some idea of where it was when you..."

McHughes closed the door firmly.

Grace stood astounded, looking back at her radio friend. "IA again?' she asked.

"Nope," he shook his head. "We won't get anywhere with that yahoo. This time let's move on up the ladder."

"Chief Stone?" she queried.

"Sounds about right."

**

Grace was beginning to feel like a broken record; she was becoming a repeat performer at the APD headquarters.

"Sergeant, we'd like to speak to Chief Stone," Dent said in a businesslike tone.

The desk officer looked up from his paperwork, regarded them suspiciously, looked at Jankowski's camera and picked up the phone. He spoke in hushed tones and hung up. "Someone will be right down," he announced and returned to his administrative task.

"Here comes the roadblock," Dent murmured softly to Grace after a few minutes wait.

She understood what he meant. Aretha Herrington was approaching. Grace knew from their previous encounters that she would not be sociable.

After the episode in Vivian Ellis' office, Grace had asked

around to find out more about the public affairs spokesperson for the largest police department in the state. Everyone she queried seemed to have a story about her difficult disposition. From those conversations, Grace also concluded that Herrington had weathered some personal storms.

Aretha Herrington was born in 1970 and named after singer Aretha Franklin. Her mother, never married, was music pastor of the Mount Zion Baptist Church in Winder, Georgia. She had named Aretha's older siblings for musicians, too—Stevie, Dionne and Ella. She taught all four of them to sing, and when Aretha was five they formed a quartet. They sang at church functions and occasionally on the local radio station.

But Aretha's brother, twelve years her senior, left home before finishing high school, went to California, got into trouble and ended up in jail for dealing cocaine. Her two sisters moved out—one was pregnant and settled in South Carolina with her boyfriend, and the other enrolled in cosmetology school in Atlanta.

Despite her mother pushing her in talent shows as a teenager, Aretha never quite had the chops, nor the desire, to make it in the music business. Attending the University of Georgia, she entered the Miss Georgia pageant her sophomore year, sang *Amazing Grace* for the talent portion of the competition and finished third runner-up. But she had decided to major in journalism, and in her senior year she was editor of *The Bulldog*, the school's newspaper.

After graduation, Aretha landed a job as a staff writer for the *Mobile News Daily*. Two years later, she signed on as Metairie bureau chief for the *New Orleans Times-Reporter.*

Her mother became sick in 2004 and was taken to Piedmont Hospital in Atlanta with a severe case of pneumonia. She was put on life support, and doctors pronounced her prognosis grim. Her kidneys were failing, and her weight ballooned because of edema.

Aretha asked for, and was granted, a leave of absence to

help her sister put their mother's affairs in order. Dionne was immature and unreliable. Aretha single-handedly arranged for her mother to sign powers of attorney and execute a will.

While she was in Atlanta, the newswoman stopped by the *Atlanta Daily Post* to see an old friend from college—Terrance Newberry, who was assistant managing editor. Terrance had been her associate editor on *The Bulldog*, and together they had fought the usual wars with the school's administration over stories.

"You should come to Atlanta permanently," Newberry told her when she stopped by his office.

"What would I do? I have a good job in New Orleans," she replied.

Terrance grinned. "There's an opening here, and it's perfect for you. Beat writer on politics, public policy issues and covering city hall."

Within a month, Aretha had the job. She was on the road, pulling a rented trailer with her possessions, when her cellphone rang.

"Mama passed this morning," said Dionne, barely audible to Aretha as she sobbed.

After they buried their mother, the two sisters rarely saw each other, though they lived thirty minutes apart.

After five years on the *Daily Post*, Aretha applied for a civilian opening on the city police force and was hired. It was an exciting position. She managed all employees of the public affairs unit. They responded to Open Records Act requests, managed emergency communications, enacted outreach programs and oversaw internal and external messages.

In the first six months she managed several crises. One involved allegations that four police officers had beaten an unarmed man to death during a public disturbance. In another, two officers had covered up the inadvertent shooting of an informant when a drug sting went awry.

Aretha received accolades from the chief for her hard-nosed handling of the media during those events. But media people covering the city weren't so kind. She developed a reputation among reporters of pushing back against what they considered legitimate requests for information and interviews.

As Grace and Rick approached her, with Steve trailing, his camera off, Herrington pursed her lips and gestured no. "Chief Stone is in meetings. He can't see you today. Sorry."

"Aretha, this is significant." Grace appealed. "We're not just asking to see him about how you handle overdue parking tickets. You have an officer on leave with a serious facial wound, and his pistol has disappeared. All of it right after the Nick Pontellis shootout. We don't want to draw any premature conclusions."

"Just ask Chief Stone some legitimate questions," Dent added.

Herrington shook her head no, her dark eyes narrowed. "You need to go see Internal Affairs about something like that. I can set it up."

Rick uttered a guttural laugh. "Are you kidding? You're the public affairs person and even you probably can't get any information out of that doofus J.D. Woods."

"I guess you could interview me," she offered. "That's as far as you're going to get today."

"How about the chief first thing tomorrow morning?" Grace begged.

Herrington shook her head no again. "He's leaving for Chicago in the a.m. Has a conference."

"All right," Grace conceded. "Spokesperson Herrington it is. Steve, let's get your camera rolling."

Steve turned on his lights. Aretha winced as their brightness hit her eyes and bounced off her chocolate complexion. Meanwhile, both Grace and Rick extended their microphones in her direction.

"Ms. Herrington, you have an officer named Douglas McHughes who has been mysteriously on leave. Can you tell us what his circumstances are?"

"No, I can't," Aretha stated emphatically. "We are prohibited by law from discussing personnel matters."

"But this appears to be an unusual situation. We saw McHughes today, talked to him. He has a serious wound on the side of his face, and he claims his handgun has been stolen. Shouldn't Internal Affairs investigate, rather than buy his story that he's home with the flu?"

The public affairs woman smirked. "First, I didn't say he claimed to have the flu. I said we cannot disclose personnel matters. Second, our Internal Affairs department probes every public complaint or internal problem that has merit. I might add that according to the Citizen's Committee on Civil Rights, the number of cases that have merited investigation are lower than the average metro city of similar size."

Rick leaned in a little closer. "Isn't that because your IA office is perceived as biased toward not investigating? And your processes for reviewing its activity are almost non-existent?"

Herrington's voice grew strident. "That's an untrue and offensive accusation, Mr. Dent. We're not getting anyplace. I've answered your questions, and we're through here." Aretha Herrington spun around and strode away.

Grace looked at Rick and then Steve, half-smiling. "Well, that was certainly productive. Let's go write a story for my show tonight. I want you on the air, Dent."

The radio reporter's face morphed into a circus clown grin. "You're going to make me a star? Your management would never go for that. It's not done, mixing the TV and radio news sides."

"I'll talk to them."

He scrunched his rubbery face into a dubious squint. "Good

luck with that."

"What about your management?" she asked.

"I'm pulling good ratings on my reports. They will see it as an advantage—you know, cross promotion as the promo guys call it."

**

Vivian Ellis was standing behind her desk, hands on her hips, in an obvious defensive posture.

"I told you over the phone, no," she said sternly. "You can't bring a reporter from the radio side onto our news set."

"Is there a good reason why not?" Grace normally made an effort to be more tactful, but Vivian's instant negative response to the idea bothered her.

Ellis frowned. "It's not done," she said. "Harvey won't allow it."

"Can we call him?" Grace snapped.

"Too late," Vivian gestured toward the door where Silver was approaching. "I already asked him if he'd join us."

"What's up?" the station manager sounded cheerful.

Grace was ecstatic they had caught him in a good mood.

Ellis nodded toward Grace, as if to say "You're on."

"I want to interview a somewhat unique guest on the news tonight."

Silver grinned. "Let me guess…Justin Bieber. Taylor Swift."

"Rick Dent."

Harvey paused, thinking for a moment. "Dent. The radio news guy?"

"That's right," Grace answered. "Rick and I have worked to-gether on much of the property theft story. And the Pontellis murder. We've helped each other out a lot. And as you know, with both our brains working on it, we are out in front of the APD."

"That's true," Harvey agreed. "But bringing Dent on your set? We can't do that."

"You hired me to break new ground. I've been doing that. Here's another chance. Rick can share insights from the perspective of a seasoned reporter who's been on this scene a long time and knows where the bones are buried. Especially at the police department."

"That's what is the most worrisome," Silver responded, scratching his head thoughtfully. "We get crosswise with the Atlanta force, they can make it hell for us. You've already learned that the hard way."

Grace seized the opportunity. "Meaning I've earned this opportunity."

She waited hopefully. They stood in silence.

"No," Harvey said with finality. "I don't like it."

Grace's shoulders sagged.

"I say let's do it," Vivian chipped in.

Grace and Harvey jerked to attention.

Vivian appealed to her boss, "You told me to hire someone who's not shy about taking an incursion into uncharted territory, somebody who thinks outside the circle. Grace does that—is doing that. We're not talking war here. Let's let her bring the guy on her set."

"Is he really that good? He'll add texture?" Harvey inquired.

"I haven't encountered a newsman with such cogent insights in a long time." Grace let herself feel a little hopeful.

The station manager shrugged. "Okay. As long as his supervisors are all right with it." He turned around and was gone.

Grace stared at her boss, her mouth half open.

Ellis smiled warmly. "You'd better go call him."

As Grace raced to her cubicle and dialed Rick, her mind spun with confusion about the many contradictory facets of Vivian Ellis.

**

The battle lines had been drawn. Grace and Rick had gone

into the day willing to listen and learn, give the city the benefit of the doubt. But after their encounters with a giant whitewash, two and two were not adding up.

On the set, as the cameras rolled, Grace moved to the giant screen. She touched an icon and the video showed Major Woods recoiling from her questions.

"We are looking into all aspects of the Pontellis murder," the officer said. "I'm sure you understand our policy is that all information to the media must come from our public affairs officer. So I have nothing else to add to your story."

"Let's bring in my radio collegue, Rick Dent, who is working with me on this story," Grace said into camera one.

Dent strode to the counter and propped up on a stool. "Grace, the resistance we're getting from the city police is unbelievable. Not only would the Internal Affairs leader not go into any depth on McHughes' situation, but we were denied access to the chief of police."

Grace pulled up the Aretha Herrington interview. "We are prohibited by law from discussing personnel matters."

Grace turned to Rick. "So there were no answers to our questions?"

"That's right," he answered. "More than that, it became obvious after we did our own investigation they might not have a clue what is going on."

Grace reached to another icon, touched it, and the video at McHughes' house revealed a wounded officer peering out from his doorway.

Dent continued, "Policeman Doug McHughes has been on leave ever since a shootout in the stylish neighborhood of Riverwood Heights. The owner of a nightclub was killed in that fray. The officer might have the flu, but there's something else obviously wrong with him."

"I had an accident," McHughes said on the screen.

"We heard you lost your service pistol." Rick said on the video.

"I didn't lose it. It was stolen."

McWherter signaled, and camera two zoomed in on Dent for a close-up. "Here's what we know," he said. "Nick Pontellis was killed in a melee in his garage by unknown intruders. Police have not named a suspect, let alone two or three. Some suspect the shootout, indeed, a whole host of robberies and burglaries, are the work of gangs related to the drug trade. Yet we have a mysterious situation involving a city policeman who suffered a facial injury and whose pistol was missing shortly after the garage killing. Grace, ordinarily these facts would prompt an investigation by the APD's Internal Affairs Division."

Grace nodded toward the radio reporter. "Thanks, Rick Dent. We'll continue to pursue this story." She stared sternly into the camera lens. "The Atlanta Police Department owes us some answers. We can't help but wonder, do the chief of police and the higher-ups in city government know how incompetent this string of crimes is making our police force look? I'll keep demanding answers. This is Grace Gleason, and you've been watching 'Crime and Corruption.'"

MaryAnne McWherter drew a finger across her throat as the camera light went off. "Great job, Grace," she cheered.

Grace sagged against the counter, relaxing for the first time all day. She had been going non-stop and was exhausted. She knew the pace would only get crazier.

25 BOOKED AND PRINTED

CHARLIE'S VOICE WAS becoming too familiar, making these calls to Grace's home from the night assignment desk.

"Thought you'd want to know, we just got a tip from someone over at the APD about another robbery."

She knew he was just doing his job, but on Sunday night? "Charlie..." she began.

He cut her off. "I know, I know. I was going to contact Matthews, but I thought you might want first crack at it, given your increased interest in the subject matter. They didn't provide details, but it seems like those other heists, kind of an epidemic now. It's your call, Grace."

"All right, Charlie. I guess I have no choice," she sighed heavily.

"The cameraman on call is Norm Baker. He lives in Henry County, so you'll get there before he does. Be sure to wait in your car until Norm shows up."

"Got it, Charlie," she rolled her eyes.

He gave her the address of a convenience store near the zoo. It was not the worst section of town, but not one she would normally venture into after dark. *At least I haven't dressed for bed yet,* she thought. Grace turned off the television and pulled her shoes on. She stuffed her electronic tablet into her bag, checked her hair in the mirror, grabbed her car keys and headed out the door.

**

Twenty minutes later she drove past Grant Park. She made a turn at Confederate Avenue. The firm and comforting voice inside her GPS announced, "In about one-tenth of a mile, you will have reached your destination on the right."

She turned the system off and cruised ahead, scanning the seedy neighborhood. She saw a mixture of poorly kept bungalows and vacant lots dotted by hair salons, auto body garages, bars and tiny markets. Streetlights were far between and dim, if lighted at all. The only business signs still aglow were the bars.

Grace found the store, but it was dark. One car was sitting in front, an old sedan with mismatched fenders, but there were no squad cars in sight. Subdued light radiated from a nearby tavern's neon "open" sign, but its cave-like entrance was dark and gloomy. No one was going in and out. She could hear hip-hop music playing with a prominent thumping bass beat.

Grace parked next to the sedan. *Charlie said wait for the cameraman, but I can't just sit here,* she thought. She walked to the convenience store's front window, peeking in, puzzled there were no signs of life. *So much for convenience,* she thought, mildly annoyed. *Maybe they're around back.*

Without another moment's thought, she went to the rear of the building. It was shadowy there, too. An old rusted-out pick-up teetered on wheel blocks next to the trash dumpster.

Damn. Either Charlie got the address wrong, or someone played a bad joke on us. She theorized it could have been a drunk from the saloon next door.

She returned to her car and called the night desk.

"Charlie, who phoned that robbery in?" Grace questioned. "It looks like a false alarm."

"Our intern took the call. Said the guy was Sergeant Tread-way from APD," Charlie said, angry. "I'll call back over there and find out what's going on."

"I'm going home," she reported. "This place is giving me the creeps."

Grace double-checked her door locks, wheeled a u-turn and headed back the way she had come. In about a minute, she pulled over as her cell rang.

"Desk sergeant at APD says they don't have a Treadway there," Charlie reported. "Sorry, Grace. I'll chew out the intern. He should have known to call back and confirm."

Grace tried to hide the displeasure in her voice. "See if you can catch Baker before he drives all the way up here."

She drove down Boulevard Avenue, a welcome sight that would take her back to the interstate and a comforting view of lights, traffic and the downtown skyline.

A sudden flash of blue in her rear-view mirror startled her.

No! her brain screamed.

**

She sat, paralyzed, waiting for the officer. Finally, in her mirror she saw him open his door and approach her car. He was a large man, early twenties, with broad shoulders and an extraordinarily thick neck. She rolled down her window and looked up at him expectantly.

"License and registration, please," he said curtly in a deep voice.

She could see fog from his breath in the chill March air.

"What's the problem officer?" she asked, handing him the documents.

"You failed to maintain your lane. Just remain in the car, please ma'am," he said. Not a request but an order. As he turned to walk to his cruiser and run the check, he dropped her license.

"What's this?" she heard him say as he stooped next to her car.

"What?"

"Something. Something stuck under the edge of your wheel well."

"Don't know," Grace answered. "Mud, maybe?"

As he stood, his eyes met hers, serious. "Please step out of the car, ma'am."

"What?" she said, astonished. "What for?"

He took a step back. "Step out of the car, please, and keep your hands where I can see them."

She began to panic, gripped by this bizarre moment. Her emotions were turning from anxiety to seething anger.

"Ma'am, is this yours?" he asked brusquely. He held out a plastic bag he had pulled from a small magnetic box. She had covered enough drug stories to know what it was.

"Of course not, officer." She tried to maintain her poise. "I'm a news reporter out here on a story."

"It was under your fender. Did you put it there?"

Now she was furious. "I told you no. That bag is not mine. I don't know how it got there."

A slight grin crossed his lips and disappeared as quickly. "Know how many times I've heard that? Turn around and face the car."

"Wait, wait, wait. This is crazy. That's not my bag. I told you." Her voice was a few decibels below a shout now. "Officer, I'm a reporter with Channel Six. I was sent here to cover a story. You can call my news desk if you want. My station ID is in my handbag."

A stray dog passing by began to approach, barking noisily as if protecting his territory. The officer made a guttural sound as he stepped toward the animal, and it skittered away, it's tail low. It was beginning to rain, adding to Grace's annoyance. *What a pain in the butt,* she thought.

"I don't care if you're the queen of Sheeba," the cop said with a glare.

"You don't have to..." she started her complaint, hands defiantly on her hips.

But he cut in on her, "Ma'am, you don't want me to book you for resisting arrest. Please turn and face your car."

She shrugged, turned and leaned weakly against the driver

side door. She felt the cuffs scrape around her wrists. *I can't believe this is happening to me,* she thought.

"Okay if I search your car?" the officer asked. She nodded yes as mixed emotions of wrath, embarrassment and horror collided in her head. As he searched the console, glove compartment, under the seats and all the other places where suspects hide drugs, she glanced around the area, thankful they weren't someplace where she might be recognized.

As the officer returned to her side, she said, "You do know who I am, don't you?"

"I don't care," he said. "I'm going to take you in. You have the right to remain…" He continued to read her rights as he led her gently by the elbow toward his car.

I know my Miranda rights, for heaven's sake, she thought as they walked. *"I've heard them a thousand times covering crime stories in the streets.* Grace knew her lawyer would tell her never to say anything, but it was so much harder to do now that she was the suspect.

It seemed as if she had been sitting in the back of the cruiser for hours when the wrecker showed up. The policeman, who had said nothing to her since placing her in the back seat, got out and spoke to the driver. Within minutes, her car was winched onto the flatbed trailer. As the officer returned, she could see the truck pull away. Its yellow blinkers illuminated the area in contrast to the squad car's blue lights, which had flashed the entire time.

Grace squirmed uncomfortably with her hands cuffed behind her. Her arms and wrists began to ache. "Officer, seriously, this is silly," she pleaded. "Whatever you've got in that bag was placed there by someone other than me."

He half-turned and frowned as he pressed the accelerator and turned north on Morehouse. "Lady, please sit there and be quiet."

"But look," she continued her protest. "You have to know who

I am, and you know this trumped up charge won't stick."

"Ma'am, I'm warning you for the last time, don't say anything. If you keep it up, I'll add resist to the charges."

She sat back, humiliated and confused. She would have to stay in a cell overnight. In one of the most notoriously scary lock-ups in the state.

She had never seen the Grain Street jail in Northwest Atlanta. Getting there was intimidating in itself. The patrol car weaved through dark, pot-holed streets. When they finally turned onto Grain, appearing they were headed toward a vacant lot or dumpsite, the sprawling, fourteen-story high edifice suddenly loomed before them.

Grace thought it looked like an imposing, sand-colored, lop-sided wedding cake surrounded by a massive brick fortress of a wall.

She knew from other reporters the top floor was reserved for the worst offenders—murder and rape suspects, violent inmates, serious criminals. The lower floors were where they held suspects charged with lesser crimes. *That would be me,* she thought helplessly.

The arresting officer led her to booking on the first floor, where a policewoman removed her cuffs and searched her.

"Put all your personal items in this," the woman said, handing her a bag. As she placed her jewelry, purse and other belongings in it, Grace's senses were swimming wildly, silently crying out, pleading for something rational in this night of unreason.

The officer led her through a maze of hallways and doorways, opening the door of a holding cell. "They're pretty busy in booking right now. It'll be a little while. You'll stay here until someone comes to take you to processing."

Grace sat alone in the cell for twenty minutes, shaking. Every clang of a cell door opening or closing, a drunken arrestee shouting, groaning or vomiting, a cop barking instructions, echoed through the corridor and bounced around the hard surfaces of the depressing jail.

Finally, an officer arrived and yanked the door the open with grim authority. Without a word, he motioned for her to follow him.

She knew the process, had done stories many times over the years about the fate of detainees who had been put through it. Now she understood why they stumbled through the answers to questions fired at them—full legal name, address, date of birth.

Her heart stopped momentarily when the booking officer asked, "Name and number of an emergency contact?"

She couldn't tell them Megan. "Harry Hamlin, attorney at Channel Six television," she finally answered unsteadily. She expected a surprised reaction from the booking officer, but he didn't even look up.

The policeman then led Grace to a small area where he fingerprinted her.

"Stand right there and look into the camera," he instructed.

The camera flashed.

"Now turn sideways."

It flashed again.

Throughout these methodical procedures, she kept thinking, *My car must be in impound by now. God forbid if anything else is found inside it. Of course, why should it? I've never taken drugs, everybody who knows me would recognize instantly this is a set-up.*

Grace had covered enough drug arrest stories to know that less than an ounce in a possession case was a misdemeanor, but more than that became a felony drug charge punishable from one to ten years in prison. In some jurisdictions, possession arrests had become so common, the police merely wrote a citation and moved on. *No such luck here*, she reflected.

Her mind returned to Megan. She hoped her daughter didn't find out before she could tell her the whole story. She remembered Megan was pulling an all-nighter at the university, racing the clock to complete a critical project. She breathed easier, realizing her daughter would be insulated from the news long enough for her to get out and talk to her.

Even so, she would be embarrassed.

Someone—she wasn't even sure who, because everything was happening in such a warped blur—handed her a wipe to clean the ink from her stained fingers.

This might clean my hands, but it will take forever to wash this nightmare out of my memory, Grace thought.

A deputy led her down a hall to a cell. Its bare, sterile walls and stark lighting announced she had no choice, no way out of this horrendous mistake. As the cell door slammed shut, she thought about how differently everything looks when you're the one peering out from behind bars.

"When can I make a phone call?" she asked in an exhausted half-whisper. "I need to reach our station lawyer. I was on an assignment when that guy stopped me."

The deputy fixed unsympathetic eyes on her, the ten-thousandth time he had answered the same query. "You can call whoever you want in the morning. Tonight you're not going anywhere." Then he was gone. She was alone in the tiny compartment. Grace sat down on the small cot against the wall, her fingers running over the blanket folded there. Her head pounded and her heart raced, but something inherent in her natural stubbornness told her to stay calm, keep her wits together.

She was thankful they had let her keep her own clothes. Wearing one of those jailhouse jumpsuits would have pushed her to the edge.

She went back over the events, what the policeman had said to her, how she had answered. Grace knew she would need to remember it all in detail.

Tomorrow's going to be a long day, she thought. She self-consciously used the toilet, stretched out on the thin mattress, pulled the blanket up over her and curled her knees up in a fetal position. She felt the tears coming, slowly at first and then flowing, uncontrolled, in a torrent of anguish and disbelief.

And then, mercifully, before another thought could crawl into her mind, she slept.

**

The physical discomfort of incarceration was troubling enough. Unless you're a hardened criminal, it can't compare to the embarrassment. When Grace awoke, she ached from sleeping on a narrow cot but was exhausted from the totality of the humiliating experience.

It was the clanging of a deputy unlocking and opening her cell door that woke her, intensifying the headache that woke her off and on all night.

Hank Hamlin stood behind the officer. He entered her cell and sat beside her as she rubbed her eyes and smoothed her clothes.

"How are you doing?" he asked in a serious tone.

"How do you think?" she responded testily. "Sorry, but I've never been in jail before."

He laid a hand on her arm. "We're going to get you out of here right away."

"How did you know I was here? I haven't used my Constitutionally granted one phone call."

"We have friends down here. We're going to get you out soon. Don't talk to anyone. I've spoken to the district attorney, and he's willing to accept that the arresting officer might have made a mistake in his report."

"About?"

"The amount of marijuana in the bag. The DA will stipulate it was under an ounce."

Grace wrinkled her brow. "That would make a huge difference."

"All the difference. Between a felony and a misdemeanor."
She nodded.

"You haven't made any statements, have you?"

"Just told them who I was, what I was doing there." Seeing him frown, she added, "Sorry, Hank. I've never been on this side of the story before, and I can't tell you how rattled it makes you."

He smiled for the first time. "No problem. I'll get the police report on my way out and see what the officer had to say. But there's another thing."

"What?"

"Being on the other side of the equation. The station is going to have to report on your arrest."

"What?" she exclaimed, jumping up in surprise. "Why?"

Hank motioned for Grace to sit back down, held a hand out as if to shush her. "It's going to be on the other outlets. And in the paper. Beating them to it will give us a chance to paint you in the most innocent light."

She sighed heavily, near tears. "I can't believe this is happening."

"You were on station business. That's why I'm here to post bail and get you home. Grace, there's more."

She waited. Her head hurt. She wanted a hot shower and her own bed.

"The station will have to suspend you until this is resolved."
"Suspend?"

"It's policy. You've been charged with a crime."

"But Hank, I didn't do it. Don't you believe I didn't do it?"

He stood up. "Of course I do. We all do. Harvey, Vivian, me, all of us. But you can't go on the air until your case is resolved." He leaned toward her, lowered his voice. "Grace, no one believes you put weed under your wheel well. That's just plain stupid. I can get the prosecutor to dismiss the charges, but I have to figure out the best way to do it. Understand?"

She nodded agreement. "What happens next?"

Hank picked up the brief case he had set on the cot. "As soon as I can post bail, the judge should release you. Or there's a good chance you'll be released on your own reconnaissance. There might be an arraignment this afternoon. If there is, I'll be here to represent you."

"Should I waive a preliminary hearing?"

"Definitely not. There are rules about when the police are allowed to stop you. I want to challenge the officer's right to detain you in the first place, and the prelim is the time to contest it. Plus, the prosecutor will have to reveal the evidence, and we can make mincemeat out of that." He laid a reassuring hand on her arm. "Hang in there for a few hours. It might take a while, but you'll get out of here as soon as possible, I promise. Anyone you want me to call?"

"No, especially not my daughter. I don't want my problems to interfere with her studies. I'll let her know all about it when I get out. So, no. No one."

He turned to go.

"Except," she tossed out, "would you call Rick Dent? Let him know, would you?"

"Dent? Why?"

"No big deal. We're working on a story. I want him to know where I am."

Hamlin nodded. "Deputy," he called out. The officer came and opened the cell door. Hank stepped out and smiled reassuringly at Grace. With another bang the door was locked and the lawyer was gone.

Grace sank back against the hard wall of the cell, feeling dirty and dejected.

**

It was nearly evening when she saw Hamlin again. The deputy let him in, and he sat beside her on the cot.

"How are you holding up?" he asked.

"You try being locked up for a day with this awful food," she said. "And all the idiots passing by here, drunks, prostitutes, wild-eyed crazies. This place is disgusting."

"Well, you won't have to worry about it. You're getting out on bond right now."

"What took so long?" she asked.

"I'll tell you when we're out of here. It's good news."

He nodded at the deputy who had waited, and the officer opened the door. Hank smiled and put an arm around Grace, squeezing her shoulder, as he walked her through the door and down the corridor.

She was released. Grace felt the tension in her shoulders ease, the pounding in her brain ebbing.

It was dusk and misting outside. Hamlin held an umbrella over the two of them and opened the passenger door of his Mercedez-Benz SUV. She turned and shielded her face from the blowing spray.

She took a deep breath and smiled as he climbed in beside her. "Thank you, Hank. But I have to ask, why did it take all day to get me out?"

He flashed his pearlies. "It wouldn't have, except your buddy Dent and I did some detective work. We discovered something interesting." He watched her face grow curious. "The bar next to that closed-up business you were called out to...turns out they have a surveillance camera." He paused.

"And?" her heart pounded as she waited.

"There's an image of a man hanging around your car. After you went behind the building. Looks like he put something under your wheel well."

224

Grace's eyes widened. "I knew it. It was planted. But...hat would mean the arresting officer knew about it!"

"No kidding," he smiled at the obvious. "I've already discussed it with the district attorney. We're going to get you off the hook without charges being brought. I think we can even get the judge to waive any court appearance at all if I show the DA the tape. We'll find a way to learn what Officer Grant Madison knew and didn't know."

They pulled away from the station house, wove through some streets and headed north on Piedmont Avenue. It was nearly devoid of traffic. She was tired and miserable, yet paradoxically happy to be out of that abyss. How could such a thing have happened? Was Hank right—that she would now be able to get out from under this mess without a record?

The lawyer steered around a subtle curve on Piedmont and cranked a left onto Tenth Street.

Suddenly, a powerful thunk ripped through the silence.

Thunk! Thunk! Thunk! Grace ducked as glass exploded above her head. She felt her body lurch forward violently against the seat belt as the vehicle fishtailed on the wet pavement, spinning in her direction and tipping so precariously she felt certain they would roll. She could hear tires squealing, moving away from them.

In a few split seconds Grace's world burst, whirling around her. The SUV skidded to a sudden stop and rocked forcefully. She heard the snap of Hank's seat belt. And then the attorney's heavy body was spread over her, pushing her down toward the floorboard, splayed across her like a mother bear over a frightened cub. The Mercedes shook one more time, then settled in utter stillness.

"Are you okay?" Hank's voice, sounding a mile away, had a frantic quality. He pulled himself off of her and peered over the dash, looking out through the windshield for further danger.

"I think so," she responded, bewildered, her nerves rattled. She reached to her head and felt tiny shards of glass in her hair.

Hank opened the door and crawled out, crouching behind the door as he pulled his cell phone from his pocket, dialing nine-one-one. "There's been a shooting. Piedmont and Tenth...No, just my car...Hurry."

**

A paramedic from the fire department carefully removed glass particles from Grace's hair and cleaned up and treated small cuts and scratches on her forehead.

Great, she thought, as he pressed a bandage over the worst wound. *Now I'll catch it again from Megan about how many chances I take in this risky work.* She felt an old familiar guilt. It was impossible to protect her daughter from every danger Grace confronted in her career. Tonight, like many times before, she was caught between doing a treacherous job and telling Megan the truth about it.

The paramedic walked her to a waiting squad car for her ride home. Hamlin followed; he would leave in a separate cruiser. A tow truck operator activated a cable that yanked Hank's car onto its bed. Police wanted it for forensic evidence.

"I'll call you tomorrow," Hank said. "They're going to watch your house tonight."

"Wait. They...they were shooting at me?" In the frenzy and commotion, it hadn't occurred to Grace she was the target, not the lawyer.

"You'll be safe tonight."

Tonight! What about tomorrow? she pondered as the officer drove her home. *And the next day?*

26 SUSPENDED

HANK CALLED GRACE the following morning at ten, waking her. She didn't know how she could have slept, given the ordeal she had been through. *I must have been completely exhausted from all of this,* she thought. *Well, better dead tired than simply dead.*

"Are you all right?" Hamlin asked, his voice a bit tense.

"I think so. I can see a patrol car sitting across the street, so they must have been there all night."

"They won't be able to stay. Why not go and hang out with your daughter for a while? Meantime, I'll be working with the authorities to see if we can get to the bottom of this."

"I wouldn't dream of exposing Megan to this kind of danger."

"No, I guess not."

"Besides, somehow I have to gather myself and get in to work."

"Oh, no, Grace. You can't do that."

"What? Why?"

"You don't remember my telling you that you've been suspended?"

"Sure, but I assumed that has changed now that it's obviously a frame."

"In theory, maybe. But technically you're still under arrest on suspicion of possession until charges are dropped. That could take a day or two, and then you'll be reinstated. But meanwhile, you can't go to work."

"That's a bunch of bull, Hank. You know my arrest was an invention. Tell Silver and Ellis…"

He interrupted, "It's standard procedure when an employee is charged with a crime. It's not personal."

"Maybe, but I'm taking it personally."

"Just relax," he advised. "I'm working on it."

She paused. Her head began to ache, and her nerves felt shattered. She hadn't experienced this kind of torment from doing her job since a day in Dallas she was almost killed by a murderer she was covering. Grace wanted to climb into a hot shower and stay there for hours.

"Why, Hank? Why are you doing this for me?"

"You were arrested on company time. You were working. I represent the station in such matters. Besides..." there was a long hesitation.

"Besides?"

"I probably would do it anyway." She waited, not knowing how to respond. He continued," I like you. I like your work. You're a good person."

The praise relaxed her, and the absence of any further declaration from Hamlin was a welcome relief. A cup of coffee was what she needed.

"Thank you, Hank," she said simply, eager to end the conversation.

**

Rick Dent stopped by at noon.

"Did you see who it was?" he asked.

Grace shook her head no. "It happened too fast."

"I have some news," he announced. "Just got a text from a source over at APD. They finally got off their fat asses and arrested Doug McHughes. Word is the grand jury returned a true bill."

"What charges?" she asked, anxious.

"Grand jury is secret, as you know," he grinned. "I hear he'll be arraigned for multiple accounts of murder during felony, assault with intent, firearms violations, a slew more. The source said he's singing like Lady Gaga about the robberies, too."

"Why did they finally focus on McHughes?"

"My little birdie said it had something to do with the APD's Office of Professional Standards being goaded by a couple of aggressive news reporters. IA was finally cornered, about to be shown up as the lazy dolts they are, so they decided to get busy. When they pushed back, the first stop they made was the home of one Officer Douglas McHughes. Seems like the guy was on official leave with some mysterious ailment."

She laughed as Rick lightened her mood.

"It's ironic," she said. "Officer McHughes could have been in county lock-up at the same time I was. Worse yet, he might have been the one behind my arrest in the first place."

"Could be," Rick said.

"He might have tried to have me killed when I got out."

"They haven't turned up any witnesses, at least not yet. But what he tells the investigators will provide a huge picture. Grace, I know you went through hell and back, but I'm feeling pretty good right now. We pressed those guys into getting serious about this mess. Dirty cops? Looting Atlanta businesses? Think of the stories we're going to have."

"I can't wait," she told him, growing excited. "As soon as I'm reinstated, I'll catch up with you. But don't slow down, Rick. I'll simply jump on the train while it's moving."

"You won't have to wait, if you don't want to," Dent said.

"What do you mean?"

"McHughes' initial court appearance will be this afternoon. Go with me."

"I've been suspended. I can't go," she said, her voice full of disappointment.

"I'll take you," he grinned mischievously.

"How?"

"Big Six News doesn't hold all the cards. They can't stop you

229

from going as a concerned citizen."

She laughed like a teenager being asked on a first date. "That's right. You're on, Richard Dent."

**

The Fulton County courthouse, sitting in the shadow of the state capitol building, was a white concrete and smoked glass structure. They went through security, their cell phones and other items from their pockets and bags placed in one of the trays for x-ray.

"Damn it," Rick muttered as he set off the alarm. A deputy pulled him aside and wanded him. When the squeal went off, in the vicinity of his pants pocket, Dent pulled out a pocketful of change and showed it to the officer. The deputy gave him a "you idiot" look and waved him through.

They were the only ones on the elevator. "This won't last long," Dent said. "Word on the street is McHughes will plead not guilty but his lawyers are negotiating a deal for a guilty plea to save his butt."

"Will they reveal it in his arraignment?"

"Not likely," the radio man answered. "Probably haven't hammered out details yet, but he'll squeal before the pre-trial conference."

"He'll hang the other two out to dry?"

"More than two."

"You think there are others?"

Dent registered surprise as they stepped off the elevator and walked quickly toward the courtroom. "You don't believe the three yahoos who hit Pontellis were the only ones pulling heists, do you?"

"I haven't seen anything to the contrary," she answered.

"Smell the coffee, Gleason. Those guys cut a broad swath through the metro area, one job on top of another. There had to be more."

"Then who...?"

"Don't know." He paused, then grinned wryly, "But McHughes does. We'd better get in there. I'll go first. If my management has any

- The Blue Wall - Reichardt & Oscar

idea I'm here with you, they'll give me a hard time."

He disappeared into room Six B. Grace waited a few beats, then followed. Inside the courtroom, a huge crowd of onlookers, media and uniformed police officers were stuffed into the benches and lined against the side and back walls, creating a raucous air. Two attorneys from the D.A,'s office sat at one table, while the defense lawyer who would represent Officer McHughes, Travis Mendenhall, leaned against the court clerk's desk, chatting amiably. The clerk cackled noisily at something Mendenhall said as she printed out and handed him some papers.

Grace squeezed into a crowded bench at the end of the back row. *It's a pretty jovial atmosphere for a place where a man might put his life on the line in a few minutes,* she thought. She scanned the room, spying Jasmine Pontellis seated near the back with Bret Larkin.

Dent had joined several other reporters in the second row. He found a space next to Scott Matthews, who glanced curiously at him and then across the room at Grace. Scott was at the end of the bench, and Steve Jankowski manned a camera on a tripod in the aisle next to him.

Grace had already covered several hearings there and was struck by the varying style of the judges. Some were stiff, structured and precise in how they ran their courtrooms. Others were laid back, conversational, less disciplined in the process and more prone to easy-going back-and-forth with the counselors arguing cases before them.

Grace had seen Judge Marietta Byers on several occasions and knew her to be the former. She was abrupt and controlled her court with an iron hand.

The court reporter, a rotund, white-haired woman, entered and settled at her station between the judge's bench and the prosecutor's table.

"All rise," the bailiff announced. "The court is now in session, the Honorable Marietta L. Byers presiding."

The cacophony immediately hushed except for the collective sound of dozens of people standing in unison. Defense attorney Mendenhall grabbed the records from the clerk and scrambled to his table.

Superior Court Judge Byers entered from chambers and quickly slid into her chair. "Everyone please be seated."

The judge was middle-aged, thin—almost tiny—with short blonde hair. She wore a pinched expression, as if she intended to run a tight, no-nonsense ship. There was no levity in Marietta Byers' proceedings. Lawyers who tried to banter in cases she presided over became the object of her steely-eyed stare.

The bailiff continued, "Case number 22PX27976, the people versus Douglas D. McHughes."

A deputy ushered in McHughes to the podium. His lawyer stood and met him there. The suspended officer wore a blue suit and striped tie. Grace noticed the jacket looked even bulkier than normal, almost lumpy, on the muscle-bound cop. She realized he was wearing a bulletproof vest beneath his clothing.

Judge Byers addressed the crowd sternly. "I appreciate the fact that you have all come here out of your specific concerns, one way or another, about this case. You have every right to be here. Having said that, I expect absolute decorum to prevail in my courtroom at all times."

She turned her focus on the defense attorney. "Counselor, does your client waive the reading of the charges?"

"Yes, your Honor," Mendenhall answered.

Judge Byers perused the file for a few moments and looked up again. "Mr. McHughes, have you reviewed the charges against you, and do you understand them?"

"My client has read and understands the charges, Judge," Doug's lawyer answered.

"How do you plead?"

"My client pleads not guilty, your Honor."

"Any motions to file at this time, Mr. Mendenhall?"

"Not at this time, Judge."

She looked across at the assistant district attorney, Carolyn Woodson. "Counselor?"

"None at this time, your Honor."

"Defendant will be held without bond in an isolated cell in the Grain Street jail. Does Mr. McHughes have anything to say at this time?" she asked.

"My client has nothing further, your honor," the defense attorney answered hurriedly.

"All right," she said. "Pre-trial conference is set for two weeks from today, nine a.m."

"Thank you, your honor," the lawyers for both sides responded, and the deputy ushered McHughes out.

Judge Byers rose and disappeared as the shuffling noise of dozens of people rising filled the courtroom. Just as quickly, the courtroom emptied. Suspended policeman Douglas McHughes had not uttered a single word.

Matthews approached Grace as she walked toward the exit. "What are you doing here?" Scott asked, his question thick with curiosity.

"Wanted to see the opening salvo," Grace answered brightly.

"But...but I heard you were suspended."

"I'm just here as an interested citizen."

Her mischievous answer drew a wry chortle from Scott. "Sure you are," he said. He hesitated for a moment. "I'll have to tell Vivian you were here, you know."

Grace shrugged. "I don't care if you tell her I testified for the defense," she responded, not trying to hide her annoyance about the suspension.

**

The next morning, Grace and Rick repeated what was becoming a nearly daily ritual—coffee and a bite of breakfast at the diner. As usual, Dent was already there, waiting with her coffee and bagel.

"That had to be a world's record for the shortest arraignment ever," Grace said.

Rick smiled. "The lawyers had it greased with the judge. They know McHughes is going to cop a plea after they have a chance to review the discovery."

"Turn state's evidence to avoid the death penalty."

The radio man nodded.

"What today?" she asked, stirring her coffee, wondering why he had ordered it in a to-go cup.

"I'm on my way out to a crime scene. Want to join me?"

"Of course. What scene?"

"I just got a text message from a source. Police are converging on the lake at the Armstrong Park golf course."

Her curiosity was immediately peaked. "What's out there?"

Rick shrugged. "They didn't say, but it must be a big deal. There are several cop cars, plus a crane."

"A crane? Then it's not a body."

"Could be that some drunk drove his car in there last night. It's been known to happen. But I don't think that's it."

"Why not?"

"My friend was cryptic, but said Truman Brown was one of the cops arriving at the scene."

"Brown?" she exclaimed. "The detective who is heading up the Pontellis investigation."

Dent smiled. "My turn," he said and threw a ten dollar bill down on the check. He stuck the lid onto his coffee cup, wrapped a napkin around his bagel and slid out of the booth. "Going with?"

"You betcha."

"I'll have to drop you off a block away."

"I know. I'll just hang around the periphery and keep my eyes open."

**

Armstrong Park is a winding, forested neighborhood near Midtown. It is a section of classy older homes resided in by third-generation Atlantans and less impressive remodeled brick bungalows claimed by newly successful singles, gay couples and young families.

A small, aging shopping center defines one edge of the neighborhood. Just past the mall, on Montgomery Ferry Drive, sits the nine-hole Armstrong Park public golf course.

Dent let Grace out at a corner of the mall and drove on down Monroe Drive. It took her ten minutes to make the walk. Along the way, she marveled at the well-kept common grounds that announced each enclave of homes. The succulent, natural areas were flush with dogwoods, Eastern redbuds, big-leaf magnolias and crepe myrtles, hydrangeas, juniper and cleyera shrubs. Skittering among them in and out were nuthatches, red-headed woodpeckers, Carolina chickadees and Eastern gray squirrels.

Grace was genuinely embarrassed that she had so buried herself in her work she had neglected the raw beauty of this arboreal city.

She passed a long, flourishing row of mature Leyland cypress that bordered the golf course and hid it from view until she was almost upon it. As she arrived at the end of the tree row, she could see a half-dozen police cars parked randomly around one portion of the course's lake. A blue heron, interrupted from its morning fishing expedition, flapped across to the far end of the pond as an operator moved a huge crane into position.

Grace could see Dent, his power pack slung over his shoulder, microphone thrust in the direction of Detective Brown who gestured toward the lake.

Two television trucks arrived, one from her station. She imagined she would see Scott Matthews step out with a photographer.

The derrick's long cable dangled down toward the part of the lake where two police divers treaded water. One of them reached up and grasped the huge hook on the cable, while the other motioned to the operator to lower the boom.

The divers disappeared. Everyone on the scene waited, watched.

Within minutes, the divers reappeared. One of them motioned at the operator to raise the cable. As he did, slowly, the boom jerked and balked, jerked again, then raised a safe above the surface. It dangled momentarily while bystanders emitted a collective gasp.

Grace watched Steve Jankowski move in on the discovery with his camera. As he shot, Scott Matthews hurried toward Detective Brown, with his rival from Channel Twelve trying to elbow past him.

Grace watched the incredible scene unfold, certain that the safe must be connected to the burglaries. Her heart ached. She should be conducting the interview, gathering notes for her show, directing Steve toward the shots she wanted to use that evening. Instead, Scott Matthews got to cover it. And Jackson Davis would undoubtedly have it on his newscast.

She had to get past this suspension, this dark cloud hovering over her head. Grace was not one to hide behind cypress trees, skulking around like a wanted criminal, while one of the biggest stories in a decade played out without her.

27 EXONERATED

A DAY PASSED, and Grace puttered aimlessly around her condo, tending to some houseplants she had neglected, reading, watching news shows. Her Type A personality ate at her. It wasn't in her nature to while away the time.

Late in the afternoon, her phone rang. "I have some news to discuss," Hank Hamlin told Grace on the phone. "I'll pick you up and we'll have dinner."

"I have my car back," she responded. "I'll meet you some-place."

"All right. La Scala on Peachtree. Seven-thirty?"

La Scala was one of those exceptional restaurants people thought of at special occasions—wedding anniversaries and birth-days and Valentine's Day. It was situated in a quiet, reserved sec-tion of Buckhead, not the more rowdy area that houses the late-night nightclubs. This bastion of culinary delights oozed with elegance, old money and good breeding.

The lawyer was waiting inside as the valet took her keys and whisked her over to the doorman.

"I've never been here," she admitted to Hank.

"You're in for a treat." He guided her by the elbow down the darkened corridor to an elevator, which took them downstairs into the room appointed with brass and dark wood. There was diners' chat-ter and the sounds of service all around, but somehow it seemed magically muted—mere background music for the décor featuring expensive leather wall coverings and scented candles adorning each linen-clad table.

The maître d' led them to a small table near the corner. A server immediately appeared, poured water and handed them menus.

Hank scanned the wine list. "We'll try the Argentine Malbec," he said.

"Excellent choice," the sommelier nodded gracefully and disappeared.

Grace's patience was running out as they sipped the red and made small talk. She wanted Hamlin to get to the point of their meeting.

"You have your job back," he said triumphantly, raising his glass. She froze, waiting. "I reviewed the surveillance tape with the DA himself. We met with the judge in chambers. The prosecutor said he was going to drop the charges. But Judge Hopkins went into a rant about how unbelievable the discovery of the evidence had been and how bad this looked for the city PD and wanted this whole thing to go away, given you're the news media and all."

Grace clung to every word.

"His Honor said he wasn't going to require you to appear at a hearing. I'll be there, and the charges will be formally dismissed. Hopkins will request that Internal Affairs carry out an investigation. You'll be a free woman."

"I can't thank you enough." Grace paused. "You and I know the city will only go through the motions. When one of their guys screws up like this, they throw up a blue wall."

He cocked his head sideways.

"We call it the blue wall of silence. They protect each other, even when they're wrong. Or worse." She sighed. "If we're going to find out who's behind this, we'll have to dig it out ourselves."

"We will?"

"Oh, I don't mean you, counselor. Rick Dent and I. It will make a juicy story, don't you think?"

He lifted his glass toward her in a salute, drained it and began to pour them each another. Grace held her hand over the glass. The last thing she needed was another police stop with too much alcohol in her blood. "I'll switch to tea," she told the waiter who had arrived to take their orders.

The server brought their *vitello tonnato* and *insalata La Scala*. They talked about their childhoods and families and places where they had worked. By the time they traded bites of *tiramisu* and *pana cotta*, Grace all the while "mmmm-ing" and "aaaaah-ing," a comforting mellowness had set in.

As she took her last forkful, Grace instinctively checked her watch. "I can't believe it's already eleven," she said.

"When you're having fun..." Hank chuckled.

"I have to go in tomorrow. I want to give management a piece of my mind for abandoning me."

He looked alarmed. "They were just following policy, Grace..."

"I was joking," she laughed. "But seriously, I have a lot of work to do." She said it with the urgency of someone who was sitting in the dugout while the teammates got to play the game.

Grace went to the restroom while Hank paid the check. They met in the darkened corridor where they would ride the elevator upstairs. Grace reached for the button, but the smooth, firm grip of Hamlin's hand stopped her.

He stepped toward her, drawing close. "I can't tell you how much I've enjoyed this," he said in a low voice. "I was hoping we could stop by my place for nightcap. It's only ten minutes away."

He moved closer, and Grace placed a firm hand on his chest. "Hank, I've enjoyed dinner," she responded awkwardly. "And the unbelievably good news. But I'm going home."

"Are you sure?" he persisted, staying close despite her resistance. "I can't get over what it felt like, being close to you the night we were shot at."

Grace recoiled. "Are you kidding? We were almost killed, and you were getting heated up?" Her voice assumed an edge of anger.

"No, no, nothing like that," he flustered. "I just...just felt close to you. And now, tonight, it's been such a pleasure..."

He pulled her close and bent to kiss her. She resisted and pulled away abruptly, aggressively punching the elevator button. It opened immediately, and two couples stepped into their space.

They rode to the street level in silence and gave the doorman their valet tickets. Grace was thankful her car was delivered first. She barely glanced at Hank as she turned to leave.

"Sorry," he offered feebly from behind.

Over her shoulder, she said, "You should be, Hank. See you at the office."

Then she was driving home, not realizing she was speeding. The events of the night swam in her head, confusing her.

She was embarrassed at how she had reacted to Hank. Despite being slightly angered by his presumptuous approach, she realized he had awakened emotions she hadn't felt since moving from Dallas.

Grace left behind a heart-broken young cameraman, Matt Robertson, she had grown close to. Not only had they been professional colleagues, but Matt had come to her aid when she needed it most. A suspected murderer had tried to kill Megan, and Robertson went to her rescue, barely escaping death when he fought the guy.

Her ensuing romance with the young hero did not end well. Grace realized the disparity in their ages and backgrounds was too great for her to accept. The Atlanta position had come at the perfect time to say goodbye.

Now Robertson was gone, just a memory. Hank Hamlin presented a new, disturbing dilemma. He was brash and forward, and she wasn't emotionally prepared to be courted. Yet as her practical side took over on the drive home, she realized the lawyer was trying to support her, as Matt had. Hamlin's touch at the elevator might have troubled her, but it paradoxically kindled a forgotten pang of attraction. She decided to keep the Hank Hamlin door ajar.

As she turned into her driveway, she blinked hard, returning to her real world and relegating Hamlin's overture to the sidelines. *I'm reinstated!* She thought. *There's so much to do! I can't wait to get started in the morning.*

240

28 NOTORIOUS

AS MUCH AS GRACE disliked morning staff meetings, this time she felt relieved and delighted to enter the conference room and see the usual suspects gathered around the table. Scott Matthews, MaryAnne McWherter and Midge Rodriguez nodded toward her, but otherwise it was as if she had not been gone.

Christina wasn't there, and that seemed odd to Grace. Vivian was absent, too, meaning things would potentially move along smoothly.

Tom ran down his list of non-descript stories and then opened up the discussion with, "What've you got?"

"Rumors that another indictment might come down in the Pontellis murder and robbery case," Matthews jumped in, tapping on his tablet to retrieve his notes. "I haven't been able to get a name. McHughes is still the only one charged, but it appears that's about to change."

Tom scowled, "We've got to get out ahead of the competition on this."

"Kind of hard to do when you're on sabbatical," Grace mumbled sardonically to Rodriguez sitting next to her. Midge giggled, but Tom overheard and shot an icy glare over his reading glasses.

Jackson Davis crowed, "Just wait until the prosecutor announces he's going to seek the death penalty for McHughes. That will flush out the quail."

"The wife, Jasmine, said she had seen three guys running into the woods from an upstairs window in the den where she was hiding," Grace told them.

Jackson Davis looked like an ambush victim. He glanced at

Scott Matthews who shrugged ignorance. "How do you know this?" Jackson asked in a supercilious tone

"I have a source. Talked to him last night," Grace answered.

"Think the widow might have information?" Tom queried impatiently.

"I want to check another lead out first," Grace said. "Then I'll see about Mrs. Pontellis."

"What about Scott?" Davis barked. "He's been on this story for days. He deserves to pursue it."

Tom interjected, "Gleason and Matthews, you two work it out."

When Tom wrapped it up, Grace was first out the door, hurrying down the corridor.

Jackson Davis scrambled to catch up. "That's it, Miss High-and-Mighty. Barge right back in like you owned the place."

She searched his ruddy face for an inkling of playfulness, but there was none. "Are you serious?" she struggled to keep her tone low.

"Hell, yes," he blustered. "Matthews has been dogging the cop shenanigans, and I've been reporting them pretty much daily. Now you sweep in and want to take it over."

Grace resisted the temptation to snap back. She had been through too much to get testy with this fool. "We're just doing our jobs, okay? I'll make peace with Scott. By the way, where's Christina?"

Davis dropped his combative insolence. "The hospital. A nurse saw Eduardo's eyelids flutter this morning, so she rushed over there, hopeful there was more to come. So far, that's all there is."

Grace had been alarmed by Jackson's hostility, but she was encouraged by the news about Cruz. She rifled through her files, trying to remember where she had been when time stood still, when fate had dealt her several body blows one after the other. She couldn't concentrate. She knew she had to talk to Scott Matthews. She quickly left the station. There was research to do, and she could accomplish it more easily at the quiet little coffee shop down the street.

**

As she closed her laptop, she realized it was lunchtime. She ordered a sandwich and pulled the morning *Atlanta News Chronicle* from her briefcase.

Halfway through both the BLT and the paper, she heard her cellphone buzz. Her eyes rolled. It was a text from Harvey Silver asking her to see him.

"I thought you wouldn't want me in your sight today," Grace quipped good-naturedly as she stuck her head in his office door.

Silver laughed and motioned her in. "When the wind blows in Grace Gleason's world, it's a not a storm, it's a hurricane. I want you to see this." He retrieved his tablet from a desk drawer and pulled up a YouTube video. She quickly recognized the logo of one of the major cable news networks, then the image of Willis O'Neill, a regular commentator who often opined about media issues.

"Last week," O'Neill said, "I criticized Marjorie Smith, whose show airs nightly on one of those other networks, about how brazenly she interjects herself into countless none-of-her-business issues, using them to her broadcast advantage if it's handy and profitable. I decried how she admonishes judges and juries, and her use of speculation, hype, sensationalizing and other similar tactics to injure reputations and deprive people of their rights.

"Tonight I'm going to show you how that same sort of unethical and self-serving journalism is not just happening at the national networks. Local stations are sliding down the same unruly path. Here's a case in point."

Grace gasped as her image, taken from her program, flashed on the screen, She glanced at Harvey, whose eyes were fixed on the screen. The part of the program being shown was her criticism of the Atlanta PD and its reluctance to move on the robbery ring.

Her monologue taking issue with Chief Omoro Stone's news conference came on, then after a sentence or so the commentator faded in. "Big Six, as the number one Atlanta news station is known," the analyst continued, "is airing a new feature hosted by Texas transplant Grace Gleason, called Crime and Corruption. This news segment has ostensibly a noble objective—to expose wrongdoing in the community. Gleason pulls no punches in exposing criminals. But her reporting has gone awry. When a newscaster, even an opinion pundit, goes to great lengths to interject himself or herself into the story, not for the story's sake but for glory's sake, it's a travesty for all journalists.

"The vitriolic Ms. Gleason weighs in on meaty subjects such as drug wars and city corruption. But this reporter has no use for waiting for the facts to emerge. Woe be to the politician or lawyer who believes in innocence until proven guilty—he or she will feel the wrath of this wannabe prosecutor. Don't let the police department do its job in a methodical manner—let the irascible Gleason decide whom you should charge and convict. She purports to want justice done. But is it justice when she decides innocence and guilt regularly on her news spot, citing her own biased interpretation of the evidence?

"The ratings for programming like 'Crime and Corruption' are going up, and that's not good for objective broadcasting. Reporters such as Grace Gleason are growing in popularity, so you might want to take cover in your home town."

Grace watched the entire attack standing beside Silver as he held the tablet, then slumped into his side chair, stunned and mortified. Harvey laid the device on his desk and walked around to his chair, watching Grace.

"I don't know what to say," she muttered.

"Say it's a great day for Channel Six," he chirped.

"Are you kidding?"

"No, I'm not. This piece is going viral. Tens of thousands of people have already viewed it, and in a couple days I'll bet it'll be a million. We couldn't buy that kind of advertising."

Grace blanched at the comment. "Mr. Silver, you're missing the point. He's accusing me of practicing sensational and crude journalism without regard for truth."

Harvey sat down, his squinting eyes signaling his impatience. "Get over it, Grace. Who gives a big damn what Willis O'Neill thinks about your reporting tactics? My job is to boost ratings and get advertisers. That's it. Nothing complicated like..."

"...like doing it ethically?" she interrupted.

"Are you saying he's right?"

She stood and paced across his office. "Of course I don't think he's right." She was growing indignant. "He's making an accusation. A lot of people will believe it."

Silver leaned back and put his feet up on the desk. "What the hell do you care what 'a lot of people' say? Not me. Not Vivian Ellis. You should only care what your own viewers think of you. We have Dave Williams collect every viewer email and categorize them. Your messages have been voluminous lately, and they're four positives for every negative. That's all I care about—that and the growing viewership."

He stood, walked around to Grace and led her to the door. "Come on. We've got work to do. This guy is full of crap. You're doing a fantastic job."

She searched his eyes for sincerity. "The other day you were ripping me up for ticking off the police chief and mayor. Now I'm your golden girl?"

He grinned. "That's a different story. I have to live with those guys. Now get out of here."

As she left his office and walked to the newsroom, she felt as if she had been through a cement mixer. How could Harvey Silver so readily take her to task for aggressiveness and then just as readily express pride when someone else criticized her for it? She would never understand management's whimsical mindset, blowing in the ratings breezes. She needed to be around people who were grounded in more solid values.

She thought of Rick Dent. Ned Moore. And Megan. Grace needed a sanity fix, and her daughter was the one who could provide it.

29 AWAKENING

MEGAN FINALLY HAD some spare time. She had turned in her mid-term projects and planned a spring break get-away to Destin, Florida with several of her friends. She would leave the next day, giving Grace a morning to spend with her. They drove together to the Atlanta Zoo.

"I can't believe I haven't been here yet," Grace remarked as they drove on I-20.

"Mom, you haven't gone anywhere. All you do is work. And get arrested."

Grace eyed her daughter with a warning look. "Watch it, missy."

Megan laughed musically. "Honestly I couldn't believe it when you told me. My mom, the straight and narrow Grace Gleason, busted for drugs."

"I'm glad I got to you before the news did. You would have had a cow."

"I did anyway when you told me what happened."

They drove up Boulevard Avenue toward the zoo entrance, winding through an older neighborhood that had gone through some hard times but now wore its remodeled houses and manicured lawns and hedges with renewed pride.

"They say this area is in transition," Grace said, "but I think it's arrived. I understand the prices her are going up-up-up."

Megan pointed in the direction behind them. "Back that way, two or three miles, are some of the toughest communities in the city. Yet they've plopped a huge shopping mall right in the middle of it. Farther on is one of the funkiest shopping districts around. You'd love it, Mom, because you can get some fantastic outfits for next to nothing at the consignment and thrift shops."

"Used clothes?" she frowned at her daughter. "You wouldn't catch me wearing someone's castoffs."

Megan rolled her eyes in response.

"You've been there?" Grace asked.

"Mostly to get jeans."

They pulled through the stone entrance into the half-full parking lot. *We're not much more than a mile from where I was arrested,* Grace shuddered at the memory. She decided against mentioning it. Megan would lecture her about the dangers of her profession.

They walked past the building housing the civil war exhibit. Grace bought their tickets, and they strolled up a path bordered with lush plantings of aucuba japonica, midnight ginger, contorted tea camellia and bottle palms.

They watched the giant pandas chew bamboo shoots for a while and made a stop at the grand patio, where Grace bought them lemonade.

"It's peaceful here for such a public place," Megan said, watching the sparse stream of visitors drift past.

"The children are all still in school. This weekend it will be lively around here. I know you've told me about this place you're going to, but I want to hear it one more time."

"The condo is owned by Bradley's classmate's aunt and uncle," Megan said, some irritation in her voice despite her calm demeanor, an obvious effort to be patient. "Every spring they invite some of the college students to come down, and the condo owners—I think they're in their forties—open their home up to visitors. The beach is right across the road, and the students spend most of their time on the sand by day and exploring the pubs and restaurants at night."

Grace smiled and relaxed. "Sounds like fun," she said. "Just be careful. Remember that Alabama girl who disappeared in Aruba?"

"I know," Megan answered. "Don't worry, Mom. My friends

would never leave me to fend for myself, and I'd never allow myself to be vulnerable like that. After all, look who raised me. Besides," Megan interjected wryly, "you're the one in this family who lives on the edge. You follow cops around, participate in drug busts and interview gangsters in Mexico. You preach safety to me, but you don't practice it."

"Hey, let's not forget who's the mom here," Grace said caustically.

"Sometimes I feel like I am," Megan retorted. "You take so many foolish risks."

"Part of the job. Let's go." She rose from the bench and started toward the exit.

Megan chased after her, pressing the conversation. "That part of the job almost got you killed. And me. Remember that psycho killer you were covering in Dallas who tried to kill us both?"

"Now I have this." She fished into her purse and pulled out a canister of mace.

"I hope you never have to use it."

"I hope not, too," Grace reassured. "I'm thinking about getting a gun permit."

"Mom!" Megan began a protest, but it was interrupted by Grace's cell phone message chime.

"Saved by the text," Grace said.

It was a terse message from Christina. "Come to hospital ASAP." It sent a shudder down Grace's spine.

She dropped Megan off at her apartment. "Here's some extra money for the trip." She reached into her purse and pulled out fifty dollars. "Call me when you get there."

"I will," Megan promised and was out of the car, bounding toward her front door.

**

Eduardo had been in a coma for weeks. Every time she had visited, there was no change. She feared the worst. In fifteen minutes, she arrived at the monstrous old Grady Hospital where her officer friend fought valiantly to revive.

She knew the floor, ward and room number by heart. Her heels made a hollow click-click in rapid-fire on the concrete-and-tile floor down the corridor.

As she slipped inside the room, she first saw Christina and Jackson sitting by the bed. Christina was talking to Eduardo as she had so often, trying to educe a response. But this time, Grace's hand went to her mouth and tears formed immediately. She could see Eduardo's dark eyes were open, his mouth moving slowly as he spoke with his sister.

She gasped and rushed to the side of the bed opposite Christina, reaching out to take the young officer's hand, wrapped in tape to hold needles and tubes in place. Eduardo turned his head slowly toward her, and she felt him trying to squeeze her hand.

"Grace," he said in a soft, raspy voice.

She looked across at Christina who was choking back sobs. "You made it, Eduardo," Grace said, wanting to scream it out but knowing she had to keep control. "How do you feel?"

"Not so hot," he said, his voice a hoarse whisper. "Confused. Groggy."

"Want some more water?" Christina asked. He nodded, and she held the glass and straw to his mouth as he struggled to swallow.

Eduardo raised his hand slowly toward his sister. "I want...I want to talk to Grace," he managed.

Christina narrowed her eyes curiously.

"Alone."

"But..." Christina started.

"Please," her brother insisted weakly.

Christina gave Grace a reprimanding look. "Five minutes." She and Jackson left the room, pulling the door shut quietly behind them.

Eduardo motioned for Grace to come close. "I want to tell you something," he said. "Jackson told me about Doug McHughes getting charged. There was another guy, Bret Larkin from the Riverwood force."

"The security man at the Silver Rush?" she uttered, incredulous.

Eduardo paused for a long time, his breathing labored. "I was there, too," he finally managed.

"What?" Grace exclaimed.

"Not the Pontellis thing," he assured. "But some other...other jobs."

Grace recoiled, unbelieving. "No, Eduardo."

He nodded weakly. "They said it was drug money. I'd be doing society a favor. I got sucked in."

Her heart was breaking from astonishment and anger, and all she could do was stifle a cry.

"I know it was wrong," he whispered.

She felt incredibly torn. This man who had been her friend, who had helped her set the bar for her reporting in a new city, admitted to the ultimate sin. Disloyalty. Yet here he was, wounded, emerging from the deepest sleep, in pain physically and mentally, confessing to her. "How could you do that?" she half-shrieked. "To me? To your wife and children? To the public you're supposed to protect?"

His eyes closed slowly. A solitary tear ran from the corner of one, wending its way slowly down his sallow cheek. He motioned her closer, breathing unevenly, "Do not judge, or you too will be judged."

"You can't hide behind scripture."

"When I grow strong again, I will turn myself in. Until then, please don't tell Christina and Jackson." The words came out in desperate gasps. A pained expression crossed his face, his eyes still closed, and she knew it wasn't from physical hurting. "It was a mistake," he managed. "I wasn't thinking straight. I got caught up in their promises that we could bring down the gangs."

Grace had been overjoyed that her friend and confidant had survived the worst, but the flood of betrayal washed over her. She had to run, to leave Eduardo's devastating news behind in this musty room.

She released his hand and rushed out, fighting back tears. Christina and Jackson stood across the hallway from the door, astonished as Grace dashed past them without a word. Christina panicked. She slammed against the door and darted inside, gazing at Eduardo, desperate to know what had motivated Grace's sudden departure.

Grace sat in her car in the parking lot for a long time and sobbed. Her own words came flooding back, "...the public you're supposed to protect." Any other time, they might have seemed corny in retrospect. At this moment they made perfect sense. She realized immediately they came from her earliest memories.

Her upbringing in Chicago had been difficult. She was the only child of a demanding father and a mother too far down the alcoholic road for responsible parenting. In that dysfunctional setting, she tenaciously clung to the snippets of advice her father doled out day-to-day. They served as her life lessons.

One day when she was six, as he walked her to elementary school with her mother hung over in bed, a police cruiser passed them.

"To ser...ser..." she tried to read the words on the side of the patrol car.

"To serve and protect," her father filled in. "That's the cops' motto."

"What does it mean?"

"It means they're always there for you when you need them," he responded gruffly, as if he had expected her to know. "If anyone ever bothers you, yell real loud for the police. Or call nine-one-one. That's their job, to help you when you need it."

The message stayed with young Grace, and she tested it when she was fifteen. The routine after school rarely varied—she would arrive home to find her mother stretched out on the couch in a drunken stupor. It was up to Grace to clean up the empty liquor bottles and start dinner.

One day, however, Grace returned from band practice and found her mother on the floor in a pool of vomit. A horrible shudder ran through her. Was her mom dead? Wincing from the stench, Grace pulled at the woman, trying to lift her onto the couch, but her lifeless body was too heavy.

Grace rushed to the phone and dialed the emergency number. "Please help me. I think my mother has died!" she shouted hysterically.

Within minutes a police officer arrived. "The paramedics are on their way," he advised as he kneeled over the prone woman. "Your mother is breathing. But she smells like a brewery and she's in real bad shape. When the guys get here, they'll take her to the emergency room."

The cop stayed with Grace until her mom had been strapped onto a gurney and the ambulance had left. He called Grace's father and calmed the scared young girl's shattered nerves until he arrived home.

Grace never forgot the incident or its message. In high school, college and later in the workplace, her respect for men and women in blue was unshakeable. As a news reporter in Dallas, working on a murder story, her regard for Detective Ned Moore bordered on hero worship.

Now she realized in horror that the recent events, crowned by Eduardo's incredible admission, had fractured her faith. She knew the majority of cops out there were honest. Yet she would never look at them the same unquestioning way again.

"Damn it, Eduardo," she muttered mournfully.

She searched her memory for clues she had missed, but there were none. She fished for a tissue in her purse and wiped her eyes.

Grace drove home in disbelief and grief. She couldn't bring herself to think about what action she should take. Then she realized she would do what she always did when faced with uncertainty, take a hot bath and go to sleep.

Tomorrow morning, she would know what to do.

30 GONE

GRACE HEARD THE RAIN before her eyes were open, a constant rat-tatting against the tin flashing on top of her chimney. It was normally a welcome and soothing sound, often lulling her to sleep like some Debussy melody. But this morning, after so devastating a night of restless sleep, she needed sunshine. Birds singing. Hot coffee on the back porch with a gentle breeze drifting the aroma of honeysuckle in her direction.

She groaned quietly as the phone rang. *What now?* she wondered. *A bombing at the airport? Assassination of the governor?*

"I have some bad news," Vivian said.

"I'm not sure I can take any more," Grace said, immediately realizing her boss couldn't know what she meant.

A long pause. "I just heard from Jackson. It's Eduardo Cruz. He died this morning."

"What?"

"I'm sorry. I know he was more than a source to you."

"What...what happened?"

"Jackson said he took a turn for the worse overnight. Don't worry about coming in this morning. Do whatever you need to do. Go see Christina, his wife and kids. Take your time."

She had the coffee and the porch, but there was no sunshine, no honeysuckle smell. Just pounding rain and despair. Eduardo, gone!

Grace had awakened knowing what path she should take, but now that he was gone, how could she soil his legacy with an ugly truth? She held her face in her hands. The only thing that would save her from coming unhinged was to get ready for work. She would pay her respects at the proper time. Right now, for her own sanity, she would shower, do her make-up, dress and go do what she always did—pursue a story.

She knew the day would be "a plodder," as Jeff used to call the dull and heavy ones. But the familiar site of the diner, even in the drizzle, brought a little relief.

Rick was in their booth.

"I already heard," he said as she slid in across from him. He motioned toward the ice tea he had ordered for her.

"It's as if someone punched me in the stomach."

"You just have to get busy, get into your work."

"I know," she replied. "There was something I was going to do today, before…" Her voice broke off.

He waited.

"I have a second name from a reliable source. Bret Larkin," Grace said.

Dent sat back. "Riverwood SWAT."

"Right," Grace confirmed. "There's something else. A fascinating call last night from a guy I know, a minion in the DA's office. He phoned from a bar and sounded pretty lubricated, but I think he knew what he was doing. He wants me to unearth something from Pontellis' wife. McHughes has lawyered up and is probably holding back."

Rick squinted at her to gauge her true disposition. "There's something we can do if you feel up to it."

She sipped her tea, waited.

"I've been thinking we should pay a visit to that club where all those guys train. Impact something or other," Dent said. "We know McHughes and Larkin were fanatics about going there regularly—dedicated body-builders. Whoever else was involved, including the third guy at Pontellis' massacre, maybe even the guy who shot at you and Hamlin that night, probably worked out with them."

She realized Dent couldn't have known Eduardo Cruz had also been on that list. "It's a place to start," she answered.

"Then let's go."

Impact Workouts was not a huge establishment. It didn't cater to those with a casual attitude about getting into shape, only the smaller crowd of serious body builders.

As they entered, Grace glanced around, noting the wall-to-wall, floor-to-ceiling mirrors. There were some machines, mostly for cardio training, but the place was dominated by lifting equipment.

It was barely ten o'clock, but already the place was buzzing with the clanking sounds of free weights being hoisted or dropped to the floor, the grunts of lifters pushing their limit, the "Come on, one more," encouragement of spotters. And the sight of grown men admiring their biceps and triceps and pecs and lats in the mirrors.

"Can I help you?" the completely ripped young man at the desk said, eyeing the two skeptically, as if they were mistakenly looking for a restaurant.

I'm sure he knows we're not signing up, Grace mused.

"We're with the media," Rick said. "We'd like to talk to the manager."

"Hold on." The attendant disappeared into the back, and within a minute Big Sam walked in, dressed in shorts and a tank top with muscles bulging everywhere. Grace couldn't remember seeing anyone so bulked up since watching the Olympic Games weight lifters on television.

"What can I do for you?" the owner asked briskly.

"Grace Gleason, Channel Six," she stepped in, believing the proprietor more likely would recognize her than Dent. "This is Rick Dent, with our radio sister station."

Sam examined them distrustfully for a moment, then without a word motioned with his head and they followed him into the rear corridor.

His office was the first door. He ducked into it, flopped down behind the desk and motioned toward two chairs. "What's this about?"

"We're looking for some information about officers Doug McHughes and Bret Larkin," Grace told him, watching his expression visibly harden into a clenched jaw and furrowed eyebrows. "We understand they work out here," she added.

The owner hesitated, as if searching his mental customer list. "A lot of guys do. Even if I recognized the names, I wouldn't tell you anything. I don't give out customer information. My clients know I respect their privacy."

Dent persisted. "We're simply interested in who worked out with them."

"Why?"

Grace scooted to the front of her chair. "We're not asking you to give up any protected customer data—just to give us an idea of who their associates were. All we need is the names, we'll pursue it from there."

Big Sam stood up, inflating his considerable chest with a huge breath. "I don't know them. Sorry."

"Surely you do. They're regulars," Rick countered.

"As I said, I don't divulge customer names. Period. My clients trust me, and this conversation is over." He picked up the phone and began to make a call. Glancing up, he dismissed them. "Have a nice day."

Rick shrugged, looked at Grace, and led her out of the office.

They were near the front door when Grace hesitated. The young man who had greeted them was wiping down a stair stepper near the exit, and she approached him.

"Excuse me. Doug McHughes and Bret Larkin are regulars here, right?"

"Sure."

She was slightly shocked by his immediate response. "Who works out with them, regularly?"

"Several guys. One in particular is here most of the time, guy named Drake, can't think of his first name."

"Is Drake a cop?" Dent asked.

"Don't think so. Used to be, like our owner. Now he's a security consultant, I think, because I heard him and Larkin talking about a system he was installing for Bret at some strip club. Don't remember the name of it."

**

Outside, in the car, Grace and Rick exhaled heavily as if they had won the lottery.

"I can't believe that guy gave up all that information with no hesitation," Rick hooted.

"That owner, Big Sam, clammed up because these were his cop buddies."

"The blue wall of silence," Rick Dent stated matter-of-factly.

"We have to tear it down," Grace acknowledged. "No one else is going to do it."

Rick started the car and put it into gear. "Any idea what strip joint he was talking about?" He smiled impishly at Grace and began to steer the car toward Peachtree Street and the Silver Rush Showbar.

31 THREATENED

THE SILVER RUSH had not changed—the depressing inte-
rior, the pounding beat of the music, the dispassionate expressions of
the two dancers who gyrated around a pole on the stage. The scene
immediately brought back the memory of that day when Grace had met
Nick Pontellis. It felt weird to return after his brutal death.

A manager met them near the bar. "Mrs. Pontellis is here," he
told them. "She comes in every day. I'll see if she will talk to you."

Jasmine Pontellis looked tired as she walked toward Grace
and Rick. She had tried to keep the club open after Nick's murder, but
judging from the dark shadows under her eyes and worry lines in her
forehead, it had become too much.

A wisp of a courteous smile crossed Jasmine's face. "I saw
your coverage of Nick's murder."

"I'm sorry for your loss," Grace offered. "This is Rick Dent from
ninety-eight point seven radio. We're following up on a story about your
husband's death. Do you mind a few questions?"

Jasmine nodded toward a booth in the corner of the room.
Grace had hoped they could talk in a more quiet environment, but she
guessed Nick's wife wouldn't be comfortable in her late husband's office.

"We're trying to find out about a security consultant—a guy
named Drake," Dent said, raising his voice over the intruding music.
"We'd be off the record, following up on a possible story."

"Carter Drake," Jasmine Pontellis confirmed. "I know who he
is. I've been through the books since Nicky died, and there are paid
invoices from Drake's company."

"What were they for?" Grace asked.

"He designed and installed part of our security system. Bret
Larkin was Nick's head of security, and he hired Carter. Nick approved

the invoices."

"So Drake and Larkin were business associates?" Dent asked.

"They were friends. My manager, the one you just met, told me they worked out together at some body building club."

"Mrs. Pontellis—again, we're off the record—do you think Carter Drake might have been involved in your husband's murder?"

Jasmine Pontellis sucked in her breath and sat perfectly still. "All I know is I saw those three guys charging across our grounds like a grizzly bear was after them. One was limping and the other was holding his face, but even so, I've never seen grown men move that fast in all of my life. They were big guys, huge shoulders and backs. It wouldn't surprise me if they worked out."

Grace looked at Rick. "I think we'll go pay Carter Drake a visit."

"Why don't you go to the police?' Jasmine asked.

"Have you seen how slow afoot the APD has been on this case?" Dent challenged.

"Yes, I have. I told them everything I knew about Nick's killing, and I still don't know if they tracked down the leads."

"There you are," Rick confirmed.

When Dent dropped Grace off, he said, "Let's go see Drake at his office tomorrow morning. We'll catch him before he can get called out on a job."

Grace nodded.

Later, having dinner at a small cafe on the way to her house, the idea of waiting gnawed at her. Her curiosity was too great. She decided to drive by Drake's business, since it wasn't out of her way, and see if there was any life there.

Drake had a shadowy past, and it had caught up with him when he became a sworn police officer. Pledged to serve and protect, the young man instead looked for ways to game the system. It came naturally to him. His bipolar mother and heavy drinking father provided a socially impaired Atlanta suburban household in which Carter and his twin brother fended for themselves.

They learned at an early age to fix their own meals, dress in their friends' cast-off clothes, sign each other's report cards and stay out of their parents' way when the arguments grew violent.

By the time they reached high school, they had learned how to skim money from the till at football game concessions and alter their grades in the school's computer system.

Carter's brother disappeared when they were rising seniors. He knew his twin had been dealing dope in the hallways, so he wasn't surprised when his sibling and a buddy dropped out and hit the road for California. Carter stayed in school and joined the ROTC. He liked the military experience, and they taught him to handle weapons.

Shortly after graduation, he applied for the police department. Several divisions were woefully understaffed, and Chief Omoro Stone had emphasized rebuilding the force. Carter Drake passed the test, went through the interviews and background tests, and was tendered a conditional offer of employment. After passing the physical, psychological tests and waiting two months, he was hired.

But policing didn't agree with Drake, and vice versa. He stuck with it for a while but was written up several times for minor infractions. Then as he approached his three-year anniversary, still a beat officer, he met a security expert while investigating a robbery. They became friends.

Drake had just finished patrol one afternoon and stopped for a beer at a local pub when his friend spotted him at the bar.

"Long, hard day?" the consultant said, sitting on the stool next to Carter.

"They all are," the policeman said.

"Pay's okay, though, right?" the man asked. Carter gave him an ironic glance.

The consultant laughed. "Why not come work for me? I can use someone who knows the routines of the bad guys."

The next day, Carter called him. "Were you serious?" he asked.

"Sure was. I could start you on Monday. Pays nearly twice

what you make chasing losers."

"Done."

Carter Drake quickly demonstrated he had an affinity for the business. During his childhood, his natural computer proficiency and knack for getting into and out of rooms and buildings to survive a dysfunctional family life, served him well.

He had his own business in less than five years. But he maintained his friendship with some of the cops he had worked with. They worked out and went to ballgames together, and occasionally Drake helped them with a security problem.

Grace had the street number Jasmine Pontellis had provided, and after some searching she found the front of Drake's business in a small strip mall. She parked, and as she approached Grace noticed three-inch-high letters, "Drake Security" on the front glass.

She saw a light burning inside. As she peered through the door, a face staring out startled her.

The door jerked open. "Something I can do for you?" Carter Drake was in his forties, salt-and-pepper crew cut. His most noticeable features were gigantic shoulders and a thick neck bulging against his shirt.

"Carter Drake?" Grace asked tentatively.

The door opened wider. "Yeah."

"I'm Grace Gleason. I..."

"I know who you are," he cut her off. "I recognize you. What are you doing here?"

"I want to talk to you about your friends, the police officers you lift weights with."

He held onto the door, not inviting her in. "You doing a story about them?"

"I'm not sure. Can I come in?"

He hesitated, then swung the door a little wider and motioned her in with a nod of his head.

The office wasn't much—a desk, telephone, table lamp, computer and a few file cabinets. There were no accessories. No pictures on the wall except for a framed business license.

"What's the story about? Everyone has already covered Doug McHughes." The consultant's voice was deep, his words punctuated with arrogance. He sat down at his desk and motioned her to a chair.

"I didn't say I was doing a story," she responded. "I said maybe."

"So, what will the story be about if you do one?"

Grace was uncomfortable with the way this had started out. She needed something to melt the ice, a way to ease the barricade of stiff suspicion.

"We can't get anyone to tell us why McHughes went on leave, and what happened to his service pistol. And who his accomplices were."

"So? Ask the department. Ask his lawyer. The guy's in jail, isn't he?"

"No one's talking. I thought, since you work out with him, you might be able to shed some light."

Drake glowered at her. She had seen people quick to anger before. But watching his snap reaction to her questions, she sensed this man was a smoldering volcano. And she might have lit his fuse.

He leaned forward, his unibrow knitted. "What the hell do you think I am, some kind of spy?"

"It says on that wall you're a security consultant."

"Damn right. That's all I am. Not a source to feed your half-baked hunches."

The disconnected diatribe was sending her mind spinning. She had asked Drake a simple question, and he was reacting as if the DA had charged him with murder. It didn't add up, and she could feel her insides churning.

"I'm not sure what I said to anger you, Mr. Drake. I'm just trying to find out what is going on over at the APD. That's all."

"And you think I know, right?" His ire continued to build, turning his mammoth neck red. "You go to hell, Gleason. Get out of my office."

She started out of the chair, feeling flustered. "Look, Drake, I didn't mean anything. You're a former cop. You know these guys and see them all the time. You were a natural person to ask, that's all."

He stood up, circled the desk, and pulled her chair back. As he did, he leaned in so close she could feel his breath in her right ear. "Time for you to go, reporter. You shouldn't be here in the first place. You should know better than to snoop around at night where you don't belong. Especially around people who are expert at handling weapons."

Grace turned, looked into his fuming eyes and felt his wrath. She moved quickly toward the door. She jerked it open and sped on her way.

That could have gone very badly in one more minute, she thought. *It took every ounce of self-restraint for him not to snap my neck.*

On the way home, Grace's hands shook as she clung to the steering wheel. She had once felt this kind of danger and distrust in Dallas when she met a man who later was revealed to be a murderer. She remembered confronting the man in a darkened strip club parking lot, and he assaulted her. She felt lucky Carter Drake hadn't done the same. Grace wasn't sure what compelled her to make incursions into dangerous situations late at night, alone. She only knew as news leads unfolded and fermented in her mind, she had to act anytime and anyplace the impulse appeared.

Could Carter Drake be the third man in Pontellis' garage? Or the one who had shot up Hank's SUV? Were there others she needed to track down?

It was two a.m. before Grace was able to doze off, all keyed up. Even then, sleep was fitful as the idea of Drake's veiled threats haunted her dreams.

32 DUST TO DUST

DENT WAS FURIOUS the next morning. "What were you thinking, Gleason?' he half-shouted, small pieces of his scrambled eggs ending up on his lower lip. We were supposed to go together. You know, in broad daylight? When it might have been safe? That was stupid, stupid, stupid."

"I know."

Rick brushed his napkin across his mouth and took a swig of coffee. "So the guy didn't offer any help, huh?"

She smiled and relaxed. "Not much. He did his best to scare the crap out of me, though."

"And did he?"

"He did a pretty good job. Rick, I could feel it—Carter Drake is knee-deep in this thing. He might have been the third man at the Pontellis garage, or at least knows who was. He could have shot at me the night I got out of jail. He might have used his APD connections to get me arrested in the first place."

"Whoa, horsey," Rick warned. "Let's take this one allegation at a time, shall we?"

"I know. We can't rely on my intuition. There has to be proof."

He nodded.

"Although, you know, my intuition is usually right." Grace snickered and then looked at her watch. She became somber. "It's nearly time for the funeral. You coming?"

He shook his head no. "I don't like funerals. And I didn't know Cruz. You go on. I want to do a little snooping around over at the APD.

I have a friend who works in the DA's office, and he knows someone who knows someone who's close to the chief."

"Good luck. I'll call you after it's over."

**

For Grace, Eduardo's funeral and then burial at the cemetery became one long, excruciating blur. Saint Ann's church in Shoreville overflowed with family, friends and uniformed fire, police, homeland security and search-and-rescue officers. She entered and made her way to one side where pews were roped off marked "Press." She sat in a daze.

"We remember a man, a brother, who never questioned his duty to protect the people of Gwinnett County..." memorialized a fellow officer.

Another rose to praise him, "We always wanted to be around Officer Cruz, he was one of the good guys..."

The Gwinnett County chief rose, spoke for a few minutes and closed with, "...He understood the dangers of his work, yet he performed it willingly. He gave his life to protect his fellow citizens. Today we retire the badge of Officer Eduardo Cruz, to be placed at headquarters next to those heroes who fell before him."

Grace held a handkerchief over her eyes. She barely heard their words. She looked sadly at Christina, Raul and Juanita, Adella and the children, a family gripped by disbelief and sorrow.

The ceremony ended and the family and dignitaries filed out. Scott Matthews asked, "Want to ride out there with me? You don't look too good."

"No," was all she answered. She followed the throng of suits and uniforms outside, toward the mayhem in the parking lot. Three limos pulled away first, then a long, black hearse followed by a procession of police and fire department vehicles.

It was a two-mile drive to the cemetery. Grace saw rows of onlookers who lined the streets. Some had doffed their caps in respect. Small groups of school children held banners that said "Our Hero," and "Officer, Rest In Peace." Two squad cars were parked at each intersection to keep traffic from getting through.

At the entrance to the graveyard, hundreds of officers stood at attention, grim and reverent. From her parking spot, Grace trudged up a slight hill. She stopped when she saw a horse-drawn wagon delivering Officer Cruz to his resting place. A bagpipe played a solemn hymn. The startling report of a three-volley rifle salute split the air. There was a mournful blare of a bugle blowing taps and the low murmur of the chief speaking to Adella as he presented her with the tri-folded flag from his casket.

Then it was over. Eduardo Cruz was lowered into the ground.

The honor guard, the dignitaries, the swarm of uniforms, filed out. Grace sat in her car, alone at the roadside, staring up the hill at the tent shielding Cruz' coffin from the sun as grounds workers wrestled to take it down.

Her conscience burned with the realization she had failed to reveal Cruz's participation in the very scheme she was trying to expose. What would be the point? How would she feel about her laxness in the months to come, when the emotions had drained away and there were only facts to judge by? She didn't know, and that she didn't ate at her.

Grace needed to hear a familiar voice. She called Rick Dent. "It's done."

"How do you feel? You okay?"

"Empty," she said.

"I know," he said. "I'm sorry. Look, I've dug something up. Let's talk about it tomorrow."

"No, today," she insisted. "Come to the station. I'll meet you in the lobby."

"You sure?"

"Yes," she was alarmed at how fatigued her own voice sounded.

"Twenty minutes?"

"I'll be there," she confirmed weakly.

**

Mrs. Nicholson watched them with unhidden curiosity as Grace and Rick huddled in the corner of the reception area. Delivery people distracted the receptionist. But Grace spotted her several times casting inquisitive glances their way.

"My guy over at the DA's says they've confirmed the second Pontellis killer," Dent said excitedly, his usually squinty eyes open wide behind his thick spectacles.

"Shh," Grace warned him, noting Mrs. Nicholson's interest in their conversation.

Rick dialed down the volume. "You already had it--it's no surprise. Bret Larkin."

Grace sat back, considering. "So now we have an Atlanta cop indicted, and a Riverwood SWAT team guy about to be."

"Who doubles as a security guy at the Silver Rush Showbar," the radio man added. "Larkin's been on leave with a broken leg, claims it happened at the club when he was fighting with some rowdy customers. But he actually took a bullet in the shoot-out. McHughes apparently ratted him out."

"He cut a deal."

"To stay off of death row."

Grace's emotions began to churn. She knew if Larkin pulled the trigger on Pontellis, rather than McHughes, he could very well have been the shooter who nearly killed her and Hank Hamlin. After all, he worked at the club and would have wanted to scare her off the story.

"When's Larkin going to be arraigned?"

"A day or two," Dent replied. "They took him into custody while the funeral was going on."

Grace rubbed her eyes. The day had taken its toll. "I'm going over to the APD. I think it's time for a showdown with Chief Stone."

"I'll join you," Rick offered.

"Let's go for it, shake things up." She smiled for the first time all day. "We just have to get by that stone-waller Aretha Herrington. She's going to protect the chief like crazy now."

Dent beamed broadly. "We could do it the hard way."

"Ambush?" she returned his devilish smile.

"We're veterans at it. The poor guy won't feel a thing."

"I'll see if Steve's available," she said, energized. "Meanwhile, you call the chief's office and confirm he's in town. If you can squeeze anything out of them about his schedule, do it."

**

They parked in one of the three-dollar public lots across the street from the police headquarters building and walked hurriedly to the crosswalk, lined with bail bond businesses and small restaurants.

"Where does he park?" Grace asked Rick as they approached the entrance.

"Employees use that adjacent garage," he told her. "But I don't think that's where the chief's car is kept."

She looked askance at her colleague. "You mean you don't know where we can waylay him?"

"Don't worry. I'll find out," he said and disappeared into the front door of the building.

Grace and Steve waited nearby. She was happy no one passed, so she wouldn't have to answer questions.

Several minutes later, Dent burst out of the building. "He's over at the municipal courthouse," he shouted over his shoulder as he hurried past them, sprinting in front of the headquarters. As he ran, Rick pointed across the street. "That's his car parked in front."

The reporter, still amazed at how Rick weaseled such information out of people, scurried to catch up with him. Jankowski was right behind Grace, and they dashed across the street.

"He's supposed to leave at two o'clock for a meeting at city hall," Dent said as they stopped at the justice center's domed entrance. "We'll wait here for him to come out."

Grace thought Rick always seemed to have his radar in gear. "How do you find out this stuff?" she marveled.

"I've been around this chicken coop for thirty years. I have my ways."

She laughed and checked her watch. "He should be here any minute."

They had only been there a few seconds when a uniformed driver stepped from Omoro's waiting car and walked slowly toward

them. Grace felt they must have looked overtly obvious—two reporters with microphones and a cameraman huddled near the municipal
court doorway.

"What can I do for you?" the cop asked in a booming voice.
He was a hefty man, well over two hundred pounds. He walked with
a swagger made more pronounced by all of the police gear strapped
to various parts of his body.

"Grace Gleason, Channel Six," she said.

"I know. I watch you. What do you folks want?"

"Sergeant, we're here to interview Chief Stone," Dent replied.

"Do you have an appointment?"

"We thought we'd surprise him," Rick said in a caustic tone,
astonishing Grace with his audacity.

"No, you don't..." he began but was immediately interrupted
by Omoro Stone exiting the building.

They moved toward the approaching chief, but the officer
stepped between them. "You're not going to..."

"It's okay, Sergeant Whitacre." Omoro Stone reached out and
brushed him aside. "I'll talk to them."

Whitacre shrugged and returned to the vehicle.

Grace motioned for Steve to man his camera. "Chief, we now
have two suspects, Douglas McHughes of your department and Bret
Larkin of the Riverwood SWAT force. Are there others involved in the
Nick Pontellis shooting?"

"Officer Larkin is being held for questioning but hasn't been
formally charged. The short answer to your question is we aren't sure.
That's all I can say. You know we don't comment about ongoing investigations."

He moved toward his car.

"Why did it take you so long to identify McHughes and Larkin as suspects?" Grace asked.

He flashed her an exasperated expression but didn't respond, opening the passenger door of his vehicle.

Rick joined in, "Weren't there three shooters in that garage? Who's the third?"

The chief stopped short and stared at the reporter for a moment, then slammed the car door and the driver fired up the ignition. Within seconds, the chief was gone.

33 DOWNFALL

LESS THAN A WEEK later, Bret Larkin was charged with felony murder and the next day Mayor Ronald Walker announced at a news conference the city's chief of police would step down. Grace was elated to be back in action. She wouldn't have wanted to miss this story, one of the biggest since she had arrived in Atlanta.

The lobby of city hall was cram-packed with reporters, cameras and onlookers. Their buzz rattled around the hard marble surfaces of the foyer in a whirlwind. Mayor Walker's footsteps echoed above the din as he strode to a makeshift podium with a gaggle of staff at his side. He tapped the microphone, cleared his throat and held his hands up for silence.

"Today I have received a letter of resignation from Atlanta Police Chief Omoro Stone. He has cited personal reasons, and it is with regret that I have accepted it.

"Omoro Stone has served the Atlanta force in an exemplary manner for some twenty years. He has been an asset to our city and its citizens, and we wish him well as he moves on. I am announcing the appointment of Major Harriet Hammer, deputy chief for field operations, as interim police chief. Deputy Hammer is a fifteen-year veteran of the force, having joined us after serving for six years in the United States Coast Guard. She has performed with distinction as a beat officer, as a detective, and in field operations as a zone commander. We will immediately begin a search for Chief Stone's replacement, including the review of several internal candidates. Major Hammer?"

The interim chief stepped forward from the group behind the mayor and took the podium. She was African-American, short and slightly stocky. Her hair was pulled back in a tight bun below her cap. Her uniform fit perfectly to her solid body, her shoes military-shined. She was all business.

She unfolded a piece of paper and read. "I thank Mayor

Walker for this opportunity to further serve the citizens of our city. As acting chief, I will commit to continuing the mission we have all been on—reducing crime, building the confidence of our citizenry through stronger community relations and treating our force with dignity and respect." She moved aside without smiling.

The mayor again stepped forward.

"Thank you. That's all for now," he turned to leave, as if hoping to escape the anticipated barrage of questions.

"Mr. Mayor," Rick Dent out-shouted the others with the first question, "what can you tell us about Chief Stone's personal reasons for stepping down?"

"Those motives are known to Chief Stone and only Chief Stone. Next?"

Grace returned Rick's skeptical glance in her direction and jumped in. "Mayor Walker, did his resignation have anything to do with the arrest of Officer Doug McHughes?"

"Absolutely not." He frowned at her. "I've already told you his reasons."

"Actually, you haven't," Grace muttered quietly to herself.

Walker pivoted quickly and pointed toward a Channel Twelve reporter.

"Mayor, what about the chief of the Riverwood force? Do you know if his job is in jeopardy as well?"

Mayor Walker's face began to turn crimson, and he glared at the reporter. "First of all, you'll have to ask the mayor of Riverwood about his personnel, not me. Second, I reject your premise that this resignation is somehow related to the recent events involving one of our officers and a Riverwood deputy."

A newspaper reporter in the back boomed out, "Is Stone's announcement related in any way to the arrest and subsequent exoneration of an Atlanta television news reporter?"

Grace glanced back at him and felt the hair on her neck bristle. Mayor Walker frowned at the reporter, stared at Grace momentarily and took a step back from the podium, flustered.

276

"What about the Pontellis murder?" another reporter shouted. "Was there a third shooter in the garage or not?"

The mayor's public relations director, short, silver-headed Harry Bartsdale, pulled his boss back into their entourage. He leaned down toward the microphone. "We're drifting far afield, folks," Bartsdale barked. "That's all for now. The mayor has a busy schedule this afternoon."

Mayor Walker turned and moved through the lobby toward his offices, trailed by his minions.

**

Grace missed Larkin's arraignment, to her dismay. Over objections, she had been assigned to cover a growing dispute between the Atlanta police and a loosely organized group of street vendors downtown. The controversy had simmered for years. The motley group of entrepreneurs camped out on city sidewalks near tourist attractions. Some members of the city council had railed against law enforcement for ignoring ordinances against such sales without licenses.

But Chief Omoro Stone had contended that city police, under-staffed and under-funded, had more important crimes to deal with. "Give me the two thousand bodies I need for this force, and maybe we can put some resources against the problem," he had once complained at a council meeting.

Meanwhile, panhandlers hung around the area that attracted sight-seers looking for bargains and souvenirs. The vagrants' pushy ways further rankled the city leaders.

Finally, at the insistence of the mayor, the police force had begun to crack down. Civil rights activists, including the ACLU, waded into the roiling political waters. As police officers attempted to remove vendors and beggars from the sidewalks, the protests grew. Contentious arguments punctuated the opposing points of view.

Vivian Ellis sent Grace to tell the story. Uniformed police officers were arguing with several vendors, insisting that they dismantle their makeshift kiosks.

Grace waited on a downtown street corner for the protesters to arrive. The station had been tipped off they would be there, and she knew they would clamor for an interview.

"It's over," Rick Dent called her on her cellphone. "Short and sweet, not guilty to the identical counts McHughes was charged with."

"Damn it," Grace howled. "I should have been there."

"You didn't miss anything. Just don't let your news director get you all tied up when McHughes and Larkin start giving up the others to save their hides. Things are fixing to get explosive."

"You're absolutely certain there are others?"

"Count on it."

"How do you know they'll rat out their friends?"

"McHughes fingered Larkin, didn't he? And they're both facing a death sentence. They'll do what's required to save themselves, trust me."

Grace jerked to attention as three cars swiftly pulled up curbside. "Gotta go. The posse has arrived." She hung up and motioned to camera operator Cassandra Barrett to get ready.

A small group of protestors stepped out of cars, pulled hand-lettered signs from the trunks, and headed for the fracas. There were fewer than twenty. Most were young, Megan's age, wide-eyed with excitement.

Grace thought about all the demonstrations going on in the Middle East, covered by national network news. She knew the cameras lied—that what often appeared to be thousands of shouting, fist-waving demonstrators might be just hundreds, sometimes dozens. And when the cameras went away, so did the indignant marchers.

She sighed, shrugged, and motioned Cassandra to follow her into battle.

**

The crowd at Larkin's arraignment disappeared from room Eight F of the Fulton courthouse immediately after the officer and his lawyers exited. Only a few stragglers stayed behind, friends or relatives of others attracting no media interest whose pleas and arraignments were yet to be presided over by Judge Byers.

Filing out of the courtroom, Dent spotted Detective Truman Brown crowding toward the elevators. "Detective, got a minute?" he called out. Brown waited for the radio man to catch up.

Dent lowered his voice. "Officer Brown, what about the third shooter?"

The officer gave Rick an admonishing glare and steered him into an empty visitors sitting area. "What third shooter?" he asked nonchalantly.

"Come on, detective. You can't deny there were three in that garage. And you've interviewed McHughes and Larkin over and over, right?"

Brown hesitated, then, "We off the record?"

"If that's how it has to be."

"It is," the officer warned.

Dent nodded agreement. "There might have been a third shooter. I'm not confirming or denying. But if there was, we already have his name. Listen, Dent, I can tell you there were more guys in on the action, from Atlanta and other jurisdictions. That's why the M.O.'s weren't the same in those burglaries and robberies. Don't know how many yet, and don't have all the names, but we're getting leads and pursuing them."

"So that means you're still negotiating a plea for these guys."

Truman Brown didn't react, tantamount to a confirmation.

Dent appeared astounded. "Why in the hell are you telling me this?"

The detective smiled. "I haven't told you anything." He paused, in thought. "I've known you a long time, and you've never double-crossed me. You're one of the best newsmen in town."

Brown strode swiftly down the hall toward the elevators. Dent sat and exhaled, looking astonished. "That was a first," he said to himself.

**

Back at the Big Six News Beat, Grace filed her vendor protest story with Christina Cruz for the evening newscast. She then began to create her "Crime and Corruption" script. She leaned back, trying to decide what to write. But when her fingers hit the keyboard, the words began to spill out like a white-water river:

When I began 'Crime and Corruption' nearly a year ago, I appealed for your trust. I asked you to join me as I went behind the scenes to dig out the worst kinds of treachery in Atlanta. In increasing numbers every month, you chose this station and my segments over the hundreds of options you had for spending your time.

She stopped for a moment, deep in thought as ideas continued to cascade, and she resumed writing:

But in a sense, I have failed you. I recently learned a valued source for many of my stories had in fact become part of the problem, not the solution. I can't reveal that source, because it would do more harm than good. I'm asking you to trust me on this. And I promise, if you continue to give me your confidence—to follow me through this journey for another year, and then another, I will never again hold anything back from you. What I know, and when I know it, you will know.

**

Grace sat back, surprised at how spent she felt from the emotion of writing the brief admission. But it tasted distressingly wrong. It occurred to her she was at a crossroads of a moral dilemma. If she delivered the message she had just written, management would immediately call her in and demand full disclosure. They would not only press for every scintilla of information she had about Eduardo, but they would probably fire her.

She thought about the repercussions on Christina, and Jackson, and all of the officer's family. Grace understood why Cruz had gotten involved, but she also knew it was horribly wrong. A fellow reporter in Texas had once told her, as they grappled in a staff meeting about how to report a politician's misstep, "Once you get into bed with the devil, you become the devil."

Staring fixedly at the computer, she rubbed her hands together slowly as she read and then re-read her confession. She couldn't use this! In a moment of firm resolve, she highlighted the script and hit "delete." The paragraphs vanished like vapor trails in the sky.

She would write a new script with no hint of her secret Gwinnett source. Unless the prosecutors uncovered some evidence linking Eduardo to the criminal ring, she would take his secret to her grave.

**

A few hours later, Grace stared into camera one as the red light came on. Her decision to re-write the script had given her comfort and confidence.

She expanded on Christina's lead-in report of Bret Larkin's pleading, showing some video of the officer being led away in cuffs. Rick's telephoned report had been enough to give her the information she needed.

Then she moved from the screen to her stool, sat, and paused.

"Soon we'll be celebrating our first anniversary of 'Crime and Corruption.'" She stopped, fighting to keep from choking up, thinking of what might have been with Eduardo Cruz. She glanced at Mary-Anne McWherter, who had a dazed, panic-stricken expression, as if expecting Grace to drive off a cliff.

"You have been with me every step of the way as we chased down two of the most dangerous threats to our metro area—a violent gang-related narcotics trade going on here, especially in Gwinnett County, and more recently, the most devastating betrayal our metro area has ever endured at the hand of corrupt law enforcement officials. Facts are still coming out about the string of crimes perpetrated by police from several jurisdictions and about the hands-off response from those in the highest office. We have been receiving hundreds of responses to our reports. And according to your emails, texts and twitter messages, you say overwhelmingly that Atlanta deserves more from its leadership."

She took a deep breath. "I have a nagging sense that this story is not over. Not all of the culprits have been caught. Further, there remains the consequence of a city police department that claims a strong record of honesty and integrity, but in practice establishes a blue wall of silence when we, the public, demand to know the real story. All I can tell you is if you will watch, I will continue to dig and to report to you, my ultimate bosses. As Margaret Mead said, 'Never doubt that a small group of thoughtful, committed citizens can change the world; indeed, it is the only thing that ever has.' From the Big Six newsroom, I'm Grace Gleason, and you've been watching 'Crime and Corruption.'"

MaryAnne threw the newscast back to Christina for sign-off. Grace sagged limply on her stool. She felt diminished. She had no doubt about how hard she would work to restore her self-respect. Yet at this moment, her world was crushing her like a ten-ton weight.

Grace retreated quickly to her workspace, wanting to get out of there. A note from Harry Hamlin was taped to her phone.

She read it, thought for a moment and then called Dent. "Our lawyer has passed me a note. They found McHughes' pistol. When they searched his house they scanned his backyard with a metal detector. Dummy buried it fifteen feet from his house."

"It'll match at least some of those casings in the garage, for sure. Another key piece of evidence. Do I hear the officer singing louder?"

Grace laughed. "One more thing. Even better. They've arrested two more cops. One of them is Grant Madison."

"The guy who arrested you."

"Right."

"The plot congeals."

34 ASSAULT

AN HOUR LATER, as the evening light grew dim, Grace walked from her car through the garage and into the kitchen carrying a six-pack of beer in one hand and the other arm wrapped around a bag of groceries. She struggled to work the knob, finally twisted it and kneed the door open. It felt good to be home.

It was dark inside. She fumbled with her elbow to flip on the light switch. Then she heard a footstep and the click of a lamp being turned on in the living room. She dropped her grocery bag and it crashed to the floor. Her heart raced.

"Hello, Gleason," Carter Drake said as he stepped into the kitchen. "Remember me?"

"Drake! How did you get...what are you doing here?"

"How did I get in? Is that what you started to ask?" he guffawed boisterously. She could see the pistol he was carrying.

His speech was slurred. "Have you forgotten, Gleason? I'm a fucking security guy. I can get into anyplace."

"That's how you broke into all those businesses, you, McHughes, Larkin and all the rest?"

"And your buddy Cruz. Your fellow gang-slayer."

She felt her heart stop at hearing Eduardo's name.

A sinister sneer crossed Drake's face as he moved toward her unsteadily.

**

Moments away, Megan was riding in the back seat of Bradley's old Honda Element, with Raj riding shotgun. She had told them her mom had called after her newscast and invited them for Italian food.

Her two roommates were always hungry. The only time they

would turn away a free meal was when they were crashing on a project deadline.

They turned up Pharr Road, a block from Grace's townhome.

"That's odd," Megan said immediately.

"What?" Bradley asked as he cruised toward the curb in front.

"My mom always has the porch light on for me. And she usually burns every lamp in the house." Megan looked concerned. "I only see one light on in the whole place."

**

Grace glanced nervously around the room, looking desperately for some kind of weapon. She knew she had to keep this man talking.

"It was you, wasn't it, Carter? You drove the getaway car for those guys. You were in the garage the night Nick Pontellis was killed."

"Brilliant, reporter. What else have you figured out?"

"You're the one who shot up Hank's SUV the night I got out of jail. You tried to kill us."

He laughed and staggered a bit, catching himself. "You're really on target tonight, news lady." He raised the gun slightly.

She felt her head throb.

"Tonight I get to finish the job."

"You're not going to shoot me, Drake. That would be stupid. You'd never get away with it, and you'd be behind bars for the rest of your sorry life."

"They're going to get me anyway, thanks to you. You flushed out McHughes and Larkin and they set those dogs on me. Now they won't leave me alone, hauling me downtown, asking me one question after another. You're the one who blew our whole operation open when those stupid fools couldn't figure out squat. Yes, Grace Gleason, I might go to prison. But you're going to die." He pointed the pistol directly at her head.

Grace screamed and scrambled frantically behind the cooking island, ducking for cover.

**

Raj jumped out of the passenger side. "Maybe your mother's not home yet. Let me go check it out and make sure there's nothing wrong."

"I should do it," Megan offered, opening the back door and stepping out.

Motioning for her to hold back, Raj walked to the front stoop, skipped up the four steps and rapped loudly on the door. There was no answer. He tried the door, and it opened immediately.

From Bradley's car, Megan and her other roommate could see Raj dash inside. The evening quiet was assaulted by shouting and violent commotion. Megan sprang toward the house, but Bradley caught up and grabbed her arm.

"Wait!" he screeched. "It might be dangerous."

"No kidding." Grace's daughter had genuine fear in her eyes. She yanked away from Bradley and dashed up the steps. He shook his head and followed.

Megan hurtled through the door just as a huge figure brandishing a pistol charged from the kitchen to the living room toward Raj. As the assailant fired, the young man dropped instantly.

"Raj!" Megan screamed. Her roommate sprang back up and lunged, trapping Drake's arm. He delivered a swift hand strike to Carter's collarbone, shoving him violently backward. The bigger man shook the floor as he flopped down with a heavy thud.

The Glock flew across the room from the force of Raj's blow. But Drake wasn't through. He had his opponent outsized by eighty pounds. Pulling his massive body back up, he caught Raj on the side of the head with a wild roundhouse blow.

Prakash was staggered and dazed. Drake dove at him. Raj delivered a stop-kick to Drake's knee. The security man let out a deafening howl as the joint snapped back, hyperextended.

Grace saw the frantic action from the kitchen. The furious scene instantly recalled a near-death battle she once had with the killer she had confronted in Dallas. Strictly on instinct, she ran headlong toward Drake and bounded onto him from behind.

"Mom, no!" cried Megan as her mother beat furiously at the security man's hulking back and shoulders with clenched fists. Carter threw her backward, but the distraction was all Raj needed. When his attacker turned back around, the young student was ready.

Drake threw a desperate haymaker. Prakash blocked it. He deftly swung the man's enormous arm to one side, stepped in quickly and locked it straight, paralyzing the bigger adversary.

Raj threw a quick upper cut to Drake's chin, followed by a hammer fist straight down on his throat and a sharp, ferocious punch to his ribs. As Carter started to go down, Prakash grasped his arm, grunted loudly and flipped him. Drake flew head over heels and landed with a gargantuan crash. In a skillful move, the young martial arts expert locked Carter's arm in a twisting grip.

Drake screamed out in agony, lying face up on the floor with the smaller Raj standing over him, wrenching his wrist and arm. The assailant's shoulder appeared to be dislocated, or worse, as he writhed in pain and his contorted face turned crimson.

As Raj kept his foe's distended arm behind him, Grace gasped for air, fumbled to find her phone and called nine-one-one with trembling fingers.

35 DINNERTIME

THE POLICE HAD come and gone. They had ceremoniously taken everyone's statements and carted the injured Carter Drake away in cuffs.

An ambulance had also arrived. In the excitement of the fight, no one seemed to notice the bloody crease across Raj's forehead until the dust had settled.

"It's not serious," the paramedic said. "Just a graze wound. You were lucky. An inch closer and we might be carrying you out on a stretcher." The medic applied antiseptic and a bandage.

Megan embraced Grace and then they all hugged Raj carefully.

"You were amazing," Megan said brightly. "I knew you were into martial arts, but I had no idea you could do all of that. He was so much bigger than you."

Raj smiled and sipped on bottled water Grace had brought him. "I learned to fight as a kid," he said, sweating from the ordeal. "Jiu-jitsu, karate, all that stuff. You get training in how to flip your attacker by lowering your center of gravity under his and using his own weight to throw and defeat him." A sheepish grin crept onto his face. "But I have to admit, it's the first fight I've had outside the ring."

Grace jumped in reflex when the doorbell chimed.

"I completely forgot in all the excitement. I invited someone else for dinner," she said.

When she answered, Rick Dent smiled like a shy schoolboy, holding three large plastic bags and shrugging his shoulders. The warm aroma of something delicious perked up Grace's senses.

"Sorry I'm late." Rick motioned to the bags with his head. "Had to wait quite a while for the lasagna."

As she ushered Dent in, Grace said, "Rick, this is my daughter Megan and her two college roommates."

They all shook the radio man's hand weakly, still visibly traumatized by the events.

"Nice to meet y'all," Dent said, then, surveying the stunned group inquiringly with squinted eyes behind the cola-bottle glasses, "Did I miss something?"

They recounted the events for Rick's benefit as they ate. Grace enjoyed the food and animated conversation, but she was relieved when everyone left. She was drained. She didn't have the energy for a bath before changing and falling into bed. Grace needed sleep badly, but she couldn't wait to wake up. Tomorrow at the station, there were things she wanted to do.

36 MISSION ACCOMPLISHED

SCOTT MATTHEWS LOOKED up from his computer, and his youthful face registered surprise. Grace realized she had never stopped by his cubicle, even just to chat. It was obvious to her how wrapped up she got in her own business.

"I wanted to thank you," she said.

Matthews flashed a curious smile.

"You hung in there against the skeptics, myself among them. I became obsessed with one cause, but you recognized the real story when it came along."

"We're news hounds. We can never tell where events are going to take us."

"You're wise beyond your years," she marveled. "Anyway, you didn't leave it alone until we got it right."

Scott shrugged. "You would have gotten there. You're a genuine pro."

"Back at you, Scott."

She watched him beam.

"Listen, I need a favor," Grace said.

"Anything."

"I want you to guest-host my news segment tonight. I need a long weekend to myself, drive down to the coast and rattle around in some antique shops."

"Jeez. That's a tall order, Grace. I can't get prepared."

She put a firm hand on his shoulder. "You'll ace it. The script is written, and the video's ready to roll."

"What about...you-know-who?"

"I'll handle Vivian. No worries."

"Okay then. Sure. I'm excited to do it. Uh, listen, Grace, this is going to sound really lame. But…but could we maybe have dinner sometime?" He quickly avoided eye contact, obviously embarrassed.

Her eyes opened wide in disbelief. "Mr. Matthews, are you asking me out?"

"Maybe. I don't know. I guess so."

"Scott, I'm old enough to be your…" she paused, searching for a word.

"Big sister?" he chuckled, red-faced.

"Mother." She joined his laughter.

"I don't care. We're still colleagues, right?"

She thought for a moment. "I have a better idea. Sometime when I'm having dinner with my college-aged daughter Megan, why don't you join us?"

"Maybe I will."

She grinned genially, pulled her handbag strap up on her shoulder and started walking away.

"Grace," he called after her. "I pushed you on the story. But no one could have pulled it all together like you did."

She turned back in acknowledgement as he went on.

"You held the guys at city hall accountable. I could never have done that. You made a huge difference. That's what you said your news reports would be all about."

Grace nodded thanks, walked to her workspace and picked up a small stack of messages by her telephone. She shuffled them, studying each one as she hurried through the newsroom. She stopped short for a moment. There was a message from Hal Slaymaker. She recognized his name as head of CVN cable news in New York. *What could he possibly want?* she wondered. She would call him back after she was on the road.

Just before she reached the door, it popped open.

"Grace Gleason," the lawyer Hank Hamlin exclaimed as he stepped in. "I was coming to see you. I heard you had a knock-down, drag-out with Drake. Are you all right?"

"A little sore, that's all."

"I'm glad nothing's broken. Leaving early?"

"I'm taking a long weekend. Driving to Savannah."

Hamlin looked around and lowered his voice. "Listen, Grace, I didn't get off to such a great start with you. I realize I overstepped my bounds a bit. But I want you to know I had good intentions. When you get back, I'd like a shot at a fresh start. Nothing heavy, maybe a drink after work?"

"Mercy, I'm hitting the jackpot today," she chuckled.

"What?"

"Nothing. Sorry, private joke. I don't know, Hank. Maybe. We'll talk when I return."

Grace wondered if she had misjudged the man at first. After all, she had been in a fragile state when they had met. He had shown genuine interest in her well being when the going had gotten tough. He was smart, intelligent, honest. She knew in her deepest heart she should give the man the respect he deserved. *Maybe, when I get back,* she thought, *we'll explore the possibilities.*

Outside, a warm spring was emerging. As she walked to the parking lot, Grace noticed for the first time the rows of crepe myrtles around The Plantation's walkway had been pruned during the winter. Colorful vincas and geraniums were emerging from the large pots defining the edge of the lawn.

Scott's words rattled through her mind. *You made a huge difference.* Then suddenly, she remembered part of a poem she had memorized when she was in journalism school in Texas. It was a verse by Treacher MacDonald, a World War One doughboy with the Second Division. He wrote it sitting in a trench during a break in the action at the battle of *Belleau Wood.* The moment she read it, she had known the last four lines would become her credo as a newswoman.

> *Who will join me in my quest*
> *For justice at the world's behest?*
> *Who will stand and fight with me*
> *Until we know all we might be?*

Grace entered the parking lot, breathing in the soft morning air of late May. She remembered, she had been nervous, apprehensive, unsure as she embarked on this new challenge. So much had happened since then. She climbed into her car realizing Atlanta had become her home.

Matthews was right—Grace had accomplished a lot in just a year.

And yet, like the poet asked, she wondered what she might be. And what grand adventures lay ahead.

EPILOGUE

SCOTT MATTHEWS DABBED at perspiration on his upper lip. He sat in the newsroom on the stool usually occupied by Grace Gleason. His eyes darted from producer MaryAnne McWherter to the teleprompter and back again.

An hour earlier, IT man David Williams had reassured him. "You won't have to manipulate the technology," Williams said. "Grace and I put together video from many of the cop stories she's covered. It'll run straight through, perfectly timed with what's on the teleprompter. Concentrate on delivering the message."

Scott had issued a sigh of relief. To this point, his only on-camera work had been occasional reports from the field and a brief guest stint on Grace's segment. He practiced the script for an hour until he could have delivered it from memory.

Then, it was time. The young newsman watched the monitor as Christina Cruz provided his lead-in. "...Filling in tonight for Grace Gleason on 'Crime and Corruption' is Scott Matthews. Scott?"

Camera one's red light switched on. Maryanne pointed emphatically and nodded.

"Good evening," Scott's voice broke a bit. "Grace Gleason is taking a well deserved day off. For months, she has kept you astride of the unfolding case of police corruption in the city. I have been fortunate to work with her on aspects of the story. Tonight, rather than report new developments, we want to provide another side of this ongoing saga that has all of Atlanta concerned. Our challenge in heavily reporting the arrest and indictment of cops gone bad has been to avoid tarring all police officers with the same brush. Before she left on holiday, Gleason penned a tribute to those men and women in blue who honor their oath to serve and protect. These are her words."

293

He turned to camera two.

"Who are they, these heroes in blue? Where did they come from, and how did they become our first line of defense? They are average Joes and Janes. They were jocks in school, science junkies, Boy Scouts, Girl Scouts, gang escapees, military brats, military veterans. They watched their fathers and grandfathers come home from working patrol. They saw their mothers break the blue-glass ceiling.

"They wrestled on their college team, drank beer with frat brothers or sorority sisters, studied political science, played video games and beach volleyball, marched in parades with the ROTC, worked part-time at the corner grocery, earned their GED after dropping high school, saved their best friend from drowning in a swollen river.

"They are all of those things and more, those all-American heroes who make sure their neighbors and townspeople sleep well at night. They break up gang fights and domestic squabbles, lecture kids about marijuana, prevent drunken manslaughter, stop car-jackings. They are the first in harm's way. They take a bullet in a shootout.

"Those are the men and women in blue. And more. Or, sometimes, sadly, less. The officers now facing serious charges were, at one time in their careers, more. Somewhere along the way they became, regrettably, less. But let us not forget those who remain steadfast in their duty. Let us honor their service.

"I'm Scott Matthews for Grace Gleason, and this is 'Crime and Corruption.'"

READERS GUIDE

1. What are the major themes in *The Blue Wall*, and how do these topics relate to life in your city?

2. What key decisions by the characters move *The Blue Wall*'s plot forward the most?

3. How do you react to the chances Grace takes in doing her job? Would you approach it differently?

4. How does Megan's presence in Atlanta impact critical scenes in the story?

5. Have you ever known a person like Eduardo Cruz? Can you relate his struggles to anything you have experienced in your life?

6. What impact does learning the truth about Eduardo have on Grace's subsequent attitudes and actions?

7. How does Grace's episode in Mexico change her outlook on the impact her reporting can have on her viewers?

8. What does Grace learn about the news business from Rick Dent? What part does Dent play in Grace's growth as a reporter?

9. What pivotal role does young reporter Scott Matthews play in the story?

10. Why do you think Grace was so unreceptive toward Hank Hamlin, the lawyer, and what eventually changed her mindset?

11. What scenes in *The Blue Wall* were most memorable to you, and why?

12. What surprised you in the book, and how did these twists and turns affect the story or its characters?

13. What is the significance of the title *The Blue Wall*? Do you think the title is relevant to what Grace encountered as the story unfolded?

14. Why do you think the authors added the epilogue? How does it enrich the story that has been told?

Made in the USA
Las Vegas, NV
22 May 2023

72425248R00177